The Visitant

By K. Booye

ISBN-978-0-578-44273-0

Cover Photo © eAlisa/Adobe Stock

Dedication:

For my Grandmother, Beverly Booye,
For telling me fairy tales when I was a little girl and instilling in me the love of stories. I wish you were here to read this one.

I love you.

Prologue

"There is nothing more we can do, I am so sorry. Take as much time as you need," the doctor slipped out of the room leaving Serena in shock.

"Oh Dad," she choked. She slipped her small hand into his large one. It was limp, weak, clammy, nothing like it had been that morning when he had squeezed her shoulder as he left for work. Blood dripped to the floor, the backboard still cradled his broken body.

"Serena," his voice raspy, his eyes fluttered open.

"Dad!"

"You have," ragged breath, "to listen," another ragged breath. "to me."

"What is it?"

"Box. There. Is a box." his words came out agonizingly slow but urgent. "A box. You must get that box." He struggled for air, "Before anyone else." His eyes closed.

"Where is it?"

"Closet." his eyes remained closed, his weak voice barely heard over the heart monitor. She leaned down, his blood soaked through her shirt.

"Closet? Your's? Mine? The hall closet? Dad? Dad don't leave me!"

His eyes opened again. "I love you, baby girl." Tears leaked from his eyes, traveling down his temple, commingling with blood.

Beep.

Beep.

"I love you." the last word an exhaled whisper.

Beeeeeeeeeeep.

***

Lilith woke up, struggling for air. Her lips were dry and her tongue stuck to the roof of her mouth. She reached for the glass of water sitting on the bedside table and saw a fly floating in it. Okay, maybe she didn't need a drink. She sat up in bed, waiting a moment for the room to stop spinning. The moon cast an eerie cold light through her bedroom window, deepening shadows in the corners. She could barely hear the whispers, but she could feel their eyes on her, watching.

They were always watching.

She turned on the lamp, and the shadows disappeared.

It all came back to her then, rushing at her. She could smell the room, the blood in it that couldn't be controlled. It was hazy at first, but she focused her mental lens, and she could see him. She could see the jagged rip in one side of his body and tubes in and out of him, just barely keeping him alive. Someone was holding his hand. She couldn't visualize the person, but she could feel the spirit, her fighting spirit. Usually, Lilith could see everyone in a room. But this one she could only feel.

She watched as the heart monitor slowed and as it did so, a hand materialized. Then an arm, and then, as the soul of the dying man finally let go, Lilith could finally see the other person in the room, her narrow body, her heart-shaped face, broken in grief. And her eyes. Her eyes gave her away.

Lilith's heart leapt within her, blowing the residual fog from her brain.

She had done it! After ten years of searching, she had finally found the one they had all been looking for.

Chapter 1--Saturday--One Week Later

Jonathan Kelly of Pleasant Hill, Oregon, passed away September 25th. He was a well-respected professor at the University of Oregon, teaching classes on mysticism, the occult and its effects on modern times.

After teaching at the University of Portland for three years, Professor Kelly took a position at the University of Oregon in Eugene for ten years, making Pleasant Hill, Ore. his home where he lived until his death.

His wife, Crystal Kelly and their daughter, Anna Kelly, preceded Professor Kelly in death. His beloved daughter Serena Kelly, 17, survives him.

There will be a Celebration of Life service held at St. Mary Roman Catholic Church at eleven o'clock in the morning on October 1.

Professor Kelly's death had shocked the university.

The cathedral filled with genuine grievers and curious onlookers. They all wondered what would happen to the Professor's daughter.

She could hear the whispers behind her as she passed row after row of pews. Her head ached, her throat was dry and scratchy, her heart heavy. She wasn't one to be pitied, and in different circumstances, she would have marched down the aisle with her head held high. But not today. Today she mourned.

Two long hours later she finally escaped the handshakes and awkward hugs. Mr. and Mrs. Youngblood, close family friends, spoke quietly as he maneuvered their car down Edenvale Road. She was exhausted as her brain grappled with the truth. Her dad was gone. Like, gone gone. Forever. Earlier that morning she watched as they lowered his casket into the ground. Then it was over. At the age of seventeen, she was the only living member of what used to be a family of four.

She sat in the back seat and watched yellow and red-leaved trees and golden pastures pass by. It had just been Serena and her dad for the past eleven years. And while his funeral service had been well attended, she felt utterly alone in the world. After her mother died, the Youngbloods were the only two people Dad trusted enough to let close. She loved the older couple, but they weren't family. Her family was now buried six feet under.

"Serena," Mrs. Youngblood said.

Dazed, Serena realized the woman had called her name several times. "Yes?"

"Did you hear what I said?"

"I'm sorry. I wasn't paying attention."

"It's okay, dear. I was explaining that your aunt and uncle are waiting for you at the house."

"Okay."

"Have you packed yet?"

"Yes. I did last night."

"Oh good." She fell into silence as Mr. Youngblood drove. Serena watched him let go of the steering wheel with one weathered hand and take that of his wife's. The couple had no children, and she had become somewhat of a granddaughter to them. Now she was mandated by a judge that she move away with an aunt and uncle she had never met. Chances were, she and the Youngbloods wouldn't see each for a long time. Serena swallowed the lump in her throat. If she started crying now, she wouldn't be able to stop. The last thing she wanted was for strangers to see her as broken as she felt inside.

The car slowed when her road came into view. The blinker clicked on as they waited for an oncoming vehicle to pass. Instead, it turned in front of them, leading the way.

They followed the Lincoln Town Car down the long gravel road intersecting her beloved meadows. At the end stood a grove of oak trees, like a natural barrier between their house and the outside world.

The car in front of them disappeared under the low branches of the first two trees, and they followed. From the road, it always looked like the trees swallowed them up. When Serena was younger, she pretended that they lived in a different realm than everyone else, protected from the evils of this world.

They parked behind the other car, but none of them moved. Instead, they stared at the cozy brick house her family had lived in, the home where she and Dad mourned their losses, the home where she now mourned them alone. A concrete sidewalk led to the front stoop and a big picture window sprawled to the right of the front door with a green hedge below.

They watched the house, listening to the ticking sound of the engine as it cooled down. Through a crack in the curtains, she could see the lights on inside. It was time to meet the family she had never seen. Not for the first time she wondered what kind of people they were. She still didn't understand why a judge had reversed Dad's will stipulating that she was to go with the Youngbloods.

Movement from the car in front of them distracted her rambling thoughts.

A tall, gaunt man with white close-trimmed hair and a deeply lined face climbed out of the driver's seat of the Lincoln, walked around to the passenger side, and opened the door. Serena watched as a sheer black panty-hosed leg emerged; a gloved hand followed. The man took it and helped the woman out. She was dressed in black taffeta and a black hat with netting and feathers. This couldn't possibly be her aunt and uncle, could it? They looked so old. Or at least the man did. She hadn't seen the woman's face, but her hair, gathered into a French twist, still looked dark auburn, and no gray was showing. She looked like she had stepped from the sixties with her dress and matching hat, like an older sister to Jacqueline Kennedy.

Serena watched from the safety of the back seat, through tinted glass that allowed her to stare unobserved, but the woman turned as if she knew she was being watched. Below the netting were the strange green eyes just like the ones she and her father shared. So, this must be her grandmother.

Her face was striking in its uniqueness, reminding Serena of the older Hollywood actresses of the 1950s and '60s. She carried herself regally as she walked to the front door where it opened for her. It was strange to watch people walk into her house as if they owned the place.

"Do you know that woman, Serena?" Mrs. Youngblood's voice was quiet.

She shook her head. "I've never met her, but I think that's my grandma." She remembered all the warnings her father gave her as she grew up. Warnings to never let her grandmother in the house if she showed up one day. Yet, here she was, in Serena's house. "Her name is Rosalie," she whispered.

Dad didn't talk much about his family. She had met his brother and mother once, at her sister's and mother's funeral, but she didn't remember much from that day given that she was only six years old at the time.

Over the years, Dad had kept his information to just a few words like, "Don't let them in the door." And he was careful to keep a close eye on her. When he returned to work each fall at the University of Oregon's Religious Studies Department, he had taken her with him. He schooled her from his office as he prepared for the classes he taught and enrolled her in his classes when she got to her sophomore year of high school two years ago. She would've graduated with her high school diploma and twenty-four college credits under her belt if her father hadn't died and these stupid people hadn't insisted on taking her to Colorado, but at seventeen, she didn't have much of a say.

Serena took a deep breath as she slipped out of the car. She led the Youngbloods up the cement sidewalk. The storm from earlier that morning had passed an hour ago, leaving behind the heavy scent of decaying autumn leaves, reminding her of the dying season. Dripping water from the trees echoed through her ears, intensifying the sound. Everything felt surreal, even the walk from the car to the front door, a walk she'd taken every day of her life. A memory flashed through her mind, a memory of her father slowly walking the same path to the front door after the funerals of her mother and sister. She remembered the way his shoulders sagged, his eyes on her but not really seeing her. He was miles away as she waited for him to join her on the front steps.

The front door swung open before she had a chance to touch the doorknob, bringing her memory to a sudden halt. A man with thick black hair, cut with precision, stood in front of her. He wore a tailored Armani suit, and his dark green eyes matched hers.

"Serena?" his voice was velvety smooth.

"Yes." A cool breeze blew past her, and she shivered once. She was chilled, but she wasn't sure if she was ready to step over the threshold.

"I'm your Uncle Simon." He introduced himself with his hand stretched out to shake hers, then changed his mind and wrapped his arms around her in a big hug. "It's wonderful to see you."

She nodded in response, then he stood her back on her feet so he could look at her.

"You look just like your mother."

"And you look like my father." Her father was rougher around the edges, but just as handsome in his own way. She knew this by how many girls took his class, feigning their interest in the subject he taught.

Simon dropped his arms sensing her discomfort and stepped aside to let her enter. Suddenly she felt like a guest in her own home. She lifted her foot and stepped onto the hardwood floor, into the living room and scanned the space which had been inviting and cozy just last week, when Dad was alive. Now it looked strange with these new people standing in it. A pale, thin woman with ivory skin, long black hair, and high cheekbones stood in the kitchen doorway. Her nearly black eyes watched her intently. There was no smile on her face. The man who had arrived with her grandmother watched her too. He stood behind her mother's favorite wingback chair that her grandmother now occupied. She didn't smile either. She glared.

"Mother, doesn't she look like Crystal?" Simon asked.

Green eyes assessed her with a calculating shrewdness, freezing Serena where she stood. "Yes, she does."

Simon moved away from her and walked to the woman in the kitchen. "Serena, this is my wife, Lilith."

Lilith's eyebrows arched higher as she nodded.

He gestured to the woman sitting in the winged-backed chair. "And this is your grandmother."

"Rosalie," the woman interrupted. "You may call me Rosalie. The man behind me is Frank."

Serena nodded a hello to the gaunt man named Frank, but he didn't respond. She felt very small, standing amongst people who didn't seem to like her. Except for Simon, he of the Armani suit. He seemed warmer than the rest.

"Who are you?" Rosalie pointed to the Youngbloods who had followed Serena into the house. They were still in the entryway as if an invisible barrier kept them from coming in any further.

Serena cleared her throat before introducing them to her grandmother. Rosalie didn't respond. Instead, she turned her attention to Serena.

"Are you ready?" she asked. "You, Simon and Lilith have a flight in a few hours and need to get to the airport."

Serena's tongue stuck to the roof of her mouth, this was it. She turned and hugged the couple who had stood by her over the last several days, months, and years. They each hugged her tightly.

"We will be praying for you," Mrs. Youngblood whispered. "Call when you can sweetie."

She couldn't speak past the lump lodged in her throat. All she could do was hug back the older woman. Simon walked back to the door, his hand on the knob, making it evident that it was time for them to go. The door shut behind them and a chill seeped into her soul. As the door closed, the lock clicking seemed to echo in the silent house. It was over now, wasn't it?

She excused herself and escaped to her room where all of her clothes had been packed the night before, along with three pictures of her mom, dad, and sister.

She leaned against the closed door, staring at the shadows of her past life. Window blinds remained closed. The twin beds with matching headboards sat across from each other; a dresser stood between them. A stack of her favorite childhood books sat on one of the corners of the dresser. *The Wind in the Willows* was still on top of the pile with a bookmark sticking out of it. Her mother had left it there the night before she died. Serena had never been able to finish it. A layer of dust had settled on it.

The tears that she had swallowed all afternoon fell then. Her face crumbled in grief and she slid to the floor as a silent sob shook her frame. She was alone, truly alone. No hands to hold hers, no one to soothe her to sleep after a bad dream, no one to argue with or laugh with or eat with. Suddenly there was a sharp rap on the door she leaned against.

"We have to go, Serena. We need to go through security before we get to the gate and you never know how long that will take."

"Okay," her voice cracked, betraying her pent-up emotions. She swallowed the rest of her tears and breathed slowly in through her nose and out through her mouth. Just like Dad taught her to. Here, in the dark room of her childhood bedroom, she whispered goodbye to the ghosts that would always haunt her memories.

***

Once they arrived at the airport and went through security, Serena walked past the row of seats in the waiting area, choosing instead to stand at the window and watch the planes take off and land. Dad had taken her with him to many of his different conferences, and he always made the plane rides exciting. Even as she got older and pretended she was too cool to enjoy them, he could still coax a smile out of her.

Simon joined Serena at the window and handed her a wrapped sandwich.

"I'm not hungry."

"Our first flight will take us to Seattle, which will take an hour and then onto Telluride. It's going to be a long trip with a couple of layovers. I know you're not hungry, but you need something to eat."

She took the sandwich but didn't open the plastic wrap. It smelled good, but her stomach was in knots at the moment.

"Suit yourself." He left her side.

Serena glanced behind her to see what Lilith and Simon were up to. Lilith sat with a magazine in her lap, but she flipped through the pages too quickly to actually be reading it. Simon was texting someone.

She looked back at the tarmac and watched a plane taxi to their terminal. Overhead a female voice announced they would be boarding in a few moments and to gather their carry-on bags. Both Simon and Lilith

8

grabbed theirs. Lilith had only her black purse and the magazine she had been looking through. She raced to the front of the line as if she was trying to put as much distance between her and Simon as possible. Or maybe it was between her and Serena.

"Come on, Serena." Simon stepped up beside her and gently put his hand on the crook of her arm. "It's time to go."

She nodded, unable to speak. She made it as far as the entry of the well-lit tunnel and then had to stop for a moment. Simon stood in front of her, watching, waiting.

In her mind, she heard her dad's voice cajoling her to keep going even if she was scared. "Come on, Serena," he would always say before making a pithy remark that would encourage her to continue. The one that came to mind this time was the last one he used. "True strength is keeping everything together when everyone expects you to fall apart."

She forced herself to take a slow breath in like he'd taught her; Pulling her arm from Simon's grip, she lifted her chin, rolled back her shoulders, and took that first step. It was time to be strong.

Chapter 2--Saturday Afternoon

First class. For Simon, it would only be first class. But this plane was small, so it was closer to business class, and Lilith could tell her husband was annoyed.

Lilith was annoyed too, but for an entirely different reason. Damn. She needed a drink.

She watched Serena walk down the narrow aisle toward her. She looked like her mother, except not. Her mother wouldn't have allowed anyone to see her in a pair of jeans that had more holes than fabric and a sloppy t-shirt that fell off one shoulder. Of course, what else could you expect when a girl grows up surrounded by college students? There were some differences between mother and daughter, no matter how much they resembled each other. Where Crystal's untamed black curls had flown freely down her back, Serena's hair was long, textured to thin out those same thick curls so that only a slight wave bent her hair and highlighted the dark purple weave. Her slender frame was similar to her mother, but where Crystal stood at 5'4 and seemed as fragile as fine china, Serena was four inches taller and possessed a magnetism that she most likely didn't realize was there.

But despite the differences, Serena still had her mother's face, dainty nose (though Serena had a small nose ring in hers) and full lips. Everything except her eyes. Her eyes and the shape of her brows were from her father. They were round with long, spiky lashes, but it was the color that arrested Lilith. It was the same jade green, with black and gold that streaked from her pupil to the outer rim like lightning. They were just like Simon and just like the matriarch of the family--Rosalie.

Maybe it was the innocence of Crystal's cornflower blue eyes that had attracted the two brothers. After he met Crystal, Lilith had lost Simon's affection overnight. *No, be honest*, she said to herself. *You lost him the year before, hadn't you?* And she knew why.

But it wasn't just the ghosts that haunted their relationship. It was also because Crystal had been everything Lilith was not--soft and kind to

Lilith's hard-edged bitterness. And as she watched Simon follow Serena past each row of seats, she could see his desire flare up once again, a craving to own his niece whereas he could never own his brother's wife.

Lilith's stomach turned inside out, but she swallowed the bile creeping up her throat, shuddering as she did so. She quickly scanned the plane, desperate for something to drink.

Lilith only moved her knees to let Serena pass by her to the window seat, then she moved over one seat so that she would be between Simon and the girl.

She met his glare with one of her own and lifted her chin to show her subtle defiance. He couldn't do anything without causing a scene, and she knew it. He gritted his teeth and sat down, pulling out the newspaper from the side pocket of his coat. Simon shook the thin paper to show her that she was going to get it when she got home. She looked away, past Serena, and out the window to the concrete tarmac.

Serena seemed oblivious to the silent exchange between Lilith and Simon, which made Lilith glad. If she'd noticed anything, payback would be worse than it already was going to be.

Once they were steady in the air, the flight attendant rolled her cart to each seat, and as she approached their row Lilith's mouth was watering, wanting, no, *needing* a drink. This had already been a long day, and it wasn't over yet.

The cart stopped beside Simon.

"Would you like a drink, sir?" she asked.

"No, but thank you."

He waved her away, and she clattered to the next row. Lilith's heart sunk. Of course, he'd do that. She'd known he would pay her back and this was his punishment. How stupid she was for angering him before the drinks were passed out. She swallowed the saliva that had accumulated since she'd seen that stupid cart and turned her head back to the window.

Chapter 3--Saturday Night

The flights from Eugene to Seattle to Telluride Regional Airport was exhausting. By the time they reached their final destination, Serena was nearly asleep.

The trip to Simon and Lilith's house was a short one, which was good. The hum of tires on concrete lulled her into a twilight sleep. When she woke, they were climbing a steep gravel road. Five minutes later, Simon stopped at a gated entry, pushed a few buttons and waited as the gates slowly opened, flanked on either side by stone and concrete and trees that hung low. Once they passed through, the view was stunning. Manicured lawn sloped up to a stately log and stone house surrounded by gigantic spruce trees. Thirteen-foot windows faced her on either side of a rock chimney centerpiece that matched the stone pillars they had just driven through. A faint wisp of smoke rose into the night. Lights from the inside cast oblong shadows onto the lawn and gave Serena a glimpse of an open beamed ceiling inside. On the left side of the house were more windows and floors and one room illuminated where the fireplace was. The other windows, however, were dark. And the siding was odd compared to the rest of the house. This siding was one of wood slats. Simon continued up the paved road. The driveway circled the back of the house and stopped between the house and a huge garage. There were three parking spots between the two buildings and Simon took the middle one.

Lilith got out of the car before he turned the key off. He sighed as they watched her plow through the double doors and slam them behind her. He hit a button on the dashboard. A faint pop of a trunk opening sounded behind her. Simon opened his door. Serena followed his lead, gasping at the cold air that hit her face.

While he pulled out her luggage, she did a complete turn, scanning her surroundings.

"Looks like it may snow tonight," Simon said.

Serena looked at the door through which Lilith had disappeared.

Lights hung below an arched brick entryway leading to the double doors of the house. Serena turned to her right and looked at the garage. That building was two stories and matched the house's exterior. At the top of the smaller building was a dark circular window. The grass behind the garage was a little longer, but it matched the front lawn, manicured. It climbed even further up the hill until it reached a natural fence of trees. To the left a sheer drop off bordered the lawn. Her stomach flip-flopped. She hated heights.

"How do you like your new home?" Simon interrupted her thoughts.

"It's quite..." she grappled with the right word, "majestic." Even to her ears, that word sounded dramatic, so she didn't blame Simon when he chuckled.

"Majestic, huh? I haven't heard that one before. It must seem a hell of a lot better than that shack you grew up in."

Serena looked at him, no longer captivated with her surroundings. "I'd take my 'shack' any day over this monstrosity of a property."

His charming smile hardened. She lifted her chin and matched his tight smile with one of hers.

They stared each other down a little longer, ignoring the freezing temperature and snow flurries that began to fall around them.

Uncle and niece.

Same eyes as Dad, she thought.

He broke the staring contest first. "Let's go inside." He picked up her two suitcases and carried them up the steps, disappearing through the double doors. She followed.

It was a grand entryway behind those double doors. A black gothic table with claw foot stands, reminding her of dragon feet, stood on hardwood flooring. Two long tapered candlesticks with melted wax at the top and black wicks stood in front of two large lamps, flanking an exaggerated oval mirror, reminding her of Snow White's stepmother.

Mirror, mirror on the wall. . .

Simon turned on one of the lamps. It didn't help warm up the ominous entrance. Instead, it intensified the dark shadows. He kept walking, and she slowly followed him, glancing at the mirror hanging on the wall. Her face was stark white and her hair disappeared into the background. Something caught the corner of her eye, and she turned to see what it was. Nothing but the door stood before her.

A warm glow beckoned her away from the eeriness.

The clean, earthy scent of cedar filled her senses as she breathed in deeply. The large floor to ceiling windows she'd seen from outside flanked the stone fireplace making it even more stunning. A wood mantle stretched across the fireplace where a roaring flame warmed the room and her insides. Two more candles stood on either side of the mantle. Another oval mirror hung at a slant so that it reflected her and the room in which she stood.

Wide wooden stairs matching the outside steps circled upwards to a second story. Another set of stairs climbed from that floor to a third story. A large leather sofa sat facing the fireplace. It matched the two Victorian-style overstuffed chairs, but they were older than the sofa with their dark wood frames and claw-feet, marrying the long-ago style with the present day.

The living room was stunning in its own right, but her eyes were pulled to the view beyond. The snow flurries from only a few minutes ago had turned into large clumps that fell to the ground as if they each had coal inside of them.

Whispers behind her made Serena turn around. Lilith stood in the kitchen. She continued her low whisper as she pulled out a platter of cold cuts and crackers from a refrigerator. Serena's stomach growled in response.

"It looks like Claudia was here today," Simon said.

"Claudia is always here," Lilith replied. She glared at him as he stood in front of the fire, warming his outstretched hands. "Not that you would know that."

"You don't live here?" Serena asked Simon.

"No, I live in Santa Barbara where I run the family business."

"Oh? What is the family business?"

"I'll tell you about it later. Back to Claudia," he said. "A little word of advice: Don't bother her when she comes to clean on Saturdays."

"I take it Claudia is your housekeeper."

"Try live-in maid," Lilith said.

"She lives in the wing where you will be. Her bedroom is just above yours, so if you hear footsteps, that's her.."

Lilith interrupted, "She's also very private about her space, so do not go up to the third floor. That's her living quarters. If she finds you up there, she'll make your life a living Hell."

"Stop it, Lilith. She's not that bad."

"You don't live here, remember. You're not around when she's in one of her moods. She's only calm when you're here."

Simon rolled his eyes. "Don't listen to her. She can be a bit histrionic. I'll take your suitcase to your room."

Serena turned to find food on the counter behind her. She snagged a cracker and a cut of roast beef. Lilith pulled out two shot glasses and a bottle filled with dark liquid from the cabinet. She poured a little bit of the alcohol into both glasses with a shaky hand and slid one of them to Serena. She tipped her glass and said, "Cheers."

"Drink it," she added when Serena didn't pick her cup up. "Trust me, you'll need it."

"Is Claudia really that bad?" Serena lifted her glass and swirled the liquid around.

"Worse." Lilith poured a second glass and threw that one back too. "She loves Simon, so she hates anybody who takes his attention away from her."

"How come you haven't fired her yet?"

"Because she came with the house."

"What?"

"She was Simon's nanny when he was growing up." Lilith swallowed another shot. "He'll never throw her out."

"Oh."

"Now, drink little girl. It's the only thing that'll keep you warm tonight."

Following Lilith's example, Serena took the glass, threw back her head, and swallowed the liquid. Only half of it went down. She choked on the rest as it flamed down her throat. She sputtered and ran for the sink as she coughed most of it up. Lilith laughed behind her, then she drained her fourth shot in one swallow. She put it in the sink, then walked past the stairs, disappearing into a room beneath them.

Serena shook her head. Who gives a seventeen-year-old whiskey? She set her glass in the sink next to Lilith's and left the bottle on the counter. The log stairs seemed steeper when looking upward. She could feel the heat of the little bit of alcohol she'd had spread to her fingers, toes, and soul with each step.

At the top of the stairs, she stopped. She was met with two hallways, one to her right and one to her left. The one to her right continued into sheer black. The one to the left had a light at the end of it. Every few feet was a window that connected the ceiling to the floor. She turned back to look down the other hall. Why was that hall so dark? Were there no windows on that side? She tried to recall the house from the outside, but she couldn't remember. She shrugged and turned left toward the light.

She stepped out of the darkness and into a lamp-lit room. Her eyes scanned the bedroom: high ceiling with open log beams and a stone fireplace with a window seat to the right. It was almost an exact, albeit smaller, replica of the massive stone fireplace in the great room. Wooden slats closed her view to the outside world.

A wrought iron double bed stood to the right, next to an antique dresser with an oval mirror above it and a low seat next to it. Another taller dresser was on the left with drawers out, next to it, her open suitcases. She could see Simon hovering over them, though his back was to her. She stood and watched, curiosity outweighing the vague eeriness of watching someone go through her things.

Simon had already pulled out a few of her sweatshirts and laid them in a drawer. He froze when he pulled out a picture frame, then stroked the glass, as if it was the face of someone he loved. Serena shifted her weight. The wood floor creaked, startling Simon. He dropped the picture inside the suitcase and spun around. He gave her a charming crooked grin that would've made any woman weak at the knees. It only touched Serena's because it reminded her of dad.

"Hey," he said.

"Hi." She couldn't bring herself to take the last step into the room.

"I was helping you unpack," he said as he drifted toward the door, "but you're probably old enough to do that yourself, huh."

"Yeah, I think I can do it." Her legs wanted to give out from sheer exhaustion. She put her hand on the bedpost to keep herself upright as well as to look nonchalant. "Thanks, though. I did have a question. Why won't my cell phone work? Is there no signal up here?"

"Not a strong one, it comes and goes. Give me your phone, I'll get it set up for you. If that doesn't work, I'll get you a new one."

She pulled out her phone but hesitated. If she gave it to him she suspected she wouldn't see it again. "No, that's okay. I didn't have many friends back home anyway. I'll keep it."

"You sure? I can do it right now. I have the password here in my noggin." He tapped his temple like he was knocking on a door.

"Okay." She unlocked her screen and handed it to him.

He tapped in the Internet password and handed it back to her. "Bear in mind, this signal is iffy. If it's snowing, like it will tonight, you probably won't be able to use it."

"Thank you, again." Maybe she had him wrong. Perhaps he wasn't a bad guy.

"No problem." He brushed by her and gave her arm a comforting squeeze. His footsteps sounded down the hallway but stopped halfway. A disembodied voice said, "I'll be gone in the morning. Lilith will get you registered for school on Monday. Have a good night's sleep, Serena." His steps faded down the hall. She shut the door behind him.

Her room was quite cozy, with a large sky blue throw rug over the polished wood floors and the bed was under a gilded picture frame of a woman from another century sitting at a dresser much like the one in her room. Her face in the mirror seemed to look past it as if she was watching Serena. She looked away, ignoring the picture and the chill in her heart.

The bed was covered by a white down comforter and large blue pillows that matched the rug. A china doll, dressed in blue, rested against them. The doll's eyes were closed as if she were sleeping. Serena's breath caught in her throat. She always liked china dolls and the artistry used to make them look real, but she didn't want one lying on her bed.

She picked up the doll to set her aside, and the eyes opened. Serena almost dropped it. *Just a doll*, she reminded herself. Her father taught her that the mind could play tricks on you when you're tired like she was at that moment. At the thought of her dad, she went to her suitcase and pulled out her pictures of her parents and sister.

She propped two on the dresser. The one of her father she held to her chest as she went back to bed. She just wanted to lie down for a few minutes before she finished the unpacking. In a minute she fell into a heavy dreamless sleep, completely unaware of the one who covered her with a blanket.

Chapter 4--Saturday Night/Sunday

Simon lay in bed, arms folded behind his head, and watched the snow continue to fall. His mind was upstairs in Serena's room, thinking of her mother's picture. It had been nearly 12 years since the accident, an accident that shouldn't have happened but did. He had been crushed when she was suddenly gone, her infectious laughter no longer to be heard, her bright smile no longer to be seen. So, to have Serena in his home, almost a carbon copy of her mother, was surreal.

What wasn't surreal? Lilith. She was still very much there, haunting every hallway and every room, if not physically, then mentally. They slept in separate rooms with the living room between them. He wondered if leaving Serena at the house was a good idea. Would Lilith harm Serena while he was gone? Worse yet, would she turn Serena against him? He couldn't have that. He hadn't searched for that girl for so long just to lose her now. He had plans for her.

Lilith was not the only one he had to worry about in this house though. According to his wife, Claudia was becoming a nuisance, a very real and dangerous one at that.

He threw back the covers and began his yoga ritual. The stretching and balancing pose connected his mind to his body. When he finished with his last stretch, he settled down and assumed the lotus position, centering his spirit within his physical form. He could hear better that way. There was another dimension within this home. The spirits of that dimension would often relay their secrets to him when he was most relaxed.

He traveled through the living room into Lilith's room. She was in a deep sleep, a drunken stupor rendering her incapable of doing anything malevolent. At least, not tonight.

Next, he traveled up the stairs, down three hallways, pausing only to glance at the dark door across from Serena's room.

"Remember our deal," his mind projected. He felt the agreement confirmed. Then he traveled toward the other bedroom and through the door.

He found her asleep, huddled under the pile of blankets that left her head and face barely visible. He looked around the room. She had locked the door behind her. He saw the pictures of his brother's family staring down at Serena. Even in the dark, he could feel his brother's eyes upon him. He looked away from Jonathan's photo and turned back to Serena. He drifted closer to her bed, wishing he could touch her. Long dark lashes fluttered lightly as if she was waking up, but she wouldn't, she couldn't. Her breathing continued in a steady rhythm. She would have a headache when she woke up a few hours from now.

Above the room, he heard Claudia's heavy footfalls. What was she doing up this early in the morning, prowling around her rooms? He supposed she could be readying things for her husband to come home. Rosalie often took him with her to pose as her driver or stand-in husband whenever she left her New York home. Claudia hated her for that but was powerless to stop her. Sometimes he felt sorry for the woman who had practically raised him once his mother had become far too busy to do so, but Claudia had changed since he was young. The years had not been kind to her, both in mind and body.

He turned his attention back to Serena, whose eyes were beginning to open. How was she doing that? He had cast a spell that put her in a heavy sleep.

A ticking clock sounded in the distance; it began pulling him away from Serena. What was happening? He always had control, but the pulling sensation was too intense to ignore. He felt his soul being sucked back through the door, the halls, stairs, and bedroom, slamming him into his body. His eyes shot wide open as he gasped. The stupid ticking on the small clock pounded in his head as if it were a loud gong. What just happened? He always had control of when and where his conscience roamed, especially in this house, on these hallowed grounds.

His jaw worked, clenching and unclenching — three o'clock.

The alarm on his phone began to vibrate on the bedside table. It was time to leave.

He grabbed the duffel bag sitting in the corner and threw it on the bed. His thoughts went back to Serena as he dressed. Would she be safe here? He'd wanted to bring her to Santa Barbara with him, but Mother had put her foot down.

He sagged back down to his bed. Would Lilith go after her one night? She was more than capable of it. He knew that from personal experience. But it wasn't just Lilith that worried him. It was also Claudia. Claudia could be as sweet as apple pie, but she could also be volatile.

He shook his head and stood up. He'd have to visit more often to make sure they didn't all kill each other. He packed the rest of his clothing and then put on his heavy boots. He'd need to change halfway through the flight since he'd be arriving to sunshine and balmy temperatures. He couldn't wait.

Before walking out the door, he left a few hundred dollars on the counter and a brief note telling Lilith to take Serena shopping. She wouldn't have the right clothing for this weather, and he didn't want her walking around in ripped jeans unless they were designer ripped jeans.

The brisk walk across the driveway woke him up even more. The girls would be snowed in today unless Henry, the groundskeeper, would drive them.

Speaking of Henry, he stood at the car door waiting to drive Simon to the airport. As the SUV engine warmed, Simon looked back at the house. It was gigantic, with many secrets he hoped Serena would never discover. Between Claudia, Henry and Lilith she wouldn't be able to leave without someone knowing. Mother was right, maybe it was better to keep her here. He grimaced. He hated it when Mother was right. He glanced at his wristwatch. Time to go. He removed his coat and climbed up into the car. He saluted the silent mansion. "'Til next time."

Henry pressed the gas pedal down carefully; the tires caught traction propelling them down the road at a snail's pace.

Chapter 5--Sunday Morning

Serena woke thirsty with a pounding headache. Light peeked through the wood slat blinds at the windows. What was creepy the night before was now just a cold bedroom.

She eased out of bed, her feet dropping a few inches onto the fluffy white rug beneath. She didn't remember the bed being so tall last night, but everything seemed different in the light of the day. She crossed the floor to the windows and opened the blinds. It was still snowing, and the mountains above, beneath and surrounding the house were all dressed in white.

Her need for the restroom and a drink of water pulled her away from the stunning scenery outside. She took care of her bathroom duties and ventured out into the hallway once again. She stood, looking down the opposite hall from her room. There were windows in that direction too, but the light seemed to be dimmer than her side. The bathroom door closed behind her, making her jump.

Serena shuddered, and hugging herself, she walked down the hall that lead downstairs. A scuffle of footsteps behind her made her stop. Slowly she turned around, but no one was there. She gulped and began to walk more quickly this time.

She stepped onto the balcony looking over the great room. The windows across from her revealed a scene much like the one from her bedroom, but these were more expansive and set off the mountains beyond with such stunning clarity, she gasped at the view.

Her eyes traveled down to the ground floor where the scene was much less spectacular. The curtains were closed, a dying fire sparked and sizzled in the fireplace, and a sleeping form was on a couch so large it seemed to swallow her up. It had to be Lilith. Serena followed the stairs down to the ground floor and walked to the kitchen. Her feet froze from the stone slabs that covered the ground. She'd have to remember to wear socks or slippers the next time around. A box of whole wheat cereal sat on the counter with a room temperature carton of soymilk next to it. She decided on the leftover platter of cheese, crackers, and cold cuts from the night before.

"Did you sleep well?"

Serena looked over to see Lilith sitting up and facing her.

"Yeah, I did."

"Hmmm." She rose from the couch and began stacking wood that had been on the hearth into the mouth of the fireplace. Serena watched Lilith's tall, wraith like frame. Her shoulder blades were sharply defined beneath the black turtleneck she wore. She stuck wadded up newspapers in the crooks and crannies of the stack she was making then she struck a long match and lit each wad. The flame gathered energy, growing larger with crackles and sparks giving the living room life. Serena gradually began to thaw from the inside out.

"There's coffee in the pot and creamer in the fridge if you'd like some."

"Thanks." She searched for the coffee mugs and finally found them. They all matched, unlike the ones at her house, where all of them were mismatched and from different places. Suddenly very homesick, she swallowed back the tears. Not here, not now. Her hands shook as she poured the coffee.

Lilith pulled back the curtains to allow the light in and settled back on the couch.

"Would you like some coffee?" Serena asked.

"Hmmm. Yes, coffee would be good."

Serena warmed a second cup. "Black or with cream?"

"Cream and some sugar." Her voice was barely audible.

Serena brought her the cup, steam floating up to her nose. She handed her aunt her cup and then sat beside her, sipping her coffee, feeling the warmth seep in. Lilith sat beside her, sipping her coffee, one leg crossed over the other, her eyes glued to either the fireplace or the snow. Serena couldn't tell which.

"Simon's gone," she said.

"Oh good," Serena replied, but then caught herself, unsure if she should've said that in front of Lilith.

Lilith gave a mirthless laugh, "That's what I thought too." She took another drink. By now their coffee had cooled down, so she finished it in one last gulp. Lilith stood and walked to the kitchen, put her mug in the sink. Without saying a word, she went back to the door behind which she had disappeared the night before and vanished once again, leaving Serena alone. So much for bonding.

With nothing else to do, Serena drank the rest of her coffee. She glanced at the fridge. She should eat, but she had little appetite.

She walked to the spiral staircase and ran her fingers along the satiny railing as she climbed the stairs. Her room was on the second floor, but the stairs continued its climb to the floor above her.

Who was this Claudia? Serena's interest was piqued from the night before when Simon and Lilith warned her about the housekeeper. Was she as scary as Lilith made her out to be? She couldn't be that bad. Right?

Serena continued down the rest of the hall and turned left, ignoring the mysterious door at the end. It was the late night and exhaustion that had tricked her eyes into thinking there was something spooky down there.

When she entered her room, she found it completely clean. The bed was made like it had been the night before, the suitcases were gone, the pictures stood on the dresser that held her clothing. Gooseflesh traveled up her arms. The idea that someone had been in her room left her chilled. She didn't want to be in the room any longer. Needing a shower was a good excuse to leave it. She grabbed clean lounge pants and an oversized t-shirt.

The wood floor creaked under her feet as she went down the hall to the bathroom. Again there was shuffling of feet behind her. She flipped on the bathroom light and turned, but still found nothing but darkness. She gulped then shut the bathroom door and locked it.

A fluffy white towel hung next to the claw foot tub. She showered and dressed in clean clothes and went back to her room. The makeup dresser did make a good place to comb her hair. She sat at the vanity and pulled gently at the snarls. The girl facing her did the same. They looked identical but different somehow. Serena felt weary, but her reflection seemed alert and skeptical as if judging herself. Or was the look more accusatory? The guilt of turning off the machines haunted her again.

"I didn't have a choice."

The girl repeated what Serena said, but her stare was unrelenting and unforgiving. She was at fault for her father's death.

He'd been coming home to see her and tell her something important He had called her and to tell her she needed to pack and be ready to leave. She had been arguing with him on the phone when his car left the road and ran head-on into an old garage.

Serena shut down her mind to the memory and climbed back into bed, waiting and hoping for sleep to take her away. Just as she drifted off, Lilith interrupted with a short rap on the door.

"Time to get up," she said.

"Huh?" Serena sat up, foggy headed.

Lilith stood in the doorway putting on an earring as she spoke. Her hair was pulled back into a bun, and she wore a simple black turtleneck tunic that showcased a long silver chain and large oval locket, and black trouser pants.

"What are we doing?" Serena asked, rubbing her face.

"We're going into town to buy you new clothes." Lilith walked briskly to the dresser and opened the second drawer. She pulled out a pair of jeans and wrinkled her nose. "And it's no wonder. Where did you find these? Some second-hand shop?"

"As a matter of fact, I did." Serena hopped off the bed. Angry, she stomped over to Lilith and pulled the jeans out of her aunt's hand.

Lilith smirked at her. "That's why we're going on a little shopping spree. You have twenty minutes." She walked past Serena to the door and looked back to say something else when her gaze stopped on one of the pictures. Serena followed her stare and saw her mother's picture. Lilith's hands tightened into fists. A look of disgust replaced the smirk. She turned and left the room.

Serena went to her door, meaning to slam it as hard as she could when she saw Lilith stop at the bathroom. Instead of turning to go downstairs, she stood facing the dark hallway. Her stiff shoulders sagged downward as she sighed.

Serena knew that sound. Suddenly she didn't want to slam the door. Lilith turned to leave, swiping at the tears on her face. Serena closed the door quietly.

Thirty minutes later she finally descended the stairs. Lilith was tapping her fluffy snow boots that looked too pretty to be functional.

"It's about time," Lilith said. She grabbed her purse and walked to the front door, leaving Serena to follow. She found her slip-on ballet style shoes and wished for Lilith's fur-lined boots. A grizzled man with gray bristle on his face and a deep scowl stood waiting by a dark green Excursion.

He said nothing as he opened the door for her. She walked through the snow, immediately freezing her feet. She would get a pair of nice jeans, boots and maybe a coat if there was money left over. She had brought with her a blue pea coat, but it wasn't nearly warm enough for winter in Colorado.

Lilith sat in the passenger seat and ignored Serena completely. The drive down the mountain was slippery. Her stomach was in knots by the time they hit the main road. Once they got on the road though, she pressed her face so close to the window, that she began to fog it up. She felt eyes on her and turned to find the man staring at her.

He looked away first to watch the road.

When they arrived in town, she was surprised to see it wasn't all that big, but it was charming in its beauty. She felt like she'd stepped into a Christmas snow globe. People with coffee cups and gloves milled around, looking through the windows of storefronts.

They got out of the car. Lilith spoke quietly to the driver, and then he got back into the truck and slowly drove away.

"Come on," Lilith said. There was a lightness to her step that Serena responded to.

"I take it you like shopping," she said as she walked carefully through the snow and slush.

"Yep, it's one of the things I'm good at," Lilith said, and then under her breath added, "one of a few anyway."

Serena wasn't sure if she was meant to hear the last part, so she didn't respond to it. "Where are we going to first?"

"We're getting you a coat, boots, and gloves."

***

Five hours and three thousand dollars later, with three gigantic bags between them, they made their way slowly down the street. Snow flurries floated down around them. Serena glanced at her aunt and saw how pretty she was. Her face was peaceful, no scowl, a soft glow on her otherwise porcelain skin and her black hair was still in the perfect chignon from when they left the house. Serena glanced at her reflection in one of the windows. Lilith had been right when she said she knew how to shop well. Serena had never looked this nice before. But just as soon as the admiring feelings came, the guilt came following after. She was enjoying this, but she wasn't supposed to be enjoying anything yet. The faint smile on her face disappeared.

Her head was down, looking at the muddy slush on the road when she ran into Lilith who'd stopped suddenly. Serena followed Lilith's gaze. A young man stood across from them. Serena couldn't figure out his age. His black hair was short on the sides and long on the top, some of it falling into steel blue eyes. And they were just as cold as steel too. His jaw was clenched even from across the street

Lilith, however, looked like she'd seen a ghost. The porcelain skin of just a few minutes ago was now ashy gray. Her look wasn't one of anger though. It was one of disbelief. What was going on? If Serena didn't know any better, she'd swear they had had a lover's quarrel, their looks were that intense. Either that or they always hated each other. Her head

25

went back and forth from her aunt's face and the boy in the Doc Martens and bomber jacket.

After a few minutes of giving Lilith a death stare, he finally glanced at Serena. This time it was his skin that went completely gray, as he looked her straight in the eyes. He stared questioningly at Lilith and then back at Serena. Serena looked at Lilith too. Instead of glaring back at him, the older woman seemed defeated.

Lilith turned away first and began marching further down the sidewalk, demanding that Serena catch up. But she couldn't. She was stuck in place, nailed there by the boy across the street. She didn't notice Lilith come back until fingers dug into her upper arm and pulled firmly. It broke the stare. A car passed by, splashing some of the muddy water on her new boots.

She followed Lilith, stumbling a little bit with Lilith's grip pulling her off balance. When she turned to look back at the boy, he was gone.

Chapter 6--Sunday Afternoon

Lilith couldn't believe it was Jesse. She'd told him to leave, but he hadn't.

She could see his surprise when he saw Serena. It wasn't that she looked like Stormy, but their eyes were exactly alike. No one could forget those eyes. Her mother-in-law, Rosalie, called them 'bewitching.' And they were.

That was why she clutched Serena's arm and started walking as fast as she dared in the snow. Lilith would not stop, could not stop until she got to their meeting place. She hoped Henry would be there. He hadn't let her down yet, but there was always a first time for everything, right?

They rounded the corner of the building and crossed the public parking lot. There it was — the black Excursion. Henry was getting out and opening the back door. She handed him the bags of clothing and took Serena's bags too.

"Get in the car," she commanded.

"Who was that?" Serena finally asked.

No answer.

"Did you know him?" She was still looking out the window behind them. Lilith watched her from the corner of her eye. Serena finally turned forward and heaved a sigh. "Never mind. You're probably not going to tell me anyway."

Sometimes no answer was the best answer of all.

Lilith continued to look forward, clasping her hands in her lap to keep them from restless movements. She ignored Henry's questioning glances. Once they arrived back on the mountain, she'd tell him what happened, who'd she seen. He knew as much as she did. He was her confidant and a bit more.

No one spoke as the large vehicle effortlessly wound its way around the slushy curves. The temperature had dropped in the short time since leaving town. It would be cold tonight.

By the time he turned onto their private road, daylight was quickly running away, as if the night had bullied it out of the sky. Henry paused to shift into four-wheel-drive and then started up the steep incline. Serena's heart calmed as they climbed higher up the mountain. The house wasn't exactly home, but it was at least a refuge from the cold weather and frigid people outside.

The parking lights at the house were bright in the surrounding darkness when the truck came to a stop in front of the garage. Henry left the engine running as he hopped out and opened the doors of the truck for their bags of clothing. Serena was right behind him, leaving Lilith alone for a moment to gather her thoughts.

***

With bags in both hands, Serena managed to open the door to the house. She glanced back, assuming Lilith was right behind her, only to find her in a heated discussion with the driver, hands waving in the air. She couldn't see Lilith's face, but she could see Henry's, and he seemed just as angry as Lilith, or maybe it was alarm at whatever Lilith was saying. Serena wished she was close enough to hear their words, but since she couldn't, she stepped inside. As soon as she cleared the entryway, the door swung closed. Was there a sensor on the door, like the ones at grocery stores? She looked up to find what looked like a video camera. It seemed odd to have one inside and not on the outside. She shrugged and continued into the living room.

The white snow beyond the windows made the open living space even more bright and airy. It was a beautiful area, with the open beams high above her head and the great stone fireplace before her. Above the mantel hung the grand, gilded mirror that looked like it was a family heirloom. It was gold in some places and tarnished black in others. Curious, she stepped closer to it, catching her reflection. She was pale, unrecognizable to herself. She saw her own eyes narrow. The accuser was back. Serena needed to move, to keep moving, or she would disintegrate into tears on the white, fur skin rug. She picked up her bags and walked up the stairs.

Her room was cold when she walked into it. She'd have to find a way to warm it during the night, although she hadn't noticed it when she slept the night before. She dropped the new clothes bags into the corner beside the dresser. She'd put them away later. For now, she needed to rest. She sat down at the window seat and stared at the snow-capped mountains. Her mind shifted back to the boy she saw on the street.

Who was he? And why was Lilith so freaked out when she saw him? The boy seemed just as surprised to see her too, only his look had

28

changed abruptly to shock when he had noticed Serena. She wished she could've seen into both of their minds at that moment.

A tinkling chime sounded just outside her closed door.

"Hello?" she called out. She got up and crossed the room. "Lilith?" She opened the door to find no one there. A deep chill spread through her chest. Again an invisible chime sounded. She didn't waste time. Barely keeping her fast walk from an all-out run, she rushed down to the living room.

The great room seemed to have gotten colder since she had left. Lilith hadn't come back inside, so Serena used her adrenaline to her advantage. She busied herself with starting the fire in the fireplace. By the time she had stacked the wood into a pyre and stuffed the paper in the crooks and crannies, she was lost in memories of her father.

***

Lilith remained behind in the SUV while Serena got out and went into the house. Jesse was not a factor Lilith counted on. Simon had wanted Serena homeschooled so there would be less interaction with others, but that wouldn't work in the long run. They had to keep up the pretenses, that meant sending her to the local high school. Besides, Lilith didn't want Serena poking around the house, which she was apt to do when she was finished with her school work. Rosalie agreed with her on that point, so the decision was made, and Serena had been enrolled before she'd even arrived. The stipulation from Simon was that Henry would drive her to school every morning and pick her up every afternoon to ensure her interaction with the other kids would be minimal. Lilith had a feeling this would backfire on him, but he never listened to her, so she hadn't bothered saying anything

Now, with Jesse in the picture, how would this affect Simon's (and for that matter, Rosalie's) plans? A part of her didn't care, in fact, she'd love to see Simon fail epically. That being said, his failure would cost her something too. No, she wouldn't allow this kid to screw up Simon's plans, but she wasn't going to tell Simon about him either. If for no other reason than for Stormy's sake.

What concerned her more at the moment though, was how to keep Jesse and Serena separated at school. As soon as Jesse had seen Serena Lilith knew he had questions. His surprise had momentarily left him vulnerable, but the walls went back up after the shock. She knew from previous experiences that he could hide anything and everything behind a stone facade. It was what kept him alive because no one knew how much he'd learned about their family and who he might have told.

A cold blast of air cleared her head, chasing away her obsessive thoughts for the time being. She took Henry's outstretched hand and climbed out, trusting him to keep her steady.

Lilith walked to the back of the car to help bring in the bags but found the job had already been done. Henry swung the barn doors shut and turned to her to hand sign his questions.

"What happened back there?" he demanded. His hands flew faster than some people could talk.

Lilith signed back, almost as fast. "Remember Jesse?"

"Yes."

"I saw him in town."

Henry's hands stopped moving for a minute, his face registering the concern she was feeling.

She went back to signing again, answering his question before he could ask it. "No, I don't know what we should do about it. I warned him. This just made our job more difficult."

His hands began to move again.

"We're just going forward with Simon's plan unless something comes up."

"And if something does come up? Because you know it will, don't you?" He pressed on the issue he knew she was struggling with, "Will you tell him about Jesse? And Stormy?"

This time it was Lilith who stopped signing. She shrugged her answer instead.

"You can't keep this a secret, Lil. You're going to have to come clean with it to Simon. The longer you wait, the angrier he'll be, but that's nothing compared to Rosalie, and you know it."

She began to sign again, this time slower. "I know. Let's do what we can before we tell them. Take her to school as the plan called for, watch her, and watch for Jesse. Our presence may deter him from coming forward."

"Or not."

"Or not," she agreed.

"What about telling the teachers in the school? They can be on the lookout for him."

"Let's wait on that for a bit."

"Why do you protect him?"

"Why do you think?"

He nodded. He knew.

"I need to go inside. Thanks for taking us to town." These words signaled to Henry that the conversation was over.

"Okay."

"You'll need to be ready for her at around six thirty tomorrow morning."

"Are you going with us in the morning?"

"I'm not sure just yet."

Lilith turned to the house and began walking, her boots crunching on snow that was beginning to harden from the cold. She could feel Henry's eyes watching her, but before walking through the door, she turned to find him gone. She hoped he was still on her side and not texting Simon with the information she had just shared.

The entryway was dark given the dimming light outside. One candle was lit, allowing her to see where she was going. She paused to take off her gloves and rub her hands together. She refused to look in the mirror. She didn't want to see the reflection that would be staring back at her.

She felt, more than heard, a creak of the wood flooring behind her. Her heart lurched her forward. She refused to run, but she moved out of the entryway quickly.

Lilith found Serena at the stone fireplace, lighting bits of paper that were tucked into the crevices of the stacked wood. The fire spread, crackling as it did so, engulfing the wood.

"Who taught you to start a fire?" Lilith asked as she peeled off her coat and hat and threw them on the chair beside her.

"My dad."

Of course, Jonathan would have made sure she knew these things. Lilith walked to the kitchen. There should be two microwave dinners in the freezer. She paused though as Serena continued.

"Our house is an older one. Sometimes the heater wouldn't work, so on really cold nights we would light a fire and sleep out in the living room. I always loved those nights the most."

Her voice was quiet, barely audible in the large room. She stood pushing the wood with the iron poker, stirring up the fire. Lilith glanced up at the mirror above Serena to see if tears were falling. There weren't any, not yet anyway. Any minute Serena would hiccup a dramatic sob, like Stormy would sometimes, but Lilith wouldn't hug this strange girl with her daughter's eyes.

However, the tears never came. Instead, Serena's gaze rose up to the mirror above her and locked eyes with Lilith. Crying she'd expected, but not this defiant stare. Lilith was about to look away but realized that if she did, she would lose any control she had over Serena. She needed to stare her down first. Serena felt the same way because she didn't look away either.

Just around the time Lilith was wondering if she should give up the battle, Serena did. Her eyes finally cast down to the fire again. She heaved a deep sigh. Lilith let out the breath of air she'd been holding too, but much more quietly. She didn't want Serena to know how this contest of wills affected her.

She couldn't remember what she was doing before the awkward stare. Dinner. That's what she was going to do next. First, though, she would need to turn on the lamps in the darkened room. The shadows were growing longer. She walked around the room turning on lights. Noise would be good. The TV remote was on the coffee table, and she picked it up. The widescreen glowed as it warmed up. She dialed in the channel number that she knew by heart. *Frasier* filled the screen, his voice filled the room.

Lilith walked back to the kitchen, pulled out two dinners and began to heat one of them. Serena moved from the fireplace and sunk into the oversized couch. She was exhausted, but Lilith refused to take pity on her.

The microwave dinged. Lilith stirred the food in the little tray and then set the microwave again to finish the cooking. When the machine dinged again, Lilith transferred the food to a plate, poured a glass of milk and brought it to Serena.

The girl's eyes were nearly closed. Lilith set the milk on the coffee table and shook Serena awake. "Eat," she said.

Serena sat up and began eating. By the time Lilith sat down in the overstuffed chair, half of Serena's food was gone. She had taken over the couch entirely. The sleep she had been fighting earlier had won.

Lilith watched the rest of the show as she finished dinner. Episodes of *Frasier* turned into the show *Friends* that turned into *Dharma and Gregg*. She didn't hear a word they said or laugh at any of the jokes. Her mind was too tired to follow the storylines. Eventually, she glanced at the clock in the corner of the TV and was surprised to see it was already eleven o'clock. She clicked off the tv and looked at Serena. Did she wake the girl up and send her to her room? Nah, what would it hurt for her to sleep downstairs tonight?

She took a throw blanket from on the opposite side of the couch and covered Serena. Lilith went into the kitchen, poured a glass of whiskey, shut off the lights and went to her room. Morning would come too soon.

Chapter 7--Sunday Night

Lilith left the lights on in her bedroom. They would stay on all night. Claudia was taunting her, coming downstairs to bother her when she knew the agreement was that she had the third floor and Lilith had the first and second floor. Simon never returned her calls or concerned emails giving detailed information about Claudia. And now she was always left with the feeling of being watched.

Lilith took off her yoga pants and put on her pajamas. She walked to the small bar in the corner of her bedroom and poured another shot of whiskey and drank it. Then she poured another and another and took the last one with her back to bed. Regardless of the pain, she would have to stop drinking the following night. If she didn't, she wouldn't be prepared for Rosalie. Unpreparedness was not an option with that woman.

Memories played on the giant screen in her mind. She remembered watching *Entertainment Tonight*, a show she didn't watch anymore.

They were covering a red-carpet event that Simon was attending. He and his business partner Azazel were becoming big names in the Hollywood Industry. She had met Aza several years earlier. He was an intense man with his dusky olive skin, deep-set eyes, so dark they could easily be black, and a clenched chiseled jaw. He had given her a tight smile and an almost painful handshake.

After he passed the cameras, Simon came into view. He was striking too, in a different way. It was not just the green eyes and dark brows that he shared with his brother and mother, nor his fit build beneath the cut of his Calvin Klein suit; it was his dynamic personality that drew the crowd in. What they didn't know was just how savage both men were. And they were not alone. The silent third party in this company was Rosalie, perhaps the most ruthless of the three.

An unknown woman accompanied Simon that night. Her overt flirting and barely harnessed cleavage insinuated her position as his assistant. Lilith had sat on the couch and cried. She knew the truth but seeing it was different. She felt Simon had betrayed their family.

She drank the last shot of whiskey, set the glass on the bedside table and lay down. The pain of finding out about Simon was still as raw as it was that night she had watched the show. She had sworn she was done with him forever. She did not call, text or email him again.

He came home two weeks later, and she came unglued. There had been a lot of screaming and yelling. He left the next morning before she woke up.

This year it would be different. This year there would be no yelling or screaming. Only quiet tears, nothing else would be permitted. This year, this coming weekend, Serena would be there, but worse yet, Rosalie would be here too. Her memories fogged up like warmth on a window on a cold winter day. The alcoholic effects passed through painful memories and settled into pleasant drowsiness. Sleep finally claimed Lilith for the night.

Chapter 8--Sunday Night

Serena's fingers dug into the rough-hewn rock, opening her skin in the process. Darkness surrounded her, making her disoriented, but she could tell from the echoing water drops and the roughness of the floor that she had to be in a cave. She also knew she was in a dream.

She stood up and turned around to face what was behind her. In the far distance, she could see a pinpoint of light. She began walking toward it.

At the mouth of the cave, she found herself standing in a meadow of dead grass. Fog ebbed and flowed through the dead stalks, waving in a breeze she couldn't feel.

"Hello?" she called. No one answered.

She turned to look behind her, but instead of a cave, it was the mansion she now called home. The house looked different though. It wasn't made of stately logs, it was made of old wood, weathered by wind, rain and in some places, fire. The whole house looked more like an old barn than a winter chateau and seemed as if it would collapse at any moment.

She felt as if she was being watched from behind. She slowly turned around. In the distance, she could see someone floating on the sea of fog. The figure of a girl, her dress flowing wildly around her, was too far away to see clearly. Her black hair whipped around her, blocking her face. The fog carried her along, and the girl's frame began to fade out from her feet up until she was only a torso.

The girl called out, but Serena couldn't understand what she was saying.

"Wait!" She waved to her. "Where are you going?"

The girl drifted further, riding on the fog bank, which was carrying her away, faster and to the edge of the mountain.

Serena screamed and pushed her legs up the hill, moving with speed she wouldn't have in the real world. "Wait!" she called out. As Serena gained ground, she was able to see the features of the other girl.

Her eyes, the shape of her brow, the same length of lashes, the same color were a mirror image of Serena. She slowed down in shock.

The girl on the fog bank screamed, her face twisted in terror, and Serena moved faster, but the fog that carried the girl away began to entwine itself up Serena's legs. She felt like she was running through tar.

She pushed herself. Serena reached out, almost grasping the fading fingertips when the ground dropped beneath the girl.

Help me! The girl screamed as she disappeared off the cliff.

Chapter 9--Monday Morning

Serena woke to a dry throat, tears on her face and Lilith standing over her, watching intently. Dressed in black, she blended in with the darkness surrounding them. Her pale face, accented by the black circles under her eyes, gave her a skeletal appearance.

Serena trembled uncontrollably, too scared to make a sound. Her teeth chattered as Lilith drew closer. The click of the lamp beside them brought light to the room. It chased away the confusion of sleeping or waking, but her heart hammered in her chest. "Having a bad dream?" Lilith asked.

"Yeah," Serena struggled to sit up. The couch cushions made it difficult to do so. Looking around she realized she had slept downstairs in the living room. "What gave it away?"

Lilith ignored the sarcasm, "You were crying out in your sleep or at least attempting to."

"I'm an active sleeper," she lied.

Lilith crossed her arms, "No you're not. It doesn't matter, it's time to get up anyway."

"What time is it?" Serena stood up as soon as Lilith walked into the kitchen.

"It's five-thirty."

"That's early."

"You're going to school, remember?" She pulled out a roll of bagels from a cupboard above her. "I figured you'd want to take a shower before leaving."

Serena headed for the stairs. "How much time do I have?"

"An hour. Henry will be driving you down to the bus stop."

Thoughts of school, Henry driving, and Lilith standing over her when she woke encompassed her mind, chasing away the remnants of the dream. She had all but forgotten it until she was standing underwater, feeling the streams of water massage her shoulders and back. She lathered her hair with shampoo. The girl's face suddenly appeared behind her closed eyes and the dream replayed itself like a movie.

One of her friends at the college told her that dreams were her subconscious giving information that her waking mind couldn't figure out. If that were the case, then she figured she'd see her father, not a strange girl, falling off a cliff. She shuddered despite the heat of the water. That dream still felt real to her.

She turned off the water and opened the shower curtain. A fluffy white towel hung on the hook beside her. She dried off and wrapped it around her body, then combed her hair.

Cold air met her when she opened the door, making it extra chilly after being in the warm bathroom. Her door was open, a lamp inside, guiding the way. She was about three feet down the hall when she heard the sound of a door shut behind her. The light from the bathroom still shed into the hall, so it wasn't that door. The only other door it could have been was the door far into the darkness. Bumps covered her arms, but for an entirely different reason.

She only felt safe when she got to her room. There would be no need for caffeine this morning with all the adrenalin flowing through her. The old fashioned clock beside the bed read six o'clock. She needed to hustle. She shut the door so she could dress. A sense of watchfulness hovered above her.

She made a 360-degree turn of the entire room. No one was there. Maybe it was the picture of the Victorian-era woman above the bed or the doll sitting straight up on the bed, her pretty blue eyes looking her. Only now, two little girls were resting against the pillows. Where had the second doll come from?

Serena whipped her towel off and threw it on the dolls. They were creepy. She opened the top drawer and grabbed her underwear and bra, and then opened the drawer beneath it. Her new clothes were already folded nicely inside. Did Claudia do that? She must have. Having a maid was nice, but one she had not seen yet was odd. She should have run into her at some point, right? Had she left the new doll this morning? Of course, who else would it be?

Serena pulled out the new skinny jeans and red-wine sweater. A half hour later, hair blown straight and make-up on, she came down the stairs. She half expected Lilith to be back in her room, but she wasn't. The fire was roaring in the fireplace. Lilith sat in one of the chairs, coffee cup in hand. Regardless of the large expanse of the room, with the lamps on and flames flickering in the fireplace, the room seemed to shrink a bit and feel much cozier.

"There are bagels on the counter," Lilith said. "Henry will be ready at seven."

Serena was halfway through her third bite when she remembered the new clothes in her drawer.

"Did you or Claudia put my new clothes away?"

Lilith turned to look at her. "I didn't."

"Yeah, I didn't think so," Serena forced down the bite of bagel. Lilith stared at Serena, her eyes round. If Serena didn't know any better, she'd say it was fear.

"You haven't seen Claudia have you?" she asked Serena.

"No."

"Huh." She was silent.

A knock on the door startled Lilith.

Clumping boots in the entry alerted Serena to Henry's arrival. He nodded at her.

"I'll be right out," she said hopping off the stool she'd been sitting on. Her new boots sat by the wall where Henry stood. He seemed to sense her apprehension of getting too close. He exited the way he came in, clumpy and wordless.

As Serena was putting her boots on, Lilith came to join her.

"Serena," Lilith spoke just above a whisper. "Don't talk about Claudia, not out loud. I don't want her downstairs. I don't want her to think she can come down any day besides Saturday. You cannot invite her into your room either. She doesn't belong there." Her voice was trembling now.

"I didn't invite her." Serena matched Lilith's quietness. "What's wrong with you?"

"Nothing is wrong with me. Just trust me on this. You don-- " Lilith stopped talking, then sighed. "Never mind for now."

Serena turned to find Henry silently observing them through the window. "Does he have to take me?"

"Would you rather walk?"

"Can't you drive me?" she pleaded.

"I do not drive."

Serena was about to ask why when Lilith cut her off.

"You're going to be late. Your bag is next to the front door. All lunches have been paid for the year."

Serena was puzzled at Lilith's abrupt change in demeanor. She was all business now; only a little fear lurked behind her eyes.

"Go on, you're going to be late." She followed Serena to the door, handing her the new coat she'd bought the day before and all but pushing her out of the house without actually laying a hand on her.

Serena stepped out in the cold air where a snowy wonderland surrounded them. The lights on the garage and set around the driveway made the outside prettier. It was still dark beyond the lights though. Henry stood next to the same vehicle from the day before, with the door opened. She didn't bother saying goodbye to Lilith, even though she stood beside her. Serena sighed, her puff of air visible in the cold. She walked across the cleared driveway then hopped into the car. She didn't look back as Henry drove down the mountain to the bus stop.

***

Lilith watched the SUV disappear around the corner. Chills ran up her arms as she stood in the foyer. She was being watched again. She rubbed her arms against the cold. Though she wanted to be inside, she wanted to be free from scrutiny. Finally, unable to stand the cold, she went back into the house and shut the door. The phone rang. Even without caller ID, she knew it would be Simon, and she knew what he wanted. She couldn't do it. She wouldn't do it. Not today.

Instead, she went to the kitchen, pulled out a bottle of whiskey and began to throw back shot after shot after shot as the phone rang and rang and rang.

Chapter 10--Monday

Serena and Henry sat silently in the Excursion. Between the still dark sky, humming motor and the heater warming the cabin she probably would've fallen asleep, but not this morning. This morning she was wide awake as they waited for the school bus. She still couldn't believe she was going to an actual high school. She'd argued with her father for the last few years to let her attend any one of the three schools around them, but he'd stood firm in his decision. She wasn't allowed to participate. He continued to take her with him to the university. Serena did her schoolwork online in his office while he taught his classes down the hall. Finally, in her sophomore year, he enrolled her in the dual credit program where she could get both college and high school credit at the same time. She was allowed to go to a couple of classes on campus, but they were in the same building as him. Any classes that took her away, even if that building was across the street, she would have to take online.

She had very few friends because her father controlled that part of her life too. Oh, the fights they'd have on the way home from school. She'd been tempted to run away. Not forever, of course, but just for the night. The problem with that idea was that she didn't have any friends she could stay with, except for the Youngbloods, and they'd call her father as soon as she showed up.

She would've never left him because the thought of leaving him alone in his house, driving to school alone, living life alone, kept her from doing anything rash. She knew his reasons for holding her close was out of fear of losing her like he'd lost her mom and sister. Despite her frustrations with him, Dad was still her best friend, or had been. Yeah, she hated the seclusion, but they did have good times too. She missed running with him around the track in the afternoons, rain or shine. Even when she didn't want to go, he'd make her. She sighed. She was still under someone's thumb. The only difference was that her father had acted out of love.

Henry shifted in his seat bringing her back to the present. Headlights flashed on the trees and road, and a large bus emerged from around the corner and came to a stop. Car doors slammed shut and two other kids her age walked to the bus. The bus door opened for them and the noise from inside traveled to Serena. They knocked their boots against the first step to shake the snow off and then climbed up the stairs. Henry sighed but still didn't speak. He stared her down. All of her previous excitement was replaced by apprehension.

She gulped and then opened the door. The chill nipped at any area where her skin was exposed. She wished she'd worn her hair down instead of up in a messy bun on the top of her head. No matter, she could fix that later. She pulled her backpack out from where it had been sitting between her legs and swung it on her right shoulder, slammed the door and stomped through the snow. She copied the other two students and knocked her boots against the first step before climbing in. The loudness she'd heard from outside assaulted her as she took that first step. She took a second step and then looked up at the driver. His mouth opened a bit in shock before it closed. He didn't address her at all. He shut the door behind her.

The cacophony of just a few moments ago became a low hum and then halted altogether as soon as she turned to stare down the length of the bus. The looks on their faces weren't so much curious glances. She expected those but ones of fear took her by surprise. She had never been stared at like this before. Her stomach twisted in response. She squared her shoulders and raised her chin and walked down the aisle. Her gaze faltered on one face in particular. He was the same guy who'd scared Lilith the day before. Of course, the only empty seat was the one next to him. She felt every eye on her as she drew closer to him. That old cliché of time standing still applied to this moment. He scooted closer to the window so she'd have a place to sit. She sat, the lights went off and the bus lurched forward. The noise stayed at a low hum, people whispering instead of yelling over each other. She was confused by the weirdness. Yes, she was new, but she didn't have two heads.

She waited for him to speak. The longer he remained silent, the more awkward it became. Of course, she could say something first. She opened her mouth to speak and was immediately interrupted by a guy a few seats up from them.

"Hey Jesse, does she remind you of anyone?"

"Shut up, man," the kid next to her responded. The other guy just laughed.

Jesse, huh?

She turned to him, ready to introduce herself and ask him about the previous day, but he'd shifted his focus to the world outside his window. She returned his silence with hers and looked out the front window.

The trees outside gave way to the empty downtown main street that she and Lilith had walked the day before. The bus continued through the town, leaving it behind, taking the road to school. The bus slowed down as it fell into line with others. By the time the bus pulled up to the school the students had already begun standing and grabbing their backpacks. She watched them file into a single line down the aisle. The air brakes released and the door opened allowing the students to escape.

Serena was frozen in place. She had never been in this position before, without an ally and completely lost as to where she was supposed to go first. She knew her father's building and the professors in it. She knew the entire school's layout. This not knowing was foreign to her. She hated the feeling. Her stomach felt like a beehive.

When the kids in the seat next to her stood up and started down the aisle, she knew it was her turn, but her legs felt wobbly. Jesse cleared his throat.

"Are you waiting for an invitation?"

"Sorry." She stood and pulled her backpack upon her shoulder, then started down the aisle. The driver didn't look or speak to her. But seeing Jesse following her, he said, "Have a good day, Jesse. Say hi to your sister for me."

"Will do."

Serena paused at the bottom step. *I think I can, I think I can.* She wasn't sure she could, but did she have much of a choice?

"Hey, it's time to get off the bus," The driver's voice forced her to move, causing her to bump into another student walking by the doors.

"Watch it." A male voice startled her.

"Sorry." She froze as a group of guys clad in letterman jackets passed her.

"Hey," her seat partner called to her. "Do you know where you're supposed to go?"

She turned to find Jesse a few feet away. He wore a long green army coat from the 1940s, a t-shirt, jeans, and Doc Martens. "The front office. I don't know where it is."

Jesse walked over to her. "Didn't Lilith give you the map?"

She shook her head.

"Of course not," he grumbled. "Why would she help anyone other than herself?"

"You don't like her, I take it."

"Do you?"

She shrugged. "I don't know yet."

He shook his head. "Come on, I'll show you where to go." He began walking toward the school and she fell into step with him. Her two steps matched his one step. He was tall. She hadn't realized it on the bus or from across the street, but he had a good six inches over her, and she was tall herself. The way he held his head high and shoulders back made her feel like a dwarf in comparison. "Do you know what your first class is?"

"No. Lilith told me to go to the front office and they would give me my schedule."

He nodded. "Okay." He led her through the front doors and down a maze of halls.

Shrill laughter from the girls and guys yelling at each other overwhelmed her. Lockers opened and slammed shut. She flinched every time. She continued walking beside Jesse. He bumped into the other kids, but they didn't yell at him; instead, they moved out of his way. He commanded respect, or maybe it was fear, from every student. She also noticed the halls quieted as they passed by. At first, she thought it was him, but then realized they were looking at her. The guys were watching her, curious with raised eyebrows, and the girls? Well, the girls were openly glaring. Fresh meat and competition. Great. She squared her shoulders that had previously rounded subconsciously and lifted her chin. She felt Jesse's eyes on her, but she pretended not to notice. He stopped at the door and opened it for her. She stepped through, grateful to be out from under the stares. The bell overhead rang loud, signaling the start of school.

As soon as the door closed the noise faded into a distant thunder. A silver-haired woman looked up from the counter. Smiling eyes met hers. She glanced at Jesse. Her smile vanished.

"Jesse. Why aren't you in class?" Serena jumped at the woman's loud bark.

"Just showing the new student to the office, Mrs. Flinch."

"You can go now." She stared him down, and he returned it.

"Yes, ma'am." His voice was just as harsh as hers, but Serena didn't jump at it. "See ya," he told her, and then he exited the office.

"Do yourself a favor, young lady, and keep away from that boy." She shuffled papers together. "Now, what can I do for you?"

"I'm Serena Kelly. Lilith told me to come here. I'm a new student."

"Aah yes, that's right. I should've recognized you immediately." She turned to a wide-screen computer beside her and began typing. "We've been waiting for you. I have your schedule and a map of the school so you can figure out where to go." The printer across the room hummed and a moment later two pieces of paper slipped out of it. Mrs. Flinch walked across the expansive office behind the counter, took the papers and brought them back to her. "Here you go. Go out this door, turn right, then left, and then right again. Your first class is in room number nine. Mr. Gordon is the teacher. Don't worry sweetie, everyone is happy to have you here. Have fun."

Serena doubted the other kids were happy to have her, but who cared? Mrs. Flinch went back to her paperwork, effectively ending the meet and greet. Serena sighed.

The halls were quiet except for the echo of her feet bouncing against metal lockers and linoleum. She followed the directions and found the classroom without getting lost. The teacher's voice could be heard through the glass-window door. She pulled it open and stepped inside.

Every eye turned to her and then the whispers began.

"You must be Serena," the teacher interrupted the non-verbal interaction between the students and Serena.

She turned to him, reached out and gave him a firm handshake like her father had taught her when she met the professors around the university. "Serena Kelly."

"Yes, I've heard of you." His voice was effeminate, and his skin, hair and pale eyes were all white. She had never met an albino before. "I'm Mr. Gordon. You may have a seat in the back over in there in the corner."

She followed his pointed finger to the only open seat and desk in the front row. A textbook was already waiting for her. She walked across the room, which seemed small compared to the lecture halls her father taught in. The chair made a loud sound as it scraped on the hard floor. She felt every eye on her when she sat down. The teacher began talking about something in Europe. There were page numbers on the whiteboard, opened books and a droning teacher. The next forty-five minutes dragged on.

Four class periods, four subjects. Geography, math, science, English. Lunch.

At lunch, she saw Jesse again.

The cafeteria was louder than the hallway from earlier in the morning. Students were everywhere, sitting on tables, leaning back in chairs, hanging off each other. She wasn't sure she wanted to eat, but knew if she didn't she'd be starving by the time she got back to the house.

With lunch tray in hand, she scanned the large room for a table, preferably in a dark corner. She spied one in the far back of the cafeteria which meant she'd have to cross in front a ton of kids to get to it, but it was the only empty one. She took a deep breath, blew it out, and started walking. Fortunately, the kids were too distracted to notice her. She sat in the shadows, facing the crowd.

The food wasn't as bad as she expected. She ate quickly and then leaned back in her chair and watched the crowd. Each table marked the clichéd cliques in high schools everywhere. The jocks at one table, cheerleaders at the next one, nerds at the next two, rebels at another, and everyone else that landed in the middle. It was the crowd of "rebels" that caught her eye. Some of the kids were Goth, some were just odd. One girl had dark teal hair that accented her features. She wore a beret and was in a deep conversation with a girl with hot pink hair, which, unfortunately, did nothing for her. The guy sitting next to her was Jesse. Serena noticed the teal-haired girl was watching him. Obviously, she liked him. He didn't notice, or he didn't care.

He wasn't talking with anybody. He was watching Serena, studying her as she studied others. She was tempted to look away but refused the urge. He cocked his head to the side. The one side of his mouth raised in a half smile. They sat there, in a staring contest until the bell rang, signaling the end of lunch. He stood and left without a backward glance. The rest of the day ran slowly.

When the last bell rang, Serena ran for the bus, taking the first open seat. When her stop came up, she was relieved to see the black Excursion waiting for her. Henry's silence was welcoming as she leaned her head against the cold window.

Day one was over. Now, she just had to get through the rest of the year.

Chapter 11--Tuesday

Serena woke to Lilith standing over her. Again. At least this time she was in her own bed, in her room.

"Jeez!" She jumped. "You have got to stop doing that."

"I always find adrenaline to be a good alarm clock."

Serena closed her eyes. "You know I have an alarm clock on my phone."

"No, I didn't realize that." Lilith's voice sounded further away. Serena opened one eye to find her aunt walking around her room, lightly touching the dresser and opening one of the top drawers.

"What are you doing?" Serena raised herself to the sitting position, every joint and muscle screaming. Her dream lingered, making her feel as if she was still in it. Memories of mornings like this came back. Mornings of waking after a lucid dream, often her dad sitting beside her, murmuring prayers as he stroked the damp hair off her face. This time she wiped her hair off her face and whatever dream she had been having left her mind.

Lilith was still, watching Serena.

"What?"

"I wanted to make sure you were going to stay awake."

Serena's phone buzzed and sang an eerie tune. She needed to change the sounds back to the classic screeching alarm clock. She reached for her phone and turned it off. "Well, I'm awake now, so you can leave."

"Coffee is ready whenever you are." Lilith turned for the door. "There's cream in the fridge and sugar in the little bowl."

"Thanks."

"I'm going to town today; let me know if you need anything." She closed the door behind her.

"Okay." Serena was wide-awake, with an odd sense that she was not alone. Every shadow in the room deepened as if the lamplight had dimmed. She needed to get out of that room, but like a six-year-old afraid of the monster under the bed she sat frozen, unable to set her toe to the floor. "Come on Serena, you have to get out of bed," she coached herself. At the count of three, she leaped off the bed. Tempted to run, she forced herself to walk in the hallway, feeling that to run would make her look like prey, which would be odd since she was the only person there. She flipped on her bathroom light when she got to the door.

"Good grief," she chided herself. She glanced in the mirror to find mascara smeared under her eyes. The extra few minutes it took to clean her face, add fresh makeup and straighten the rat's nest of curls, made her feel more grounded, reminding herself of who she was. She was still the girl from Pleasant Hill, just displaced for the time being. She'd go home though as soon as she graduated.

Back in the bedroom, she quickly changed, but instead of choosing one of the new outfits, she wanted her own clothes. She needed to be herself today. She decided on her favorite pair of jeans. Next was her favorite deep olive green tee, matching one of the colors in her eyes, with a little bulldog on the left breast that said "Pug Life." She wrapped one of her dad's flannel shirts around her waist and slipped on a pair of socks. She glanced in the oval mirror that hung above the antique vanity. Yep, that was her. And she was going to be late, just like she always was at home.

By the time she got downstairs, Henry was already there, drinking a cup of coffee.

"You are going to be late," Lilith said.

"Yeah, sorry about that. Time got away from me."

Lilith waved away the apology. "I don't care. Henry can always drive you to school if necessary. I made you oatmeal, it will keep you warm this morning."

"Hey, thanks." A bowl sat in front of a stool at the counter. She hated oatmeal but touched by Lilith's moment of caring she grabbed a "thank you" bite. She finished the entire bowl, drank some milk and then put her boots on. "I'm ready," she said to Henry.

Mute as always, Henry led the way. The truck was already running and backed up to the house. They rode in silence, and she sat feeling just as tense as the morning before. But she didn't have time to think this morning. The bus came around the corner just as they arrived and Serena stepped out into three feet of snow. She said a silent prayer of thanks for the tall fur-lined boots and the heavy jacket.

She stomped up the steps and the driver gave her a nod as she passed by. The bus quieted as she clunked down the aisle. She pushed off the hood, as she sat down next to Jesse.

"Who are you?" he asked.

She turned to look at him and found his stare to be one of genuine curiosity.

"Serena Kelly. Who are you?"

"Jesse."

He continued to stare at her. She stared right back and asked the question that she had wondered about since she'd first seen him. "How do you know Lilith?"

He finally looked away without answering her. His eyes shifted forward to the front of the bus. She waited for his answer, but he didn't give her one. She sighed and let the pent up air out of her lungs. It calmed her down. She waited.

He continued to look outside. "How do *you* know Lilith?"

She breathed in then out. Fine, she'd have to give a little to get a little. "Simon is my dad's brother. That's how I know Lilith."

"Why are you living with them?" He continued to look forward. The inside lights came on as the bus stopped to let another student climb on board.

She refused to give him an answer. "Your turn to answer: How do you know Lilith?"

He finally looked at her, surprise in his eyes. The lights turned off. He shrugged. Instead of an answer, he smirked, one side of his mouth going up in a half smile. She swallowed, thankful the lights were out so he couldn't see how he affected her. Sure she'd had crushes on the guys in class; they were obviously too old for her. But this guy? This guy stopped her heart, and it bothered her. This was a whole new game. A game she didn't know how to play because she'd never felt quite like this before.

He gave her a silent chuckle. His eyes flickered down to her mouth and then up to her eyes again. He shook his head slowly. "Huh. You look similar, but you're nothing like her."

She pursed her lips. She waited for him to explain, but he didn't say anything else. Instead, he turned his focus to the world outside his window. She returned his silence with hers and stared out the front window.

As soon as the bus parked, the door swung open. Everyone stood and began filing out in a single line. The crowd swept her along to the school entrance. She felt their eyes on her and quickly realized they'd edged away, giving her wide berth. What in the world was going on with everyone?

Serena followed the halls to her first-period class, or at least she tried to. She looked around for someone she could ask, but again, no one would get close enough.

"You must be Serena," a deep male voice startled her.

She turned.

"I'm Mr. Dawson." He stuck his hand out to shake hers.

"Hi." She put hers out too but instantly regretted it. His skin was cold, clammy and he smelled a little weird. She resisted the urge to wipe her hand on her jeans and smiled at him instead. It didn't matter what that cologne was, except that he shouldn't be wearing it.

"Are you lost? These halls can be a little confusing." She hated the idea of being escorted by a teacher. Unfortunately, she had no choice since no one would stop to even talk to her.

"Yeah, I guess I am." She shifted the backpack on her shoulder. "Here, let me show you where to go." He placed a heavy hand on her back with one hand and pointed the way down one of the halls with the other. "It's right down this hall."

With no other choice, she walked beside him. He kept his hand on the small of her back, preventing her from moving too far away. They arrived at the classroom, a different one than the day before. She was confused.

"This isn't my class."

"Sure it is." He took a folded piece of paper out of his back pocket. "This is our 'blue' day. Monday, Wednesday and Friday have one schedule. Tuesday and Thursday have another."

"Well, thank you."

"You're very welcome. I'm the computer lab teacher, by the way. I believe I have you in my class this afternoon." He nodded to her formally. "I look forward to it."

"Nice to meet you," She nodded back at him, then opened the door.

"Good morning. Glad you joined us instead of gawking through the window." The teacher stood but didn't bother with shaking hands. She wore a short skirt, professional looking, but still a little on the short side, which Serena thought was stupid given that it was freezing outside. Her blouse didn't look any warmer either. It draped her frame perfectly, but plunged a little low, giving a small peak at her fake cleavage.

"I'm Serena Kelly."

"I know. I'm Ms. Harold." She grabbed a book off the desk and handed it to Serena. "Assignment is on the board." She sat down, propped her high-heels on the desk and picked up whatever novel she was reading. Her skirt got shorter. Much shorter. Which would explain so many attentive guys in the front row.

Serena turned to find her classmates watching her. The only empty seat was in the back row, of course. In any other class, that seat would be the first one filled. Not here.

She walked around the desks, then paused when she saw who sat next to that empty seat. Jesse. He met her eyes. She set her book down and took a seat herself.

At lunch, she went through the motions of getting her food and heading for the table in the back corner. She wondered why others hadn't taken it. Everything was the same as the day before, kids talking and laughing, and she was on the outside watching and being watched as well.

She found him before realizing that she had been looking for him. Jesse sat at his table, the teal-haired girl beside him, practically hovering over his lunch tray, trying to engage him in any kind of conversation. But he wasn't listening. He was watching her. In the middle of whatever the girl was saying to him, he suddenly stood and walked across the cafeteria. He pulled out a chair across from Serena and sat down.

"Serena," he nodded his head toward her, then leaned back and propped his legs on the table, clunky boots and all.

"Jesse," She crossed her arms and leaned back.

He smirked and shook his head. "So where did you come from? Obviously, you're related to Simon in some way."

She smirked back at him. He wanted to talk now? Fine, but she would only give him as much information as he gave her. "Eugene, Oregon. And you?"

"I've lived here for so long that I don't remember being anywhere else.

She pursed her lips.

"I have a friend who moved to Eugene recently. What high school did you go to? Maybe you know him."

"I doubt it. I went to U of O."

"No way. That's cool. How did you get to do that?"

"My dad was a professor there. He liked having me close by, so he put me in a dual-credit program."

"Awesome. How did you end up here if he liked you so close?"

"He died." She took a drink of water to force down the lump forming in her throat. The raw shock of her dad's death took her breath away leaving her disoriented, the crowd's noise quieting to a muffled hum. Colorado, a cafeteria, a high school in the middle of a snowy valley. All of it surreal. A waking dream.

"I'm sorry." No joking in the guy's voice.

His voice woke her like a popped balloon. The noise of the room was back, the weird feeling had fled.

She looked up at him to find a soft, sympathetic face. She swallowed the tears, shrugged as if it didn't bother her to talk about father. As soon as she got her voice under control, she asked him something she'd been wondering about all morning.

"Why do you have a different last name if Simon is your uncle?"

"Honestly, I don't know. I have a question. Why is everyone looking at me funny?" She nodded to the kids behind him.

"Because you're the new kid in town."

"I know that. But this is different. It's like they're kind of, I don't know, distant. Like they don't want to get close. Afraid almost. They're watching us, but no one dares to join us. Even your friends over there." She pointed with her head. "What gives?"

"Well yeah, they're nervous about you. You remind them of Stormy."

"Stormy?" She prompted him. "And that is?"

"Oh, ha ha. You have a dark sense of humor, girl." He sat back as if he was waiting for her to come clean, but she didn't. As soon as he realized she wasn't kidding his feet came off the table, and he leaned forward, surprised. "You're joking around, aren't you?" His tone changed when he asked her again, "aren't you?"

She shook her head slowly. "No. Who is Stormy?"

"She's your cousin."

This time it was Serena who leaned forward in surprise. "Cousin?"

"You don't know anything about her? Didn't your families get together for holidays and stuff?"

"No. I had no idea Simon or Lilith even existed before last week, let alone that I had a cousin. They've never said anything about her."

"Wow."

"Where is she?"

This time Jesse looked away, back at the table where he'd been sitting. The teal-haired girl was openly glaring at Serena now. He didn't acknowledge her. Instead, he turned back to Serena.

"No one knows. One day she's hanging out with us, the next day she's gone. Her parents said she moved to Europe, studying abroad with her grandmother. She disappeared after a fire burned down most of her house. Lilith told me she was so traumatized that she had to move. It never made sense to us. She had friends here, but no one has heard from her since."

"When did all of this happen?"

"Three years ago."

The bell rang above them, signaling the end of lunch. Neither Jesse nor Serena moved. They studied each other, openly curious now. There were still questions, but no time to answer them.

Both of them stood at the same time and grabbed their bags.

"See you later. Nice talking with you Serena Kelly," he said.

"Yeah, see ya."

The rest of the classes went by way too slowly for Serena. So many questions ran through her head. Why didn't her dad tell her? He had to have known about Stormy. But if he did tell her about Stormy, then he'd have to tell her about Simon and Lilith.

She sat on the bus watching each student climb the steps, but none of them were him. The doors closed and the bus moved along. Deflated, she sagged against the seat. Why didn't he show up? Without Jesse there to ask questions, she was frustrated. He was the only link to her mysterious family. By the time she got off the bus, she was tired. The anticipation, anxiety, and weirdness of the day had caught up to her, leaving her exhausted and unable to think coherently. She was relieved to see the black suburban waiting for her. Henry's silence was welcoming as she leaned her head against the cold window.

Chapter 12--Tuesday

Of all the houses that Simon owned Lilith loved this one the most. Unfortunately, things change. People change. Even houses can change. And what used to be home was now a prison, and Claudia was the warden.

Lilith had grown up in mansions her whole life. Her father was one of the most wealthy men in the world, the most powerful too, so she knew how housekeepers should act. But Claudia brought new meaning to the word housekeeper. She didn't just manage the house for Rosalie, and then Simon when he took ownership of this land. She managed the people inside it as well. She didn't handle Simon or Rosalie so much, but she did "manage" Lilith, or attempted to. They had finally agreed to a middle road, once Simon had stepped in and settled things down, but he wasn't always there to make sure Claudia did what was ordered.

After Serena left for school, Lilith stood out in the snow because she didn't want to run into "The housekeeper," as she referred to Claudia. She was afraid that even Serena speaking the old woman's name had invited her downstairs on other days besides Saturday.

The house phone began to ring. She knew Simon was going to call her this morning. She reluctantly left the front porch and went inside. The phone stopped ringing as soon as she got to it, but it began to ring again almost immediately.

"Hello Simon," she said.

"No, this is Angel," a woman's voice purred. "Simon wants to know if Serena has gone to school."

Lilith rolled her eyes. She hated this woman. And she hated Simon for making her speak with her. "You tell Simon I don't talk to whores and to call me himself if he has questions." Lilith hung up before Angel could start yelling.

Thirty seconds later the phone rang again. Lilith picked it up.

"What am I going to do with you, Lilith?" Simon wasn't angry; he was barely chastising her. She knew he liked watching the power struggle between his wife and the 'secretary.' She also knew he respected his wife more because she was the one with the power, not Angel.

"You're going to start calling me yourself and not making your little slut do your dirty work for you. Honestly Simon, why are you even with her? She's a dingbat."

Simon laughed out loud. "Yes, she is. But why do you do the tango with good old Henry? To keep the bed warm at night?"

"Well, if you're doing it with your 'personal assistant,' why not Henry?"

"Touché."

"Look, Simon, we need to talk." She sighed and rubbed her forehead with her fingers. "Have you gone upstairs yet?" Simon's voice dropped to a quieter tone.

"Yes, but only to wake up Serena."

"Then we don't have anything to talk about."

"It's about Claudia,"

"Seriously? Come on Lilith. You're stronger than this."

"She's been in Serena's room."

Silence.

"You told her not to bother the girl, but she's been in there making the bed, putting clothes away, and who knows what else." The memory of her talk with Serena from only forty-five minutes ago dumped adrenalin into her system.

"You're sure?"

"Yes, I'm sure! Serena told me this morning."

"Was she upset?"

"I'm not sure about that. She seemed wary."

Silence again.

"Look, Simon, I'm not trying to be paranoid here, but I am concerned."

"No, you look. You need to handle this. I can't come back every time you get worried."

"I'm not sure what to do."

"Fine, I'll call my mother and she'll visit. Set Claudia straight on a few things. Would that make you feel better?"

Claudia or Rosalie? Which woman was worse? Rosalie was the only other person who terrified Lilith. Both women in the same house just might kill her. No, Rosalie was the last resort.

"Fine, I'll deal with it."

"Good. Now, go upstairs and search the room. It's gotta be in there somewhere."

"What exactly am I looking for?"

"Anything. Maybe a letter or a clue to where my brother hid it. I'm not sure. I know he had to have given it to Serena."

"If this is so important, and I know it is because you've explained it enough times, why don't you know what it looks like?"

"I don't have time to explain my brother or the powers he could harness. What I do know is that he was able to hide things that we've never been able to find." He sighed heavily into the receiver. "We don't have time for these questions, Lilith. You know your job, now get to it."

"Fine. But, I'm warning you, if Claudia keeps after us, I'm calling and you are coming back to deal with her."

"You need to find your backbone, Lilith."

Click.

She sat on the couch looking at the phone for a few minutes. It was now or never. She hated Simon, but he was right. She did need to find her backbone. She crossed the room and started up the stairs before she could talk herself out of it. *I can do this*, she whispered. By the time she reached the top of the stairs, she was feeling confident, but the first look down the hall leading to the reading room made her knees weak. She pushed her feet to move even though her brain seemed frozen in place. Going down this hall the previous day didn't faze her. She was on a mission to wake up Serena. Today, that mission was to search Serena's room for whatever Simon was looking for. But if he didn't know what it looked like, how was she supposed to know?

She had to get to Serena's room, look around, and get out before she ran into Claudia. The hall came to an end; on the right, Stormy's room, on the left, Serena's. There were six rooms in this house and Simon could have picked any one of them for Serena, but she knew why he chose this cursed wing. She put a mental shield in place to protect her from the debilitating memories and entered Serena's room.

Once inside Lilith could see Serena's clothes piled high on top of the bed, practically burying the doll that lay against the pillows. She hated that doll. It gave her chills to see it once again. Lilith looked away and started for the dresser. Three hard-bound books stacked on top of each other. The pictures of Jonathan, Crystal, and Anna faced her, but those didn't scare her, not like that damn doll. She searched through the drawers, pulling out underwear and socks. Nothing there. Next drawer, pajamas and lounge pants. Every drawer only contained clothes. Serena's clothes that she had brought with her. Where were her suitcases? She turned around to find the old wardrobe. Her old wardrobe. How in the world had Simon found it? She thought it was still in the attic. She glanced at her watch to see how much time she had. She had a sinking feeling that more time had passed than she expected. She was correct. It was around eight-thirty when she'd gone upstairs and it was already noon. The second floor always had its own timing--it could last longer than you wanted or fast forward in the blink. This time it had sped forward three to four hours.

She opened the double doors to find the suitcases and pulled them out. She unzipped the biggest case and searched every corner. Nothing. She put it back and did the same with the second one. Again, nothing. She scanned the room, hoping something would jump out at her. The clock surely did. Two o'clock. Seriously?

She closed her eyes and began to look with her mind. It was easier that way, but something blocked her from seeing. Her magic wouldn't work in the room. Why?

Her eyes flew open. The books on the dresser. Nah, it would be too obvious, but she had to look. She went to the dresser and opened the book on top, *The Wind in the Willows*. A bookmark between the pages fell out, and she shoved it back inside. The next book was *The Lord of the Rings*. No bookmark but there were frayed edges and dog-eared corners. It must have been read over and over again.

The third book was the Bible. It was leather with a leather tie to keep it closed. She handled it carefully as she opened it. Nothing jumped out at her except the inscription:

To Serena: May your faith move mountains and protect your soul. Love, Mom and Dad. May 5, 1995.

Lilith flipped through the pages. There was only small lettering on the edges and underlined verses, and she didn't care to read those. She shut that book and stacked the books as they had been originally. She glanced at her wrist again.

Three o'clock. She had to get downstairs before Serena got home. Dammit! Not finding anything meant she would have to come back every day until she found whatever it was that Simon wanted, and even he didn't know what it was.

She heard something scurry down the hall and all at once the room changed in temperature. She could smell her own body odor, sour from searching and fear. It was time to leave. Right now. She walked to the door and swung it open. The scurrying sound was from rats that raced down the hall. Her heart beat faster. She hated rats. There were ten of them, unafraid of her presence. Carpenter ants had joined them, large and threatening as they looked back at her.

Simon's words came back to her. *You need to find your backbone,*

Lilith. He was right, wasn't he? There had been a time when the ants or rats or whatever passing in front of her would scurry away. But these insects knew she wasn't powerful anymore. Grief had stolen that from her. She stomped her foot in frustration. It was time she took that power back, especially now with Rosalie returning. Head raised, eyes forward, she attempted to extort the power she once owned. Whether she liked it or not, she had to walk through this hall.

She stomped down the hallway. She had to go downstairs, not just because Serena was coming home, but because Claudia would be coming to inspect this floor soon, make sure all was neat, tidy and ready for its newest occupant.

Down Stormy's hall, the door creaked open, then closed again, nearly silent.

She was out of time. The housekeeper was already there, she had been inspecting Stormy's room first. Lilith quickened her step. Claudia was the last person she wanted to see. Lilith was breathing hard. Her body odor was even more intense than it was in Serena's room. She needed a shower. A glance at her wrist showed a watch frozen in time at three o'clock. She raced down the circular stairs, across the kitchen, living room, and closed her bedroom door just as the front door opened.

Chapter 13--Tuesday

Arms crossed, Simon stood at his office window overlooking the Santa Barbara coastline. It was a chilly seventy-five degrees. Most people loved this weather, and so did he, most of the time. Today was not that time. Tuesday. Three days until he had to fly back to Colorado. Three days until his mother would descend upon his house, upon Lilith, upon Serena.

This weekend was going to be Hell. What was she thinking? Never mind, he knew what she was doing. More to the point, she knew what she was doing. He only had a vague idea.

"Simon," Angel swept into the room. "Your mother wants to know when you're leaving for Colorado this weekend. So would I, for that matter."

He turned away from the view outside. Angel stood at his desk, rifling through stacks of papers. Her blonde hair was wrapped in a bun at the top of her head, making her seem taller, as did the six-inch heels that perfectly matched her haute couture ensemble. Her look was polished, her face perfect, her mannerisms graceful, and her voice airy and light like that of Marilyn Monroe.

The truth was, she was a conniving, power-hungry, catty bitch. Her voice could switch from airy to shrill in three seconds flat if all he did was look at her wrong. She reminded him of those women on reality shows about real wives. They looked pretty, until they opened their mouths and proceeded to thrash everyone.

"Leave my stuff alone." He walked to the desk and flattened his palm on the stack of papers she was searching through. "You can tell my mother I'll leave when I leave."

She flipped him off before leaving.

"Real classy, Angel," he muttered.

He would've thrown the stack of papers across the room but there was something in there that Angel wanted. He didn't want to risk her finding it. Instead, he put the stack inside one of his many filing cabinets and locked it. The phone rang through to his office. It was Angel. Of course. Transferring his mother's call.

He picked up the receiver. "Hello, Mother."

"All I need to know is when you plan to arrive."

Another shrill woman.

"Actually, all you need to know is that I will be there when you arrive. You are invited on Saturday. Are we clear?"

"Oh no, son. That's not how it works. You know that." The voice on the other end grew dark. "You may own that property by deed, but we both know it really belongs to me. I am the chosen one. I will be·there when I decide to be. I was merely being polite by telling you when I chose to visit. Next time I may drop in unannounced."

He hung up without giving her a response. He steepled his fingers and leaned back in his chair. The plan had been to fly up on Friday, but now he wasn't so sure that would be a good idea. Sooner would be better. Much better. He pulled out his phone and checked his calendar for the next few days. He had an important meeting with Aza on Wednesday. He couldn't miss that one. There was another meeting with one of his clients on Thursday morning. It would have to be that evening before he could fly out. He switched to a different app and set up a solo flight.

The weekend weighed heavily on his shoulders. A break from Angel notwithstanding, he was still left to play referee between his mother, Rosalie, Lilith, and Claudia. And somehow in the middle of all this, he needed to protect Serena.

Simon heaved a deep sigh and slumped in his chair. What was he going to do with this girl? There were so many plans he and Aza had for her, but they didn't expect her to be so strong. Breaking her down would be difficult, more difficult than he'd guessed. Aza was still intent on bringing her to their office, putting her through rigorous tests, but Simon wasn't so sure she was the right candidate. He wondered if his business partner would be as interested if he fully understood exactly what he was dealing with. Simon had in mind that Serena would be like Stormy, more pliable and demure, thus making her the right person to experiment in mind-control.

But Serena was not pliable, unlike her mother, Crystal. She'd been gentle, soft and kind. She would've been perfect for their molding. And that's who he thought Serena would be like all these years he'd searched for her. Instead, he'd found his brother's daughter.

Speaking with her the night before confirmed his earlier hunch, that he had just grabbed a cat by the tale. Like his daughter, Jonathan had been a strong force, fierce in dealing with those who came against him or his plans. Those things were why their mother had always preferred him over Simon, but those same traits would be the reason Rosalie would hate Jonathan's daughter.

Restless, he stood and paced the floor. Thinking, thinking. He would have to rely on the house to do its job. That house was built on land that could make the sanest man go crazy. It wasn't just the wind howling through the trees, it was the way it seemed to whisper a person's name in that wind. When it snowed, it always seemed that there was a being, a soul that took a form but one you could never be sure was there. And then there was the sense that the house itself was alive, a slumbering giant ready to wake at the appointed time, but no one knew what time that was. He wasn't sure his mother knew how to control it. Between all three things he often wondered if Lilith was going mad up there on that mountain.

He found himself at the window again, looking out over the ocean. The key to this weekend would be to act fast. Lilith would be a wreck anyway because of the anniversary, but throw Rosalie into the mix, and his wife could come out crazier than his mother.

Oh yes, then there was Claudia. He should've thrown her out years ago, but he hadn't. Now, when he wanted to, there was no way he could do it. He would never admit it, especially to Lilith, but he'd have to rely on his mother to do the job.

His cell phone vibrated in his pocket. He pulled it out and checked the text.

Aza: Are you ready?

He texted back: Yes.

It no longer mattered if he was ready. The time they'd been waiting for so many years had arrived.

Chapter 14--Tuesday Afternoon/Evening

Serena walked into the living room and was met by a cold, ashy fireplace. Lilith's closing door caught her peripheral vision. The scene beyond the windows was still beautiful, but she was too tired and too chilled to enjoy it. She dropped her backpack on the kitchen floor. The only way to bring warmth into her body was to start a fire.

She got the fire started. Her eyes blurred as she stood as close to the heat as possible, mesmerized by the flames, calmed by the silence after a day of clashing noise. She'd always loved this weather back home, except there it was usually rain. The outside world was only getting colder, both literally and figuratively. She saw herself in the reflection of the window and felt like a ghost herself, adrift in the land of the living, but dead to those she loved.

She pressed her hand against the cold glass and whispered, "Are you there?" Of course, he wasn't. He was six feet underground back in Oregon. Her head fell gently against the glass. The tears that threatened all day finally gave way. She missed her dad, of course, but with that feeling came confusion. They had told each other everything. *So how come he never told her he had a brother? Or that she had a cousin?*

Lilith's door opened. She would have answers. Serena followed Lilith to the kitchen and watched her place the frozen dinner tray into the microwave and start it. Lilith's back was still to her, but that was good. She may not have had the guts to ask if she had turned around and stared her down.

"Who's Stormy?" She watched Lilith shoulders hunch up and then sag down.

"You met Jesse, I take it."

"You had to know I would. What with it being a small town and all." Lilith didn't confirm or deny her assumption.

"Who's Stormy?" She repeated the question.

Lilith finally turned around and leaned against the counter, her arms crossed. "I'm sure he told you."

"Yeah, he did. I just wanted to hear it from you."

"Damn, if you aren't your father's daughter." The microwave dinged. She turned around and removed the plastic, stirred the food and restarted the microwave. Then pivoted to face Serena and took her previous stance.

"Stormy's my daughter."

"What happened to her?"

"What did Jesse tell you?"

The microwave dinged again. This time Lilith ignored the food and, instead, glared at Serena, forcing her without a word, to answer.

Serena swallowed and vowed to remain silent but against her own will, it seemed, she answered. It was if someone had sudden control of her mouth. "He said she suddenly disappeared three years ago and that they were told she was traveling Europe with her grandmother after a mysterious fire decimated the original house."

"Hm." Lilith turned around and took the dinner out of the microwave. It smelled like roast beef with gravy and mashed potatoes. "The other dinner is for you."

Serena stood and walked to the other side of the kitchen to warm her microwave dinner.

The conversation was over for the time being. Serena let it go. She took a bite of meat and chewed. It wasn't just a matter of getting an answer out of Lilith; it was a battle of wits too.

Lilith left her food on the counter and went to her room just as the phone rang shrilly. Serena jumped and then grabbed it.

"Hello?"

"Who is this?" a female voice asked.

"Serena. Who is this?"

"Is Lilith there?"

"She's using the bathroom."

"Of course she is." The voice was patronizing.

"Who is this?" Serena asked.

"Angel."

"Well. *Angel,* did you need her right away or can you be a nice friend and wait a second?"

"I'm not her friend. I'm calling because I'm Simon's assistant, you little bi--." Angel's voice cut off abruptly.

"Hello Serena," Simon purred, the sound prickling her skin. "You'll have to excuse my assistant. She's young."

"I'll bet she is."

"And in training."

"Uh-huh. So how are you doing *Uncle* Simon?"

"You know, let's just drop the whole 'uncle' thing."

"Fine by me. What's up?"

"I want you to call me 'Sir' from now on."

"Sir? Where did that come from? I think I like 'uncle' better. Let's just stick with that."

Silence.

"Hello? Are you there?"

"I'm not kidding." His voice dropped two octaves lower. "You are to call me sir from now on. Are we clear? Serena?"

She gulped. "Yes?"

"Sir?"

"Yes?"

"Are we clear?"

"Yes."

"Now, let's try this again." His voice went back to his normal cadence leaving Serena feeling off balance by the shift in his voice and the sudden control he had just taken with her. "Where's my wife?"

"She's in her room."

"Is she drunk?"

"What kind of random question is that?"

"The kind of question a man asks about his wife of twenty-five years and who knows her inside and out. Not so random, sweetheart."

Serena didn't know how to respond to that. It wasn't just his smooth voice, it was what he said. He spoke not out of judgment but from experience.

"Of course she's drinking," he said at her hesitation. "This is a hard week for her since this is the third anniversary of our daughter leaving us." She heard him take a sip of something and then the clinking of ice against glass. Was he drinking too?

"Actually, no. She really isn't drunk," Serena said, this time without sarcasm. "We're just about to eat and watch *Murder She Wrote*. She'd just left the room when you called."

"Hm. Ok," He cleared his voice. "Look, I actually phoned to warn Lil that my mother is coming to visit at the end of this week. She'd like to get to know you since my brother kept you from us for so many years."

She picked up on the slight sneer he put to the words *mother* and *brother*. Why the family discord? Why the warning regarding his mother coming to visit? It would've been an intriguing saga, except she wasn't just watching it. She felt like she had a significant role, but no lines were given, no direction, and no idea of where the story was going.

"You need to make sure the house looks nice for Rosalie. I'll be getting there on Friday night, and she'll be arriving on Saturday morning."

"Isn't that what a housekeeper is for? No offense, but don't you pay you-know-who to clean?"

He chuckled. "Normally yes, but not with Claudia. She lives by her own rules. She views the house as hers. You're the guest."

"Oh."

"You're not bothering her are you?" He took on a more serious tone.

"Nope." She found herself both afraid as well as more curious about the woman upstairs.

"Good. Okay, back to Rosalie." He paused. She heard him take another drink. More ice clinking. "Rosalie hasn't been out to the house since the fire. On her best days Lil hates Rosalie, but this weekend, of all weekends . . . I can't believe my mother is doing this to her. You have to warn her. She'll need it."

"Okay. Are you coming too? You won't make Lilith do this alone will you?"

"No, I won't make Lilith do this alone. We may not see eye to eye anymore, but I still care for her. However, now I'm coming for both of you, to protect you. I have a call coming in. See you Friday." He hung up before she had a chance to say goodbye.

***

Lilith stood behind the partially opened door, listening to the one-sided conversation. Why was this girl defending her to Simon? What did she have to gain from doing so? There had to be an ulterior motive, otherwise, it didn't make sense. But the idea of someone stepping in to fight on her behalf chipped away at her armor, leaving a chink. No one had put up a fight on her behalf her over the last few years. Though this girl had no idea who she was dealing with, she was still made of more grit then she was being credited for, which wreaked havoc within Lilith. The sound of the phone hanging up pulled Lilith out of her thoughts.

She sagged under the weight of her conflicted feelings. She wanted to remain angry, bitter, but tonight she was actually grateful, though she hated the feeling. She peeked out the door to find Serena staring down at the phone before replacing it on the charging base beside her, then she pulled her knees up to her chest and lay her head on them. She had a faraway look in her eyes. There was no haughtiness within her. She had simply done what she felt was necessary. Lilith heaved a sigh. She went

65

to the closet where she kept her extra blankets.

***

Serena clicked the off button. A few minutes later, carrying a chocolate brown down comforter, Lilith walked back into the room. She handed it to Serena as a peace offering. Serena knew she'd been listening to the call.

"Thank you."

"No," Lilith's voice was quiet, dare she say apologetic? "Thank you." She sat in her own chair; the wing-backed one. She didn't say anything else. Serena didn't push her to.

This woman confused her--or maybe her own feelings confused her. Serena always assumed that she and her mother would be close, that they would chat like girlfriends, like the show she'd see on TV. She imagined the same with her sister. Now she wondered if her romanticized dreams would've been realized. Maybe it would've been more like this: awkward gratitude, stilted conversations, or gun-shy silence.

Chapter 15--Wednesday

In fourth period, Jesse leaned over to Serena and whispered, "I need to tell you about some things, but we can't do it here." He paused and glanced up front to the teacher who was sitting at her desk. "At lunch meet me at the front doors of the school, okay?"

Her interest piqued but she held back. "I don't know you well enough to skip class. Give me one good reason why I should do it."

"Stormy."

Who was this cousin of hers? Apparently, the only way to find out was to trust Jesse.

"Okay," she said.

***

As soon as the bell rang, Serena quickly walked to the front doors. Jesse, backpack on his shoulder, was pacing in the entryway, his face calm, his eyes scanning the hall for her. Try as she might, she couldn't stop the flutter in her heart.

Their eyes met, his widened briefly, and his half-smile appeared then disappeared within a second. She made a beeline for him, fighting through the swarming students.

"When we go out the doors, you have to run fast, stay close to me."

She stopped and crossed her arms, eyeing him. "What's with all the 'cloak and dagger' stuff? This seems a little overkill for skipping some classes."

Jesse's wary eyes darted around the halls, his stance indicating he was ready to spring at a moment's notice, with or without her. He dropped his eyes briefly to hers. "Just trust me on this. You want to know about Stormy? Well, this may be the only chance you get. I can't tell you about her here, there are too many ears, and once we break out of here, chances are slim that we can do it again. So, are you in or out?"

She was in alright. She nodded her head forward. "Let's go."

He pushed the bar, letting the cold air blow in, then he was jogging outside. She followed him out. He looked behind them, then leaned close to her ear. "Okay, now we run." He grabbed her hand and broke into a flat run.

Thank God her dad had dragged her out to the track every afternoon.

Ahead sat a blue Chevy Aveo, exhaust appearing in the cold air. Windows were still defrosting, the engine, louder and more powerful than it should have been for such a small car, revved enough to keep it going. Just as they reached the car, there was a holler behind them. Jesse ignored the voice and opened the back door for Serena. She dove in as the voice yelled again. Jesse jumped in the front seat. The car lurched forward, and tires spun before the got traction. "Thanks for taking us, man," Jesse said.

"No prob. Where am I dropping you guys off?"

"Grandma's cafe."

"Who was calling for us when we got to the car?" Serena asked.

"Kendra," the boys said in unison.

"Great. Do you think she'll turn us in?" she said.

"Not if she wants Jesse to talk to her again," the guy said. "By the way, I'm Garrett."

"Serena."

"I know. The entire school knows."

The car slowed, then pulled over. "Come on, Serena." Jesse opened his door.

Serena looked out the window. They idled in front of a small but welcoming cafe. "Thanks, Garrett," she said.

"Yep." He smiled, sort of. "Do me a favor, don't act like you know me at school. No offense, but I don't want the teachers, or anyone for that matter, to know we've even talked."

"Okaayyy."

"I'll explain," Jesse said. "Let's get inside."

Grabbing her backpack, she got out of the car. Jesse shut the door behind her. The car took off, sliding only a little.

"Don't mind him. It's nothing personal." Jesse led the way up the snowy path and opened the door.

The cafe was warm and cozy. The smell of dark brewed coffee and waffles filled the air. For the first time since arriving in Telluride, Serena felt like she was warming from the inside out, not from the outside in. Sounds of clunking dishes and voices came from behind a swinging door directly in front of them, just behind a small counter and old cash register. At that moment a short, plump woman with a bouffant hairdo came out from the kitchen. She looked like Mrs. Claus in old Christmas books. Her nose, cheeks, chin were rosy and round. Her face brightened as soon as she saw Jesse.

"Honey, what a wonderful surprise!" she clapped. "But what are you doing here out of school?"

"It's lunch period, Memaw." He bent down to hug her. "I want you to meet a new friend of mine. This is Serena. Serena, this is my grandma, Victoria."

The old woman looked up at Serena. "She has Stormy's eyes. Could this be our little Stormy? Finally back home from her travels."

"No, Memaw, this isn't our Stormy. This is Serena, Stormy's cousin."

The woman heaved a sigh but took Serena's hand and gently shook it. "It's so nice to meet you. You are always welcome here, dear." She turned to Jesse. "Your booth is open sweetheart." She handed Serena a menu, then walked back to the kitchen. Voices from the kitchen were loud as she opened the door and quieted when it swung shut.

"Come on." Jesse led the way, past old wood booths with high back benches and hand made tables. In the very back, tucked away from the front door was his table. It was smaller than the rest, but she liked it the most. He directed her to the seat looking away from the door, and he sat opposite from her. The high backs of the benches shielded them both from any onlookers or visitors who might come in suddenly. As Serena looked around, noting the back exit they sat near, Jesse pulled out a laptop from his bag, opened it, and began typing.

"Are you doing homework?" she asked.

"Yeah, I risked life and limb to bring you to my grandma's cafe so we could eat waffles and catch up on our homework," he deadpanned.

She chuckled. "You're right, silly question." After a beat, she said, "I like your grandma."

He smiled back. "Me too."

Grandma walked up to the table with two glasses of water. She kissed Jesse on the forehead and went back to the kitchen. He continued typing then turned the screen around so Serena could see what he had been researching. "Serena, meet your cousin."

Thick black hair made the girl's face look small in comparison. She had Lilith's translucent skin, but her father's eyes and brow, just like Serena. Her pink cheeks and sweet smile brightened her face, her teeth covered by braces with alternating pink and purple bands. "This was Stormy a year before everything changed."

"What happened to her?"

He reduced Stormy's picture and brought up another girl. Another class picture, this one of a pretty, blonde-haired and blue-eyed girl. "This is Haley. She and Stormy were best friends since kindergarten."

"You and she were really close too, weren't you?"

Jesse didn't answer immediately. He swallowed, his Adam's apple bobbing up and down.

"Yeah, we were. Me, Stormy, Kendra, Haley, Logan and Garrett, the one who gave us the ride here, along with the rest of the gang at the table yesterday, had been friends since grade school. We went to each other's birthday parties, we played together at recess, we took as many classes together as possible." Suddenly this girl, her cousin, didn't seem like a stranger. She had been a real person, connected to this boy who sat across from Serena. "We were all friends until eighth grade."

"What happened?"

"Haley disappeared one night after a dance we'd all attended. The girls were sleeping over at Stormy's house. Something freaked Haley out so bad that she wouldn't go upstairs. Stormy asked, but Haley wouldn't tell her, she just demanded to go home."

"Didn't the other girls think this was all strange? I mean, wouldn't they want to go home too?"

"Haley was high strung to begin with, so no, they weren't all that scared. If they were, they didn't show it. Later Kendra told me that Simon and the house were creepy, especially that night."

"Didn't Stormy think so too? I've had two conversations with the man and even I could see he was scary."

"Stormy couldn't see it. He's her dad. Besides, when you grow up with weirdness around you, or whatever dysfunction you're used to, you think it's normal." He stopped talking and took a drink of water.

Jesse continued, "Besides, she barely saw him at all since he worked out of state so much. When he was home he was busy, but 'he always had time to chase the monsters away,' as she put it. She was extremely loyal to her father. For a while, at least. She didn't like Claudia much at all. I didn't go up there much, but Stormy shared a lot with me."

"So . . . what happened next?" Serena prodded.

"According to Stormy, Simon offered to give Haley a ride home. Claudia offered to go with them, so Haley agreed. Simon and Claudia's story was that they dropped Haley off at her front door and watched her go inside. He and Claudia didn't get home until after Stormy and Kendra had gone upstairs. He said they got a flat tire on the way home that they had to fix. It wasn't until late the next day when Haley's parents called to ask when she was coming home, that Stormy found out Haley never made it inside her house. The police began investigating and were looking at her dad and Claudia as the obvious suspects."

"That must've been horrible," Serena said.

"It was." Jesse swung the laptop back to him and began typing. "Stormy was devastated, of course, and why wouldn't she be? Her friend disappears, and her own dad is being blamed for it. She felt so guilty for not going with Haley. After several weeks, all charges were suddenly dropped. Simon was cleared, but no one thought he was innocent. The kids at school didn't believe for a minute that Simon wasn't guilty, but they were powerless to do anything, so they went after the next best person: Stormy."

He took another drink. "Two months after Haley's disappearance there was the fire. No one knows what started it, but Stormy wasn't seen again. The story was that she departed for Europe with her grandmother. Then there was Claudia."

"The housekeeper."

"About six months after Haley's disappearance, she flew to Europe to be with Stormy, which really didn't make sense."

"How so?"

"Well, one, Stormy once told me Claudia hated flying, and two, she scared Stormy. There's no way Stormy would want her to join her or Rosalie on their trip. We've always wondered what happened to her."

"Claudia came back."

"She did?"

"Yeah. She lives on the third floor. I'm not allowed to talk to her or about her, though. From what you tell me, it sounds like she's a real piece of work. It's no wonder Lilith doesn't like her."

"Huh," Jesse's face was thoughtful as he typed in a few words and then turned the screen back to her. A different picture of Stormy stared back at Serena. "This is a year later, a week before she disappeared," he swallowed.

Stormy stood between Lilith and Simon; her petite frame seemed fragile between the two. The smile was forced, the braces gone, as was the color in her face. Haunted eyes, eyes that Serena saw in the mirror every day, were the only color in her gaunt face. She was still pretty, striking really, but Serena was shocked at how much had changed in one year. Even so, the girl in this picture looked familiar to her. Maybe it was because Serena felt as hollow as Stormy looked.

"Of course, Stormy wondered where exactly her dad had been for those missing hours when he was expected home."

He clicked on a file and up came a news story he had saved. It was about Stormy's disappearance. It was dated three years ago.

Jesse continued with the story, but his shoulders slumped as he stared at the screen. "Stormy never stopped looking into her father's alibi. And she never stopped looking for Haley even though her father commanded her to do so." The newspaper article still faced Serena. She reached over and clicked the mouse, returning to Stormy's picture.

"A few days before the Halloween dance, the same dance we went to the year before, she found something but didn't want to tell me what it was over the phone. She sounded terrified. It was a Friday night, her grandma was coming to visit, so she said she'd tell me everything at school on Monday."

"What did she tell you?"

He flipped the screen around back to himself, then typed in a few words and returned it back to her.

"Nothing. That night her house burned to the ground. Well, most of it."

Sure enough, the picture before her showed blackened boards, mostly piled on the ground with a few rafters barely standing. The only thing remaining was the left wing of the house. It had not been touched, though there were flames etched into the side. Serena gulped. There was something about the way the house stood, hollow, and skeletal. She had a feeling she had seen something like this before. "So, what made you guys believe she had left town with her grandma instead of thinking she had died in the house?"

"Because there was nothing left of her body. If she had died, they would've found a body, right? Anyway, we went up to her house site on Tuesday, all of us friends did. We wanted to make sure she was okay. Police stood at the entrance of their property and refused to let us pass through, so we left, but none of us had a good feeling about it. When the newspaper article came out a few days later, Simon said that his mother surprised Stormy with a year-long trip to Europe and he was thankful that she had not seen her childhood home burn."

"Okay. Why would you guys not believe him?"

Their food arrived. Jesse took a bite of his waffle. After he finished swallowing, he said, "The thing is, she wouldn't have left without telling us. She would've said something, called us from the airport. Besides, she hated her grandmother. There is no way she would leave for a year and travel with her, even if that was her dream vacation. I don't buy the story, none of us did."

They both fell quiet, eating their food in silence, thinking about Stormy. Serena could see the holes in Simon's story. It just didn't make sense. As Jesse took his last bite his phone buzzed, which it had been doing the whole time they talked, but he had ignored it. This time he checked it.

"Oh shit, we've gotta go." He hopped up from the table and went in search of his grandma. Serena checked his phone to see what the problem was. A text from Kendra popped up.

"Hey asshole, they're looking for Serena." The rest of the text cut off. Then another one popped up, "Seriously! Get back here!"

"Grab your things. My grandpa will take us." Jesse shut off his computer and stuffed it in the backpack. She handed the phone back to him. He shoved it in his back pocket.

Grandma showed up at the table, keys in hand. "Here ya go, sweetie. Grandpa will meet you out there."

"Thanks." He leaned down and kissed her forehead, then exited out the back door they had been sitting beside. Serena slid out of the booth next and swung her bag over her shoulder.

"Thank you," she said as she stuck her hand out to shake the older woman's hand. Instead of a handshake, she was pulled into a bear hug.

"You be careful up there," Grandma whispered in her ear. "That house is possessed, plus it's built on malevolent land. If you stay up there for too long, it won't let you go." When she pulled back from Serena, her eyes held unshed tears. "Now go sweetheart." She led her to the door through which Jesse had disappeared.

A blast of cold air stole her breath. She felt as if she had walked out from an alternate universe back into reality. A chilling reality, one she didn't want to face.

"Hurry!" Jesse called. He was climbing into an old red suburban. She shuffled along a shoveled path and climbed into the warm car. His grandpa didn't turn around to greet her, but instead, met her eyes in the rearview mirror.

A Russian hat and bushy, silver-grey eyebrows sat above clear blue eyes. So that was where Jesse got his eyes. A full beard that matched his eyebrows covered the lower part of his face. He looked stern, if not a bit annoyed that he'd been pulled out to the cold to drive his wayward grandson back to school.

He didn't say anything to her as he shifted into drive. They started at a slow pace, the old truck grabbing at the snowing ground.

"What have I told you, boy?" Grandpa's voice was deep like Jesse's too.

"I know. She had to know about Stormy though. There was no way I could tell her those things at school."

Grandpa shrugged, reluctantly agreeing. "Don't make this a habit, you understand?"

"Yeah." They both fell silent during the ride back to school. As they approached the grounds, Serena felt her blood surge with adrenaline. Busses were already lined up, exhaust plumbing in the freezing air. Grandpa drove toward the bus Jesse pointed to. Before the truck came to a complete stop, Jesse opened the door. "Thanks, Grandpa," he mumbled. "Come on," he motioned Serena out the door.

"I'm heading back with him," he said. "I work at the cafe."

"Oh." She was disappointed he wasn't going with her. She had more questions she wanted to ask.

"And I don't think it's a good idea if we're seen together while we're at school, especially when we just cut class together. The teachers are gonna be watching us more carefully, so we can't risk it. I'm sorry." He paused, "I really am. I liked hanging out with you today. I just can't. You understand, right?"

"Got it." She felt tears gathering, so she blinked them away. So close, so very close to having a friend. She had to get away from him. She wouldn't be able to keep herself together much longer. "I better go." She shifted her bag to her other shoulder.

His voice dropped lower so that it could be barely heard above the rumbling engine beside them. "Be careful up there, Serena. I've been there myself. Something's not right with that house." He drew her close and hugged her, then let her go. "I'll see you around school."

"Yeah." She stepped away, began to turn but stopped halfway. "Thanks for telling me those things about Stormy. I appreciate it." She left him before he could respond. The image of him standing in the cold, hands shoved inside pockets and regret etched on his face, burned in her mind.

Head held high, back straight, refusing to let anyone, especially Jesse, see how upset she really was, she trudged through the packed snow. The bus was warm inside. A little too warm. It smelled of sweat and stinky feet. The back of the bus was filled, the front not so much. Kendra sat among the group. She glared at Serena. Life was too complicated to play such an immature game.

She settled into the seat and refused to think any more of it. Instead, she turned her mind back to the cafe and what she'd learned from Jesse. The girl in that picture popped up in her mind. Why had she looked so familiar? Was it because she looked like Lilith? Or was it because she looked enough like Serena that they could be sisters? Same eyes, same hair, same skin color, or lack thereof. Something was off, but Serena couldn't put her finger on it.

Jesse was right. A European tour sounded unlikely, especially one with Rosalie. But what had happened to Stormy?

Suddenly it came to her as to why Stormy looked familiar. Her lunch settled like a cold lump in her stomach as a cold chill crawled down her back. The pale-faced girl with the wild, curly hair was the stranger in her dreams, the one who kept crying out for help.

Chapter 16--Wednesday Afternoon

The same number that had rung twice before rang again. Tempted as she was to ignore it again, she didn't. It occurred to her that maybe it was Serena. Perhaps she was in trouble. It wasn't that she cared so much about Serena's health and well being, she just didn't want Simon or Rosalie coming down on her for any problems that arose. Steering the car, Henry took his eyes off the road for a moment and looked at her. She ignored him too.

"Hello," her response was curt.

"Mrs. Robertson?" the male voice asked.

"Yes?"

"This is Mr. Dawson, from the high school."

She knew who this worm-man was. She shuddered at the sound of his voice. Even over the phone, he made her feel cold, slimy even. "What do you want?"

"Do you remember me?"

"Yes. What is it?" It was all she could do to keep her voice neutral.

"Your niece cut her afternoon classes," he sounded like a tattling first grader. "According to the student who saw it, Serena left with another student at lunch."

"Has she gotten back yet?" Lilith sighed.

"I don't know yet, but Mr. Robertson was adamant that if she did anything like that that we should contact him, or you, immediately. Should I call him instead?"

"No, that won't be necessary. I'll tell him myself."

"Okay, well I hope you let him know that I'm doing my job."

She hung up on the sniveling snake. He would go on and on if she hadn't done so. Dammit, Serena, what are you doing? She could feel Henry's eyes on her again, and this time she met them. He wasn't as annoyed as she thought. He was curious and rightly so. "Mr. Dawson," she answered his unasked question. "He was calling to tell me that Serena cut her afternoon classes."

He looked back at the road and flipped on the blinker before turning into their driveway. He came to a stop just as he pulled off, shifted into four-wheel-drive, and then began their long ascent to the house. She gave a heavy sigh.

"What am I going to do with her?" She didn't expect Henry to respond. He never did. Forever mute, he never would. He would hand-sign his answers, questions, and what have you, but never speak again. She always wondered how his voice would sound if he could talk. She imagined it was deep and rich and full-bodied. Just like the rest of him. She looked back at the road like he was doing. They continued on in silence. When he finally stopped in front of the house, he put the vehicle in park but left the engine running. He turned to her and hand signed a question.

"What are you going to do with her?"

"I don't know."

"You can't tell Simon or Rosalie, but you also can't keep secrets for too long. She can get you into trouble too." He reached out and stroked her face with a work-toughened hand.

She nodded and then opened the door. She entered the house; he followed soon after, holding two grocery bags per hand. Lilith began unpacking them and putting away groceries as he continued to unload the truck. When he was finished, he left to get Serena from the bus. Even with the front door closed, she could hear the truck's rumbling motor. As it faded in the distance, the house grew silent.

There was quiet, and then there was silence. Quiet was good. Silence was not. Silence happened when something was watching you, when you had become prey to that something, and it crouched in the darkness, haunches raised, ready to spring forward in attack.

She felt those eyes on her as she put away the food. She imagined a cattail, twitching back and forth, waiting for its chance, and if she looked for those watching eyes, it would begin a relentless attack. She had done that once before, but it was such a horrific experience that she vowed never to do it again. Instead, she kept her eyes down, focused on her task, waiting for Serena and Henry's arrival. Gradually the eyes begin to shift away from her. The sound of the suburban engine crept up over the hill, dispelling the attack. She took a deep breath and let it out. Now she had to confront Serena about school, which seemed easy compared to the sense of danger she had just experienced.

The front door opened and shut. Serena walked around the corner and jumped, not expecting Lilith to be there, waiting for her, one hip leaning against the counter and arms crossed. She watched Serena drop her bag on the floor, against the wall. She leaned down and began unlacing her new boots. When she was done, she stood and crossed her arms, ready to argue if she needed to. Clearly this wasn't the way to talk to her. At least, not the way to get her to listen. Lilith dropped her arms and placed her hands on the counter.

"We need to talk," she started.

"So it would seem." Serena was still on the defense.

"Sit down."

"Why?"

"Good grief! Just sit down. I'm not going to yell at you!"

Serena gave a cynical laugh. "Aren't you doing that right now?"

Lilith sighed. "Yes, but that's because you won't sit." She crossed her arms again. So it would be this way then. "I got a call from one of your teachers this afternoon." A sense of deja vu came over her. She remembered having a conversation like this one with Stormy. Same words, same stances in the kitchen, same defiant look in her daughter's eyes. That memory and the present seemed to overlap, as if someone had laid tracing paper over the original picture. Everything was the same, only the faces were different. The vision was so vivid that it took her breath away.

"Lilith?"

And the vision popped like a bubble.

"Are you okay?" Serena asked again. Her defiance had turned into concern.

"Yes." The deja vu that was so real she could have sworn it had happened before or she had dreamed about it. "Can we sit down?" She led the way to the living room, not waiting to see if Serena followed, but she did. Serena sat on the couch.

"Mr. Dawson called to tell me you skipped your afternoon classes."

"Yeah, I did." She tucked her legs under her, Indian style and leaned back. Again Lilith had that feeling of deja vu, but it wasn't as strong as before.

"You can't do that."

"Do you really care?"

"I probably wouldn't if it were under other circumstances, but these aren't normal circumstances." She ran her fingers through her hair. "Your school, this town, is subject to Rosalie, and by default, to Simon. They will call Simon, or me in this case, and tell us what you are doing and who you are with. This time it was Mr. Dawson. Next time it might be Ms. Harold."

Serena sat up straight, her nonchalant facade dropped. "They're all in his back pocket?"

"More or less, yes. If they see you do anything that is suspect or in any way rebellious, they will call me, which is better for us than if they call your uncle. That would be disastrous. For the both of us."

"So now what? I can't breathe without them telling on me?"

"Pretty much. You also need to be careful with whom you are seen."

"What?!?"

"You were with Jesse, right?"

"Yeah," Serena fumed. "How come I can't see him? What can they do about that?"

"They can make sure he disappears." Lilith's answer stopped Serena's response, whatever it might have been. She closed her mouth, defiance gone.

"Like Stormy disappeared?"

Lilith's heart skipped like a scratched CD. "I take it Jesse told you about her."

"Yeah, he told me about her and a girl named Haley disappearing a year before Stormy."

Lilith sat back in her chair and shifted her eyes to the snowy view beyond the window. She was both frustrated that Jesse told Serena about Stormy but also relieved because, frankly, she didn't have the wherewithal to do it herself. What concerned her was that Serena would keep digging until she found out exactly what happened to Stormy. It had not even been a week that Serena had moved in, but Lilith was already seeing traits of her father coming out, dangerous traits. Jonathan's insatiable appetite for the truth was what nearly destroyed the family business twenty-five years ago. Serena's curiosity could destroy her and everyone else close to her. Even she didn't know just how powerful she was.

Lilith doubted Simon had any clue of what Serena was capable of. He would be in for a shock when he saw just how powerful his niece really was. She could either be an asset to the family business or bring it to its knees. Honestly, Lilith was not sure which she preferred.

She sighed as she turned back to Serena. She was not good at communication in the best of circumstances and was actually worse in the most intense ones. What words could she use to make Serena understand just how important it was to keep her mouth shut? Jesse. She used him when she warned Stormy, and it prevented her daughter from investigating until Haley disappeared. Hopefully, Serena would heed her advice.

"Please listen to me." Lilith sat up straight and leaned in, whispering just in case Claudia was eavesdropping. "If you keep searching, the truth will kill you." It will also empower you, she thought. "And it will kill me and Jesse and his family. Stop now. This is not up for discussion." She reinforced her last two commands with a spell. The last time she used it was on Stormy. She wondered if it would work on Serena.

Her niece looked at her, her mouth opened to argue, but no words came out. Lilith was not sure if it was because of her persuasive powers she cast or because Serena thought better of arguing. Whatever it was, it had stopped the questions that she knew were on Serena's mind, and that was a relief. She hoped her incantation would keep the girl quiet until at least Sunday after everyone left.

***

Serena listened to Lilith. What just happened? The spoken words flowed over her, touching her lightly like a feather along her arms. She turned her gaze to the windows as Lilith had done just a few minutes before, her thoughts scrambling for a retort, but what she saw frightened her. Her own, very faint reflection stared back at her, where there shouldn't be a reflection because it was still early in the afternoon. The girl in the window smiled slowly, and Serena knew there wasn't a smile on her own face. It was as if her reflection had a mind of its own.

***

She'd already eaten her meat and was about halfway through her mashed potatoes when she felt it. She glanced at Lilith, but she was thoroughly engrossed in the mystery they were watching on TV. Serena shrugged her shoulders.

She looked around the expansive room, into the rafters that were so high they disappeared into darkness, but she couldn't see anything. She looked behind her, to the spiral staircase in the kitchen and followed it with her eyes to the second floor where the "feeling" stopped. It wasn't like the feeling was gone. It just stopped, like whatever, or whomever, was watching her, stood in the shadows beyond the stairs.

She forced the mashed potatoes down. The TV went silent. Serena glanced back at Lilith and found her looking into the same shadows, eyes squinting as if she were trying to see who stood just beyond their sight.

Lilith turned up the volume again, both of them in need of noise to lessen their fear but neither willing to admit to it. Both of them leaned to the lamps closest to them and turned them on.

80

Serena wanted a drink of water since the fear had sucked her mouth dry, but there was no way she was walking into that kitchen. She took another bite of the mashed potatoes instead. At least it brought the moisture back to her mouth.

When the show ended, Lilith stood.

"Where're you going?" Serena asked. She tried not to sound panicky but failed. Miserably.

Lilith smirked. "Calm down. I have to go to the bathroom."

Serena would have believed Lilith's placid response until she saw Lilith's hands clenched into fists. She turned on the standing lamp beside her bedroom door and the light just inside her room before she went inside and she left the door open a crack for the first time since Serena had been there.

A stack of Sherpa lined blankets sat, folded up, at the other side of the couch. Serena unfolded one of them and began making her bed for the night.

"What are you doing?" Lilith asked as she walked back into the living room.

"I'm getting ready for bed."

"Not down here, you're not. That other night was a one time deal."

"What? You felt something earlier, I know you did. You're going to make me go up there?"

"I have no idea what you're talking about." Lilith was not going to budge. Serena stood, this time her hands were knotted fists.

"Seriously?"

"Yes." Lilith raised her hand with her finger pointed to the stairs just beyond the light.

"Fine." It was all she could do not to throttle the woman. Lilith moved a fraction of an inch to let Serena pass, so she didn't feel guilty for roughly shouldering her aside. She stomped to the stairs, which loomed bigger than before. She wasn't about to show her fear. She gripped the railing and stomped up the stairs. Without pausing, she flicked on the hall light and continued to her room.

***

After Serena went upstairs with anger on her face and fear in her eyes, Lilith went to bed too. She flipped on all the lights in her room, knowing that little things crawled in the shadows, things only she could see and hear. Dread filled her; no, not just dread, but terror as well. Tonight she had to sleep in the dark, she had to allow those little things to creep close, crawl up on her bed and lay next to her as she slept. Tonight there was no way to drown herself in alcohol to keep the nightmares at bay. Tonight she would have to let her soul travel.

Ever since she was a little girl, she could astral project her soul into the universe. She could enter other people's dreams or walk through walls in the house or travel at the speed of sound to the far reaches of the world, pulled to the person or thing she was looking for. That was how she found Serena. Sometimes her soul traveled without her permission. And that's why she drank, to put herself in such a deep sleep that her soul could not escape. She drank more after she found the girl, emptied her mind every night of anything that would call her out, so she could sleep. But tonight she would have to let herself go again to find the object Simon was convinced Serena had.

Lilith pulled the covers over her head like she did when she was little. Father found out she could dream walk on accident. She would wander through her house, sneaking into rooms she was not allowed to enter during the day. At first, it was a delightful game. She was led through the house by a beautiful white unicorn with a rainbow-colored mane who could talk to her. She and Dreamy would go on adventures together, exploring rooms she could never enter during the day. Other rooms were barred to her even in spirit form. That was how she found Father could do the same thing.

After two years of playing, Dreamy showed her true colors. She went dark; her eyes disappeared leaving only empty holes, a tattered, moth-eaten mane replaced the lovely rainbow, and a sharp blade took the place of the lovely horn on her forehead. Her unicorn was a nightmare horse. After that night it was Father who trained her. He was not gentle, nor kind. He was ruthless. She wished for the unicorn, but he said she had outgrown Dreamy. It did not matter now anyway. Her dream horse had proven to be false. She would not trust another one.

That was then, this was now. That girl had become a woman, more powerful in soul walking than even Father had been. If she were lucky tonight, she would meet her guide, the compassionate one that led her gently through landscapes and light dreamers, but she knew in the knotted hole of her stomach that it was unlikely she would be so lucky.

Chapter 17--Wednesday Night

Serena stomped to the stairs, which loomed bigger than before. She gripped the railing and forced her way up. Without pausing, she flicked the hall light on and continued to her room.

One of the wall lamps flickered.

She didn't give it another glance as she passed, afraid that if she did she'd lose her momentum. She used her anger to push through her growing anxiety. It was all in her head. New house, new state, no father to scare the boogeyman away.

Her fear spiked when she opened her bedroom door. Freezing air pushed past her. The hall lights should've shed some light into the darkness, the room only seemed to absorb it, not allowing the light much further than the doorway. This had happened a couple of times when she lived at home. She knew from experience that if she turned on the light quickly, the fear didn't overcome her. Not much anyway.

The lamps came on with a flip of the switch. Footsteps sounded behind her. She turned, thinking Lilith had come to check on her. No one was there. Despite the cold air, she stepped into the room and closed the door.

As soon as the door shut silence surrounded her. She scanned the room from where she stood. First thing she noticed was the bed covers had been turned down, the fireplace was dark, clean, as if it had not been used in forever, the bookshelf held some of the books she had placed there a couple of nights before, and the pictures on the dresser stared past her, except the one of her mother. That frame had shifted and was now facing the antique wardrobe. That was odd. She knew she had placed the photo so that it faced the bed. She remembered feeling comforted by the idea of her mother looking over her. She moved to the dresser and repositioned the picture before turning to the wardrobe. A mirror showed her reflection and the room behind her.

It's nothing, she told herself as she changed into her pajama pants. She turned on the little lamp next to the bed, which seemed to be on a different circuit from the other lights, and then went back to the light switch and turned it off. The darkness closed in on her, bringing back the feeling of being watched by something in the shadows or from under her bed. She flipped the lights back on, then, like she did when she was a little girl, she scurried back to her bed and climbed in. The sense of something under her bed fled. It helped that the lights were on. The shadows receded, leaving her with a sense of safety. She felt like a little girl and for the umpteenth time, she wished for her dad's presence. He would've said a bedtime prayer, and she would've felt peace like she had when she was little. Like a broken dam the tears broke through.

Her shoulders shook as she sobbed into her pillow.

How could he leave me...What am I doing here.......how can I live here... Oh God, help! Help me. Help me. Help me.

Words ran through her mind, bumping into other words, her thoughts not making sense of anything. Eventually, the tears ran dry, the shaking shoulders stilled, and the ragged sobs turned into the soft inhale and exhale of the sleeping girl.

Plop. Plop. Plop. Water drops echoed. Serena was back in the cave again. She could feel the rough rock under her fingertips and see light in the distance. This time she walked steadily through the darkness, albeit jumpy from the sound of rodents scurrying around her. It struck her just before she stepped outside that the light never entered the cave. It was simply dark and then light. Footsteps running up from behind startled her. She took two giant steps that led her into the gray mist.

This dream was like the one before. Same foggy surroundings, same hill rising up from where she stood. As she walked further up, she turned and saw the same half-burned house barely standing. The difference was the girl she had seen in the previous dream wasn't there. Instead, there was a biting cold wind that clattered the bare branches and kept the fog moving.

Serena. Serena Serena Serena.

Her name echoed across the mountains until it was just a whisper in her ear. She turned to see if someone was there, but she was alone. Yet she could feel someone nearby.

"Hello?" her voice was small, but the hills still picked it up and echoed it back.

She shouldn't be here. The thought no more crossed her mind than she was back at the mouth of the cave, with a hand on her back shoving her inside.

"Wait!" the voice called from behind.

Serena turned to find the girl she'd seen in the dream before. She stood in the distance, untamed hair surrounding a pale, frightened face. As soon as Serena took another step toward her, the fog rose and began to carry her away.

"No!" the girl cried. She struggled but couldn't move in the gray matter. "Serena! Come back!"

Serena stepped away from the cave, intending to follow after her, when the push she had felt a few moments earlier now yanked her inside.

"No!" She tried to pull herself away from the invisible hand that grasped hers, but it was an iron grip she struggled against. With each pull, she felt her wrist bones grind and tighten and pop. "Let me go!" she cried out. "I have to help her!"

A white face appeared before her. A black, tar-like substance seeped out of the empty eye sockets. Serena screamed.

"You don't belong here!" the voice was gravelly and low.

"She needs help," Serena whispered.

"She is beyond your help."

The hand yanked on hers again. Suddenly, she was falling, picking up speed the further down she went. She landed hard on her bedroom floor, gasping for air. The lights she had left on were now off. She tried to get her bearings in the dark room, dragging in air as she did so, holding her sore ribs. After a few seconds, she realized she was looking up at the rafters and her bed was to her right. She rolled to her side and found the white face in her dream lying under the bed. She screamed again. The world went dark, this time she didn't dream.

Chapter 18--Wednesday Night

"Ready or not, here I come!" Lilith called out as she walked down the hall to her daughter's bedroom.

Stormy's lilting laughter sounded on the other side of the door. "You're never going to find me this time."

Lilith smiled to herself. She knew she was dreaming, but she didn't care. Any dream with Stormy in it was a happy feeling.

She picked up her steps, eager to see her daughter's face again. She loved it when her memories of Stormy came back to her, playing out before her like a 3D movie.

"Hurry, mommy."

"I'm coming, sweetie."

The floor suddenly shifted, tilting to the left. Lilith stumbled, putting her hand out to steady herself against the wall,

"Hurry, Mommy," Stormy repeated, but she was not giggling anymore. Fear filled her voice.

Lilith picked up her pace, anxious to get to her daughter. The floor moved beneath her. Glancing down, she noticed spiders underfoot, moving faster than she could.

"I'm so scared," Stormy's small voice called to her again. "Please hurry, Mommy."

The light under the door dimmed.

"No, wait!" Lilith ran faster, willing the spiders to disappear but they remained.

Another voice whispered in her ear, words she couldn't understand. The elusive door stood solid before her. Her daughter's voice cried out on the other side.

"I'm coming, baby," she said, twisting the knob. It was jammed. She twisted and turned, but it would not give. "I'm coming, I'm coming, I'm coming."

A sharp pain pierced her fingertips, waking her. She stood at Stormy's door with her hand on the knob. Her body sagged against the door, and only then did she feel sweat trickle down her face, mingling with her tears. She turned to her left and found the light attached to her daughter's portrait. She didn't turn it on. She didn't need to. She traced the swirls with her fingertips. *Oh Stormy, I'm so sorry I failed you.*

Chapter 19--Thursday Morning

Serena woke with a jerk when the alarm went off. What was she doing on the floor? The face from the night before came back to her. She jumped up, jittery and aching from the fall off the bed. She crawled across the bed and slammed down the small off button between the two bells. The force of her hand knocked the clock off the table. It fell on the hardwood, making a cracking sound when it landed.

Serena turned on the lamp and looked down. The clock was on its face. With the light on, she braved the underside of the bed and picked it up. The heaviness surprised her. She didn't remember seeing the clock before. A large, diagonal crack divided the face into two separated parts and both hands were frozen at 5:01 am. It was an old fashioned silver framed clock with two bells on top that made up the alarm. The face showed roman numerals for the numbers and two delicate hands indicating the time. She turned it over. On the back of the clock was a dedication etched in the silver.

To Stormy with love~Mommy.

Lilith must have put this clock on her bedside table. And if this was new, what else was different from the night before?

She scanned with her eyes. Creepy doll across the room. Check. Cluttered bookshelf. Check. Pictures on the dresser. Ch-, wait, not checked. All three photos were there but turned around, facing the wall behind them.

What was happening? Trembling, she placed one foot onto the floor, and then the other. Her teeth chattered as she walked to the dresser. She was unsure if the room was extra cold that morning or if she was just that scared. She reached out and turned the pictures toward herself. They were still the same photos, nothing had been tampered with. She stroked the frame of her father's picture.

I'm so scared, Dad. Why am I here? Why did you send me to these people? Why didn't you tell me about them? She blinked away the gathering moisture in her eyes. *Why did you have to die?*

Serena sighed heavily. It was up to her to get the answers if she wanted to ask them. And did she really want to start asking? Like that age-old quote, "Be careful what you wish for."

On the other hand, did she really have the choice to turn a blind eye, to ignore the growing weirdness of Lilith or this house? The house seemed to be coming awake around her, forcing itself upon her, challenging her disbelief. She wondered if she should ignore it or would that be even more dangerous than if she began poking around the house and uncovering its secrets?

Trembling, she set the clock back on the table. She had to get ready for school, she just wasn't sure if her legs could hold her up. After grabbing a towel and shampoo, she slowly made her way to the bathroom, careful not to look too closely at the door at the end of the hall. In the silence around her, she could hear the click of the light switch as she flipped the switch. Her hands, slick with sweat despite the cold air, had a difficult time turning the hot and cold levers. She made sure the water was almost scalding hot before climbing into the tub and pulling the curtain closed. The hot water calmed her down and began to thaw her from the inside out as the soap washed away the sweat from overnight.

Her thoughts slowly unraveled as the water cleared her mind. It was odd to consider the house as a person, but that was what came to mind. It felt as if this house was waking up after a long sleep. Or maybe it had been awake already and it was she who was waking up. She wished Jesse hadn't distanced himself from her. She needed to talk this out with someone.

The water began to run cold as she rinsed off the last of the soap. The steam was thick when she pulled back the curtain. The bathroom smelled of Caress body wash bringing to mind memories of home. She pushed away the feelings and took the towel off the hook next to the tub. After wrapping her hair up, she pulled on her bathrobe. Even though she had no clock to look at she knew her shower had been too long. She'd have to hurry. On her way to the door, she glanced at the steam-fogged mirror. A finger-written message scrawled across it, condensation dripping from the letters.

Help Me

The air went out of Serena in a burst, frosty and visible. She wanted to move, get out of there, but was frozen in place.

"Serenaaaa."

Her name was drawn out, as if it had been an exhalation. With the voice came an unbearable cold that seeped up from the tiles. She forced her hand out to the doorknob and ripped it open. Her heart slammed against her ribcage as she ran to her room and slammed the door shut behind her.

With numb hands she opened drawers and pulled out the first items she could find, hoping they matched because there was no way she was going to stay on the second floor with whatever was calling her name. She pulled on her green-and-yellow University of Oregon sweatshirt and old jeans. The holes and distressing wouldn't keep her warm, but she didn't care. She had to get out of that room. Heavy footsteps sounded above her. They stopped just above her head. Serena held her breath. The steps moved away from her. She exhaled, shaking uncontrollably.

Who is this woman? she wondered. She had to be real since her room was mysteriously clean when Serena got home from school, but how come she hadn't run into the woman?

Serena ran to the vanity that held her makeup and hair supplies. She ducked down a little bit to see herself as she yanked a comb through her hair. Her reflection stared back. Fear had drained all color from her skin, and coupled by the dark hair, brows and lashes, her skin seemed translucent.

Before her eyes, her reflection began to shift slightly, and her face took on a different expression than the one she knew she had at that moment. She swore under her breath and armed with only a hair comb, headband, and socks, she ripped open the bedroom door and ran as fast as she could, not stopping until she reached the bottom of the stairs.

Lilith stood in the kitchen, watching Serena. When their eyes met, they saw fear etched in the face of the other. Lilith's face was just as pale as Serena's; dark circles stood out beneath red-rimmed eyes. Her hair was uncharacteristically tangled, and instead of wearing her usual black, she had on an oversized red flannel shirt with denim colored leggings. Serena was going to ask Lilith if she had been upstairs in the early morning hours, but she didn't have to. Lilith's disheveled look told her all she needed to know.

Lilith set down an already filled coffee mug next to a bowl of oatmeal, both for Serena, and then picked up her own cup. She leaned against the counter, still facing Serena. Her hands had a slight tremor even as she gripped her mug with both hands.

"Now you know why I drink," Lilith said, her quiet voice barely making it across the kitchen to Serena.

Serena nodded and then picked up her mug, her own hand shaking too. She had to hold the cup with two hands. The front door opening and shutting broke through their silence, their gazes dropping to their coffee.

Henry walked into the kitchen and came to a stop, looking between the two women. Serena glanced up, expecting him to give her the nod that it was time to go, but he wasn't even looking at her. Instead, his eyes rested on Lilith, his face etched with concern and compassion. And love? Yes, that look was there too, startling Serena.

Henry's hands flew up in the air and hand signed to Lilith. She answered back using her hands. Without thinking, she blurted out, "Is he deaf?"

Henry turned to her, obviously having heard her.

Lilith answered for him. "No, he's mute."

"How?"

This time Henry answered by opening his mouth wide and sticking out what should have been a tongue but was only a blunt nub. He closed his mouth.

Serena's jaw dropped open. "What happened?"

"Rosalie," Lilith said. Henry turned back to Lilith and signed again. This time she answered using her words as well as her hands, allowing Serena to know what they were saying.

"Yes, I'll go with you this morning," she said and then turned to Serena. "Get your socks and boots on. You'll miss the bus if we don't hurry." She crossed the kitchen to get her boots.

Serena glanced up at the clock above the kitchen window. She was right; it was time to go. What seemed like only minutes to her had actually been an hour. She dipped her spoon into the oatmeal and took two large bites before she put her socks on. She took two more bites before slipping her feet into her fur-lined boots.

"Here, wear this," Lilith tossed a light gray beanie with a fluffy ball on top to Serena. Not exactly her style but who cared. She brought her comb with her so she could at least put her hair up while in the car. She took one more big bite before grabbing her backpack and coat and ran to catch up before the front door shut. She had a horrible sense that if Lilith and Henry left without her, she wouldn't be able to get out of the house. As she ran through the dark hallway, she felt something watching her. She didn't dare look behind.

Chapter 20--Thursday Morning

As soon as Serena climbed up the bus steps, Lilith closed her eyes. Stormy's presence could be felt everywhere. Her presence was always there, but nothing like this. Lilith felt a significant change in the atmosphere. It was as if her daughter was clamoring back to life, her desperation palpable.

"What is it, baby?" she had whispered to Stormy's painting. She had reached up to her daughter's face and stroked the canvas. What she wouldn't give to touch her again. "I miss you so much. I'm so sorry, so very, very sorry." After saying those words, she could only weep.

Lilith's dreams had increased over the last few days, more so than in the last three years. She could feel the house shifting, the sense that the unseen was attempting to invade the seen. Was that the reason Stormy seemed so close? As if she was going to enter Lilith's world? She would welcome it, if only to see her daughter again.

Or was there another reason?

***

The bus was quiet, and mercifully no one took notice of her. She was already old news. Serena walked down the long aisle, searching for a seat when she saw Jesse. His eyes widened, he scooted over.

"Are you alright?" he asked.

"No," she whispered, fighting back tears. The terror that she had felt over the last twelve hours finally caught up with her.

"What's going on?"

Serena opened her mouth, then closed it.

There were too many ears on the bus. She glanced at Jesse. By the look on his face, she could tell he understood. After a minute of silence between the two of them, the typical voices and noises of the kids rose again.

She said, "I'm just tired, and my grandmother is coming to visit, so

I'm a little nervous." It wasn't the whole truth, but it would suffice.

She glanced at him. His brows were knit together. She wasn't sure if it was out of frustration or confusion or concern. Maybe it was all three. There was no way they could talk more at that point since the bus was coming to a stop.

When the bus parked at the school all of the students stood and grabbed their bags. Amidst the cacophony, Jesse leaned in close. His voice and nearness caused her heart to flutter as he spoke. "After our class just before lunch, follow me, just not too closely. I found a place in the library that we can talk."

Jesse walked away from her as soon as he exited the bus. She pulled back, walking slower, but thinking quickly.

Serena trudged along with the other students, feeling very much alone in the middle of the crowd. She wondered how Stormy felt at school. She had had her own group of friends, so she wasn't completely isolated, but did she still feel this way even with her friends?

Once inside the building, she walked to the nearest bathroom. She felt eyes upon her. She looked up and saw Ms. Harold following her. Unnerved, she stepped into the bathroom, taking the first open stall. Three or four girls stood at the mirror reapplying lipstick, combing their hair, and talking about her.

"Did you see her clothes today?"

"I know, right? I mean who wears those ripped jeans in this weather?"

"Only people who don't know what the hell they're doing, apparently." They all thought that funny and their laughter echoed in the tiled room. Stall doors squealed open and slammed shut, the girls continued to talk about her.

"I know her aunt and uncle totally have the money to buy her new clothing. Why don't they get her something to wear?"

"She had that new jacket you were wanting," one girl said. "Her aunt is probably one of the best-dressed people whenever she comes down off that mountain. She had to have gotten something for the girl."

"And my mom sold them those boots she's been wearing. She couldn't believe how much Mrs. Robertson had changed over the last couple of years."

"That's what I heard too!"

"All I know is that Serena is pathetic. 'Oh Jesse, I'm so alone.' She's totally weird like Stormy was."

Another girl spoke, "I thought she moved to Europe. You make it sound like she's dead."

"Who knows what she is, or where, for that matter."

The school bell rang, interrupting the girls. Within three minutes the restroom was cleared. Silence filled the room. Serena's door squealed as she opened it. She walked to the sink, her footsteps echoing against the black and white checkered linoleum floor and metal stalls. She almost preferred the chatter of catty girls to the hollow sound. At the sink, she turned on the hot spigot and let the water warm. As she did so, she looked into the mirror.

The face staring back at her was pale but didn't seem as terrified as she felt. *What am I going to do?* Hot water began to trickle out, startling her. The heat was minimal, but against her freezing hands, it felt like boiling water.

Her thoughts raced. Her father was estranged from the family. What had happened that made him leave? Did he know what was happening to the family once he left? The trickling water had increased its intensity along with her thoughts. She turned off the water. The bell rang loud in the bathroom, startling her. It was time to go to class. She looked up to either side of the mirror for paper towels and instead saw herself, but not herself.

He had to know something, you know that right?

Her reflection had a different tint to her eyes and a slight tilt to her head.

You can't trust what Dad told you. If he didn't tell you about your own family then what else did he keep secret?

The bathroom door suddenly opened and bounced against the wall. Kendra stood in the doorway.

"Serena!" she whispered loudly. "What the hell are you doing? They're looking for you."

"Who's looking for me?"

"The teachers. Who do you think?"

"What would they care? And why do you?"

"I don't, but Jesse does. Come on, we need to get to class."

Serena glanced back at the mirror, and her face was once more her own. She grabbed her bag that sat at her feet and followed Kendra out into the hallway.

Just as they reached the classroom door, Kendra stopped and looked at Serena. "Look, I know it doesn't seem like it to you, but Stormy was one of my closest friends. For that reason alone I will protect you. I think that's why Jesse does too. We failed Stormy, we don't want to do that same thing to you."

Serena wasn't sure she trusted the girl. "What about in the bathroom a few minutes ago?"

Kendra waved her hand in front of her face as if brushing the scene away. "Those were just girls being girls. I have to say things to survive school somehow. I'm already considered a freak by some people after what happened to Stormy."

"Huh."

"I know we didn't get off on the right foot, but I do care. Sort of. I care enough at least to keep you from getting in trouble." Kendra tucked her hair behind her multiple pierced ear. The door opened, pulling Kendra off balance and startling both of them. "Would you care to join us?" Ms. Harold asked. "Take a seat."

Kendra sat with her so-called friends while Serena sat in the only empty seat left, the one beside Jesse.

Ms. Harold began speaking, but Serena couldn't pay attention. What happened in the bathroom? Was she going crazy? Her reflection was taking on its own personality. Was the house making her crazy? Or was it her father's death that was pushing her over the edge? She had no clue. She felt like she had lived months since his memorial, and at the same time, she felt like it was just yesterday.

The ringing bell startled her, pulling her from her thoughts. Students were standing, grabbing their books and bags. She had no idea what Ms. Harold had been teaching, but the assignment was on the chalkboard. Serena jotted it down and then grabbed her things too, anxious to get away from the teacher who was walking in her direction. She was out the door faster than the teacher, but she still felt a slight tug of her backpack strap. Not daring to look behind her, knowing if she did, she would be acknowledging it. She swam deeper into the current, surrounding herself with students, making herself less visible. Serena only hoped that she could get across the hall to her next classroom without running into Mr. Dawson.

From class to class that morning, Serena raced through the halls, mindful of not being caught alone. She was jumpy from the extra adrenalin and a bit nauseated.

When lunch period rolled around, she was anxious to find Jesse. He came up beside her in the hall and whispered in passing, "Follow me."

The library appeared suddenly. As soon as the doors shut behind them, the outside noise subsided. Serena followed Jesse down the row of books, running her fingers along the shelves and enjoying that indescribable scent that books had, and the memories of her father they inevitably brought. She blinked back the tears.

Around a corner, they came to a small alcove with a table and four chairs.

"We shouldn't be bothered by anyone here." Jesse pulled out a chair for her and then sat in the chair facing her. "What's going on?"

He gave her a slight nod and his familiar half-smile, a lock of hair falling over his eyes. Maybe it was because he had been the only decent person she'd met in Colorado, but she was quickly falling for him. She hated herself for it. He was Stormy's boyfriend, sort of, and Stormy had been her cousin.

"What can you tell me about Claudia?"

"All I know is what Stormy told me. Apparently, she was some kind of nanny to Simon."

"Hmm. There has to be more to her than just that. Did Stormy say anything else?"

"I take it she's bothering you."

"You think?" She heaved a deep sigh. "Sorry for the sarcasm. Yes, she's bothering me. I hear her footsteps in the apartment above mine, but I never see her. My clothes are picked up, my room straightened, not that I'm complaining, but I've never run into her. The house is big but not that big. I don't know who this woman is and Lilith won't talk about her. She won't even say her name out loud."

"According to Stormy, she was some kind of voodoo practitioner. I guess Lilith wouldn't tell her any more than that either. The warning was the same, 'Don't talk about Claudia or even say her name.' Whatever she is, you don't want to mess with her. Stormy started asking Lilith more questions and looking up information about voodoo just before she disappeared. The more she read, the more she feared the woman."

"Did she tell you what she found out?"

"All she told me was that Voodoo is some kind of cult worship and that Claudia seemed to be a master of it somehow, that maybe she was a priestess of some kind, but Stormy wasn't positive. What I do know is that the more Stormy learned, the more she felt Claudia around her, in her room, leaving gifts for her, or taking some of her things. She had a necklace that disappeared. She was positive the old woman had something to do with it."

"Did Stormy ever see her?"

He shook his head, "Nope, which was also extremely odd since she grew up in that house."

Serena's mouth dropped. "Never?" Goosebumps traveled up her body causing the hairs on her arm to flare up. "Do you think...?" She couldn't finish the question.

"That she might be a ghost? That's what Stormy thought. If she found anything more, she didn't tell me. Haley went missing around that time.

Stormy stopped looking into Claudia and just focused on finding our friend."

The bell rang, signaling the end of lunch. "Don't look for her Serena," Jesse whispered. "That woman, whatever she is, is cracked, and if Lilith is afraid of her, then you definitely don't want to mess with her."

Serena nodded her head. The insides of her shook at the very thought of the mysterious woman roaming her room. Jesse stood and picked up his bag all in one motion. "I wish I had more to tell you."

"No, it's okay. At least I have a little bit of information to go on."

"I'd walk you to your next class, but I don't want anyone to see us together."

His words sliced through her. "Oh gee, thanks," she bit back the tears.

"I'm sorry. That came out wrong. I meant that I didn't want us to get caught together by the teachers. It could be bad for both of us. Some of these teachers are watchers for Simon."

"Yeah, I know. Lilith told me. If it's so dangerous then why did you decide to meet with me?"

"If you'll notice, we kind of did it where no one would look for us. Besides, I knew something was wrong. You needed to talk to someone. It was worth the risk." He looked down and fiddled with the zipper to his backpack before looking up again. "You are worth the risk."

His words and the look on his face left her unsettled. He heaved his back on his shoulder. "You go first, I'll follow."

She nodded, grabbed her bag and backtracked through the maze. Just before she walked around the last corner, Jesse pulled gently on her arm to stop her.

"I want to meet with you again, help you any way I can, but we have to be careful."

She nodded. "I'll see you around."

***

Jesse wasn't on the bus that afternoon. Again. Maybe he had to work, maybe not. Kendra sat by her friends; their conversation about the dance and what to wear came to Serena in bits and pieces. She leaned her head against the cold glass. It felt good against her forehead. She hadn't realized she had dozed off until the driver yelled at her from the front. She threw her bag over her shoulder and marched off the bus. The freezing air woke her up, and Henry's SUV was a welcome sight. She opened the door, climbed in and found Lilith was in the front seat. None of them acknowledged each other. They were each too tired, too mindful of other thoughts.

Serena watched out the front window. The road narrowed and got steeper until finally they drove between two large oak trees and the land began to clear, allowing her to see the monstrosity that stood at the top of the hill.

She scanned the front of the house for her room. She knew it faced the side of the house, but the hall she walked every day to the bathroom had evenly spaced dormer windows. Her end of the hall always seemed lighter than Stormy's end. She counted the dormer windows, four on her side. 1-2-3-4-. Her heart slammed against her ribs. A face in the window peered back at her! Serena's heart pounded in her ears as they stared at each other. The girl's green eyes were wide with fear. She opened her mouth to speak, and then she was gone. The window stood empty again.

Serena gripped the armrest, digging her nails deep into the leather, knuckles white. There was nowhere to run from this house, nowhere to hide. Pressing her back against the seat, she prayed for help as they continued climbing the road to the haunted house, a disturbed aunt, and a dead cousin.

Chapter 21--Early Friday Morning

The fading notes of a once familiar song woke Serena. A flowery scent of rose petals floated around her like morning mist. She couldn't remember the dream she was having when she woke, but there had been the foreboding notes of a music box playing somewhere in the distance. She could still hear the music, though it was quieter as she rose to the surface from dreamland.

Her eyelids felt crusty and her body sore as she became fully awake. She rubbed her eyes and opened them. Darkness surrounded her. The remnants of her dream came back to her, but she was back on her bed instead of the floor like she had remembered. Had that all been a part of a dream? A dream within a dream?

The tune that had awakened her began again. It was the same song that she remembered from her mother's jewelry music box. She had very few memories of her mom, but this was one of the clearest ones she held onto over the years. She had found the box in the back of her father's closet and opened it. The song wasn't a soft, lilting song to lull someone to sleep. It was, instead, a tune that chilled her bone marrow. Her father found her in the closet, entranced by the hypnotic notes. He pulled it from her hands. She never saw the box again. She happened to find the tune on YouTube by accident. Once again, she found herself entranced by the melody. It wasn't until the person next to her nudged her to see if she was okay that she snapped out of the hypnotic trap she was in. She hadn't listened to it since.

Sitting up, she angled her head to one side, trying to place where the music was coming from. The chorus repeated itself three or four times before she had the guts to climb out of bed. The sound was muffled, but it appeared to be coming from down the hall. She tiptoed to the door and peeked into the hall. At five o'clock it was pitch black, but then she noticed a flicker of light under Stormy's door. A shadow passed beneath the door as if someone was pacing the room, but the usual sounds of creaking floorboards or footfalls were absent. As Serena took her first step, the ominous tune deepened, reverberating in every bone, every synapse of her body. She crept down the hall on her tiptoes, the music getting louder as she approached the door. She wanted to stop, to turn around and run for her room, but she was pulled to the door. She whispered the words;

"Come little children, I'll take thee away into a land of enchantment. Come little children, the time's come to play here in my garden of shadows."

Serena tried the knob, but it was locked like it had been several days ago. The song ended abruptly, the slap of the music box lid coming down suddenly. She lifted her hand to knock when she heard footsteps behind her.

The light below the portrait clicked on at the same time as the words were spoken. "What are you doing?"

She spun around, startled and near to tears from terror. "I'm s-s-sorry, Lil--." The name died in her throat. No one was there.

Erratic heart beats thudded in her ears. The floor beneath her feet became unbearably cold. She ran to her room but turned one last time to see if she was being watched. She wasn't. Yet she didn't feel like she was alone, there was still something watching her. Shuffling feet along the hardwood floor, drawing closer with each step. Serena took the last step into her room. As she shut the door, she glanced back at Stormy's bedroom door once more. A light flickered below the door like a candle flame. Then it was gone, and she was standing alone in the dark.

Shaking violently, she flipped on the light and closed her door then ran back to the bed. What had just happened?

The clock beside her rang suddenly. She hit the button between the two bells. "What the--" The clock she had broken was now working again; no shattered glass, no frozen hands. She picked it up. Someone must have fixed it, which meant that a person had snooped through her room. Serena knew the woman was Claudia. There was no one else it could be.

She surveyed the bedroom from her position on the bed. If Claudia had fixed the clock, what else had she done? Serena looked at her pictures to see if they had been moved while she had slept. They had. Again, they were facing the wall. How could the woman come into her room without Serena hearing anything? She began her search for anything else different. Her heart beat against her ribcage with such force, her chest hurt. The third scan around the room her brain finally saw the difference. In the corner diagonal from her bed on a small window seat sat a new doll. This was a boy, dressed in gray pants and suspenders and a white collared shirt. His hair was dark, parted to the side. He too looked familiar. The dolls faced her as if they were watching her. The clock ticked beside her.

She forced her body to move. Terror had rendered her frozen, but staying on that bed wouldn't get her out of the room. She pushed herself off the bed, ran to the dresser and began yanking clothes out of the drawers. All thumbs, she pulled her hair up into a messy bun. She grabbed her makeup bag, making sure it had her toothbrush and toothpaste in it. She could take care of that downstairs. She wouldn't stay on the second floor any longer than necessary. She shoved her numb feet into socks and flung open the door, scared of what would be on the other side but anxious to get downstairs. Nothing. The light from her room cast a glow only to the next hallway. Beyond that hall though, the light could not penetrate.

Counting from three she raced down the hall. The faint outline of Stormy's door was there. She could see it just as she turned the corner. She didn't stop until she was at the bottom of the stairs. Henry and Lilith stared at her, startled from her abrupt entrance. No one spoke a word.

"Going somewhere?" Lilith nodded toward Serena's makeup bag. "Just to the bathroom. I didn't have time to get ready, so I thought I'd finish up down here." Serena walked to the bathroom, feeling both sets of eyes on her back. She brushed her teeth and added mascara and a little bit of blush just for color. Her face stared back at her in the mirror. Once again she was reminded of Stormy's picture right before she had disappeared. The longer she stayed in this house, the more Serena looked like her cousin. The half-moons under her eyes had grown even darker, her skin was paler, her cheeks more hollow. Had she only moved here a week ago? She felt as if it had been a lifetime.

"Come on, Serena," Lilith's knock on the door startled her. She left her makeup bag and toothbrush on the counter by the sink.

A few bites of breakfast, four gulps of lukewarm coffee and she was out the door.

***

The last bell rang signaling the end of the day and Serena, along with the rest of the school body, packed her books inside her backpack and left the classroom. She was halfway to the exit when she remembered her history book. She had wanted to read a part about the Druids over the weekend.

As she dialed in her locker combination, Kendra and her friends came around the corner. Their conversation was about the upcoming dance. Serena finally got her locker to open. She grabbed the book and slammed the door then turned to find the girls standing behind her.

She jumped. Kendra stood in front of them, her eyes in narrow slits.

Serena lifted her chin and glared back at her. "What do you want?"

Kendra said nothing as two girls flanked Serena on either side and grabbed her arms. One pushed while the other pulled. The book dropped from her hands.

"What the hell are you doing?" Serena said. Her voice bounced off the lockers and linoleum floor. None of them answered. Kendra's mouth turned up into a smile that didn't touch her eyes.

"We're teaching you a little lesson."

A girl slipped behind Serena and wrapped a rag between her teeth and pulled it tight behind her and then tied another cloth around her eyes.

They dragged her down the hall, her feet slipping as she struggled to stay upright and fight against them. Pushed and pulled, Serena struggled violently between them. Disoriented, she tripped. Her knees hit the floor hard and she cried out. They yanked her up, tugged her forward two more steps and then stopped.

Serena tried to pull herself away. Where is everyone? Was there no one in the school to help her or were they all a part of the kidnapping? A door squealed open and Serena felt a shove. Slamming shut, leaving her in total darkness.

Chapter 22--Friday Afternoon

Henry's SUV suddenly appeared on the crest of the driveway. Lilith's focus on cutting the tomatoes immediately dropped; the knife slipped and cut her finger instead. She hardly felt the pain as the blood came rushing to the surface. "Damn." She grabbed the dish towel beside her and ran to the sink for the cold water.

The front door opened. Seeing her hand wrapped in the towel, Henry rushed to her side, his eyes wild with fright. "Would you grab a band-aid from the bathroom," she asked. He was back thirty seconds later and helped wrap her finger. Once finished she asked the question, dreading the answer.

"What happened and where's Serena?"

He signed, "I don't know! I waited at the end of the road, the bus came and went and Serena never got off of it. Could she have run away?"

She spoke instead of signing. "Where would she go? She can't run away in this weather and she'd need help to get out of here. There's no way she could've made friends this quickly that they would help her escape."

"She has to be somewhere," Lilith said more to herself than to Henry. As if on cue the phone rang in the living room. She ran to catch it, glancing quickly at the caller ID. It was the school.

"What?" she barked.

"Serena's gone," Mr. Dawson said.

"Yes, I know. Henry just got home and told me." Then she realized something. "What I'd like to know is why he found out before you did? Weren't you supposed to be watching her, making sure she got on the bus?"

"Yes, but I was disciplining some boys, and Mrs. Flinch was busy with kids in the office. You can't expect us to babysit your niece all the time. We don't work for you."

"No you don't, but you do work for Simon and my orders for you to watch the girl came from Simon. It's your head here, not mine!"

He backpedaled. "I'm sorry, Mrs. Robertson."

"Do you have an idea of where she could've gone?"

"Not a clue."

"Okay." She slammed down the receiver. Henry was by her side. He handed her the glass of whiskey. She took a drink. It did a good job of calming her down.

Think, she told herself, but no ideas came to mind, so she took another sip, and then another. "Come on, let's go."

***

Serena's fists ached from pounding on the door and her voice was hoarse from yelling. She had already investigated the small closet. Bleach filled the air, and a bucket and mop had fallen on top of her. Disoriented, she began banging on the other walls until she found one that sounded different, less muffled.

"Hello? Is anyone out there?" she called loudly. She slumped forward and leaned her head against the door, exhausted physically and emotionally. Fortunately she had no qualms with tight spaces.

Just outside the door she could hear footsteps echo along the corridor.

"Hello?" She called out again.

"Serena?" Jesse's voice called out from the other side.

"Yeah, it's me."

He jiggled something on the door and then turned the knob. Serena fell out, face planting into his chest. She looked up to see him. He paused, holding her gaze. "What happened?"

"Kendra. Those girls she hangs out." She straightened so that she wasn't leaning on him. She watched his jaw clench as his whole body turn rigid, ready for a fight. "I thought she had changed."

"So did I." His voice was quiet and angry.

She sighed and dropped her head. "I'm so tired of this." She raked her fingers through her hair and bit her lip to distract herself from crying. His arms wrapped around her and pulled her close. She leaned against him.

"I know."

"Wait, what are you doing here and not on the bus?"

"I stayed late to set up for the dance. I was trying to find the janitor's closet for some cleaning supplies. Would you like a ride home?"

Serena blew out a deep breath. "Yeah, that'd be nice."

"Hello, you two." Mr. Dawson said. Jesse and Serena sprung apart. "Serena, what happened to you?"

"Kendra and her little friends locked me in the janitor's closet."

"Hm, I'll have a talk with them. They won't bother you anymore. I'll guarantee it. Now, why don't I escort you to the office. We can call your aunt." Mr. Dawson took her by the crook of her arm and lead her away before Jesse could say or do anything. She glanced back at him, seeing him ready to fight, his hands in fists and jaw set. She shook her head at him and mouthed the word, "No."

His shoulders sagged. Neither of them could do anything about this. It was futile to even think of it.

***

Once in town Lilith closed her eyes, focused on Serena's spirit. Like a lighthouse beam she swept to and fro across the town. A faint pounding of fists and yelling called out to her. Serena. The school. When Lilith had locked in on the girl she heard a faint ringing of her cell phone deep inside of her purse. She answered on the last ring. "Hello?"

"Mrs. Robertson, this is Mrs. Flinch. We have your niece here."

***

When Henry arrived, Serena couldn't get out of the school fast enough. Lilith didn't say anything.

Serena enclosed herself in the dark backseat. In the grand scheme of life, this wasn't the worst thing that had happened to her, but it wasn't the best either. She brushed away tears as Henry drove.

Overgrown trees on either side of the road crept overhead, their branches spreading out like claws, scraping the roof of the car. Gusts of wind pushed them back and forth, making it seem as if they were reaching for her. She could see the outline of Henry's face with the help of the dash lights. His face tensed as he pushed harder on the gas pedal, anxious to get out of the woods. By the time they drove through the two trees marking the entrance to Simon and Lilith's property, her hands hurt from gripping the seat and her jaw ached from gritting it.

The house loomed in front of her, a shadow against the night sky. She tried not to look at the dormer window above the living room, fearing she'd see someone looking back at her. Of course, trying not to look only made it the first place her eyes sought. Nothing. Just an empty void.

She breathed a sigh of relief. Once parked, Lilith got out of the car first. Wind and snow blew her black hair and it swirled around her ghostly white face. As soon as Henry moved the vehicle away Lilith stepped in front of Serena, blocking her from entering the warm house. The wind was howling hard, forcing them to yell at each other.

"Where have you been?" Her voice was tinged with more terror than anger.

"The janitor's closet. Kendra and her friends threw me in there."

"Mr. Dawson says otherwise. He told me he found you and Jesse together."

"That man has no idea what he's talking about. Jesse found me five minutes before Mr. Dawson showed up."

Another gust of wind assaulted them from behind. Dead leaves scattered across the porch. Without another word Lilith finally opened the door. Both tumbled inside. She shut the door and locked it as Serena turned on the lights.

Once in the kitchen, Lilith turned on a propane burner and put on a teapot as Serena pulled her boots off her feet.

Lilith stepped back and looked Serena up and down. "You look like her, you know."

Serena couldn't tell if she was pleased or not. "Thank you?"

"It's not a compliment." Her voice steeled.

"What do you mean? I saw her portrait. Stormy's beautiful."

"Yes, she was, but Stormy's not who I meant."

"Who then?"

"You have the green eyes of your father, your uncle, your grandmother. So did Stormy." Lilith walked to the liquor cabinet and pulled out a bottle of Scotch and a tumbler. She deposited two ice cubes into the glass and poured the amber liquid over them, then she walked into the living room where she settled on the couch across from the fire right as the teapot began to whistle.

Serena turned off the burner. A dainty cup on a saucer sat on the counter beside the burner with a teabag already inside. Serena poured hot water over it and the scent of Sleepy Time tea flooded her with memories. She sucked in her breath and blinked hard to make the tears go away. Lilith sighed from the living room, reminding Serena of their conversation. She was relieved for the distraction. She followed suit with her teacup and sat in the armchair facing her.

"You look like your mother," Lilith said after a few minutes.

"And that's a bad thing?"

"She was nice, but I didn't see what the big deal was. It's not like she was special.."

Her words struck Serena hard. She hardly knew her mother, but she'd never heard anything bad about her.

"Watch yourself, Serena," Lilith spoke quietly. "I wasn't Crystal's biggest fan, but Rosalie hated her."

Her jaw dropped. "What? Why?"

She shrugged. "She blamed your mother for taking her favorite son."

"My dad?"

"Yes, your dad. Your father was very powerful and she was counting on him for a lot of things. If that wasn't enough, he was the only byproduct of her marriage with a man she actually loved."

"'Powerful? What do you mean?"

"He could move things with his mind, he had the ability to bind magic to objects that only he or anyone he appointed could open the said item, and he could cast spells that no one could break.

"He could do all of that? Can Simon do the same thing?"

"No, he doesn't have the same intensity nor the same abilities that your father had."

"Why?"

"Simon and your dad didn't share the same father. Simon has never met his father and won't speak of him, so don't bother asking. Apparently there was no love lost between the man and Rosalie. But things were different with Jonathan's father, Bruce. She actually fell in love with him."

"What happened?"

"Things didn't work out between them."

"Does he live around here?" The idea that she had a grandfather she'd never met, who looked like her dad, interested her.

"No. He's dead." Lilith took a drink.

"Oh." Deflated, she waited for Lilith to tell her more, but she sipped her drink instead. "So why didn't you like my mother?"

"Me? Well, I hated her because she stole my husband."

Serena's heart stopped. "She would never do such a thing!"

"Oh pipe down girl." Lilith rolled her eyes. "She didn't literally steal him. Simon just became so enchanted with her that he no longer wanted Stormy or me. After Jonathan married Crystal he distanced himself from the family, When she died he cut off all connections and disappeared as only he could do with the help of a spell. Simon had become obsessed with your mother and was possibly more devastated when she died than Jonathan was."

"That's not true," she repeated. "No one was more crushed than my father."

"It's really not important who missed her more," Lilith turned to her. "What is important is that Rosalie doesn't like you. Never has. You need to watch yourself around her, are we clear?"

Serena nodded.

"She's a very powerful woman," Lilith went on. "I don't know how to explain what she does, but try not to be alone in a room with her."

"Will she kill me?"

"No, I don't think so, at least not yet, but she'll make you wish you were dead. Just stay away from her. I can't believe I'm saying this, but stay close to Simon. He is the only reason Rosalie is putting up with you at the moment."

"Can Simon do the same things Rosalie does?"

Lilith didn't answer. Serena watched her eyes glaze as she detached from their conversation. As if on cue, headlights arched through the windows and Simon's car rolled up the hill to the house. A sudden burst of anxiety filled her limbs. Serena ran to the stairs just as the front door opened. She ducked into the hallway, and paused, looking down on Simon's head. He stood still, suitcase in one hand, a snow-covered hat in the other.

"Lilith," he said. "Where's Serena?"

"I believe she went upstairs to change into her pajamas. Why?" Serena heard Lilith set her glass on the table. "You weren't expecting a welcoming committee were you?" Her voice was sharp.

"Serena?" Simon called up the stairs. She didn't answer, nor did she wait any longer. She turned and raced down the hall back to her room. The darkness seemed to close in tighter around her, but she pushed through her fear and arrived at her door just as Simon called her name again. He was getting closer. Lights in the hall flickered on behind her.

Serena closed the door silently, then locked it. She had forgotten to leave on the lamp, so it was dark in her room. A cold breeze fell upon her from above her as the ceiling fan began spinning on its own; the curtains began blowing as if someone had left a window open.

"Serena?" Simon's voice called from the other side of the closed door.

"Hold on, I'm getting dressed." She flipped on the light and found some flannel plaid bottoms and an oversized sweatshirt that she pulled over her head.

"Serena!" Simon called again. "Serena--."

She yanked open the door and stepped out into the hall. Simon stood mere inches away, still dressed in his long coat, with the markings of melted snow on the shoulders.

"What took you so long?" he demanded.

"Sorry," she said, "I was just changing."

"Next time I come home from a long week away, I want you ready to meet me at the door. And not dressed in that." He gestured to her clothing. "Do you understand me?"

"Yes, sir."

He eyed her warily. "Come downstairs."

She followed him down the stairs. She reached the last two steps that left her eye-to-eye with Simon. He inspected her from bottom to top, eventually looking her in the face.

Lilith moved slowly around the kitchen, pulling out a plastic tray from the microwave. The aroma of roast beef, mashed potatoes and corn overwhelmed Serena, reminding her that she hadn't eaten. Her stomach growled as she watched Lilith, whose eyes were empty as she scooped the dinner onto a plate. Simon's arrival seemed to have robbed her of life. She reminded Serena of a marionette, merely doing what she was told.

Simon brushed past her, walked to the door on the opposite side of the living room from Lilith's room, and disappeared into it.

When he returned, he was dressed more casually. He wore loose pants and a tight fitting shirt. He set his chiseled jaw, his green eyes watching for Serena's reaction. She could feel the heat rise to her cheeks. She cast her eyes down, not wanting to look him in the eye.

He ran long fingers through his dark hair, raking it back from his face. With his hair back, his eyes and brows were even more pronounced. Lilith didn't seem to notice him as she set his food on the counter. Serena wondered if it bothered him that his wife seemed indifferent to him.

She glanced back at Simon and realized he was watching her, not his wife. "Lilith, you can go to bed now." He waved her away and she shuffled off without acknowledging either of them. Serena turned for the stairs, but Simon stopped her.

"Where do you think you're going?" Simon's lingering gaze made her more uncomfortable with each second that ticked on the wall clock.

"To bed," she answered, anxious to leave.

"Fine," he said. She turned to climb the stairs when he stopped her again.

"Tomorrow morning I want you up bright and early. I have a specific dress I want you to wear for when my mother gets here. I'll have Lilith help you with it, your hair and makeup too."

"I know how to dress nicely," Serena glared at him. How dare he control her by telling her what to wear? She crossed her arms, looking him directly in the eyes. Lilith might go numb around him, but she wasn't going to.

He stood up from the barstool, pushing it aside, and straightened his back. "Do you want to run that by me again?" His voice was quiet, but deadly. Serena felt the air suddenly grow thick and heavy and she wilted under the sudden weight of it, unsure what was happening and why she felt so dizzy.

"Again, tomorrow morning I want you up bright and early. I have a specific dress I want you to wear for when my mother gets here. Are we clear?"

She nodded in reply and put her foot on the first step.

"Oh yes." His icy tone froze her where she stood. "You are not to see that Jesse kid again, do you understand me?"

She gulped and nodded yes, her mind racing. How did he know about Jesse?

"You can go to bed now."

She bolted up the stairs and ran to her room, locking the door behind her. Her heart knocked against her chest, sending blood racing to her head and making the room spin. She slid down to the floor, her back against the door, her breath raspy and loud in her own ears. She tried to calm herself by taking deep breaths. No footsteps on the floor behind the door. Simon hadn't followed her this time.

Still, the knob above her head rattled and turned, then stopped. It jiggled again and she held her breath, waiting.

Down the hall, the music box began to play.

Chapter 23--Friday Night

Simon stood at the window, watching the snowfall heavily to the ground. It was silent both outside as well as inside.

Surreal, that's how he'd describe this day and probably the next few as well. After so many years of looking and almost finding her, they were able to bring her home. Now was the true beginning.

Serena looked like her mother. Except for her eyes. He had hoped she would have inherited the blue eyes and fine brow arch her mother had possessed. Instead, she inherited the distinctive green eyes of his family. But maybe that was a good thing. Maybe that meant she had inherited other family traits as well.

A door shut across the living room from him and he looked out his bedroom door. Lilith walked silently to the kitchen, grabbed a bottle filled with amber liquid and a glass and carried it back to her room. Why she grabbed a glass, he didn't know. It wasn't like she would leave anything in that bottle. She never had the same grace as Crystal. Where Crystal practically floated when she walked, Lilith's entrance attracted every man's attention with her self-possession, her chin up and eyes forward. She was statuesque and commanded a room of people to look her way with awe when she passed through it.

At least she used to be. Not anymore. Now she walked with her eyes glazed over. If they did focus on him the glare was full of contempt. She used to show her true self with him, their love-making fierce, their arguments passionate and fiery, but then he became distracted by Crystal and it was no longer Lilith he saw when they made love but Crystal's face instead. That's when she pulled away. With each year that passed the fracture between them became a gulf that neither of them could cross.

Simon could feel eyes looking at him. He had been distracted by his memories and just then realized Lilith was staring back at him, a look of brokenness. Their gazes locked for a few moments more.

She dropped her eyes first, turned and walked into her room. The door shut with a small click barely audible across the large expanse. He did the same. Facing the window outside, he watched the snow fall again. The grief was sometimes unbearable.

The memory he held down, the screams of, "Daddy help me!" rushed back to his ears as if it were happening all over again. He banged his head against the window, his palms splayed on the panes, hoping the cold would stop the cries. He swallowed hard and pushed that night back down into the Pandora's box that held all the things that could destroy him if opened. He pressed the lid down, but it was getting more difficult these days to keep it closed.

He slowed down his breathing and the cries grew faint. He had to get out of this house. He hated being here. This place always brought out his weaknesses. The alarm on his phone began to vibrate on the bedside table.

Chapter 24--Friday Night

Lilith lay in bed, thinking. One trail led to another. First Simon, which led to Angel. Lilith hated that woman and had vowed many times to kill her. If only she could leave this house. Angel didn't respect Lilith the way she ought to, but she didn't know just how much power Lilith still had and could derive from sheer hatred. She knew that was one of the reasons Simon wouldn't bring Angel up to the chateau. To bring that woman to this house would be to kill her himself. Maybe someday, when he was tired of her he would do just that.

Rage against Angel brought Lilith fully awake. She threw back the covers and got out of bed and pulled on her robe. She opened her bedroom door. Across the living room was the closed door to Simon's room. She sensed he wasn't in there. She was tempted to poke around inside, but she didn't know when he would come back to his body. Instead, she went to the kitchen and turned on the light above the oven and gathered some cheese and crackers. She flipped off the light and went back to her room, pausing to look at Simon's door before shutting hers. She climbed back into bed and had her snack. The wine in the mini bar in the corner of her room beckoned her, but she refused that temptation as well.

As she took another bite, Jesse came to mind. What was she going to do with that boy? Hadn't he learned the first time that he was playing with fire by being anywhere close to their family? She had warned him, she had warned his family. She cared about the boy since he was one last connection to Stormy, but she couldn't save him this time. He was on his own. She hoped with all of her might that Rosalie would not find out about him.

Rosalie. Just her name left Lilith chilled. Her stomach rolled over. She clenched her jaw to keep her teeth from chattering. Suddenly the last two pieces of cheese and crackers no longer looked appetizing. She set the plate on the table beside her.

Of all the people in the world, including her own father, no one scared her as much Rosalie did. There had been only one time she almost lost her life to that woman and that was over Stormy. Truth be told, Lilith wished she had died. To die would be sweet relief from the agony of losing her daughter, so by keeping Lilith alive, Rosalie kept her in constant pain. Another reason she was kept alive, was that even in her weakened state, Lilith was still more powerful than any family member, and Rosalie would use her, especially against Serena.

Lilith's marriage to Simon was arranged by Rosalie and her father. Her mother had no vote, no matter how much she tried to dissuade her husband. Her father knew he could make a lot of money, gain prestige, and power by being in-laws with Rosalie. Her father, Frederick Von Latent, had no idea how gifted Lilith was. It was only by accident that her father found out. He had mentally asked a question and she had audibly answered it. From the time she was twelve to her eighteenth birthday, she was "trained" to use her abilities and cultivate new ones. One of them being that she could astral project herself throughout the house. What he did not know was how far she could actually travel. Her specialty, however, was that she could cause the most excruciating pain within people just by using her mind. He found out by experience after Lilith's mother jumped to her death from their penthouse suite in New York. He had treated her mother so cruelly that she could live with herself no longer. Lilith made sure her father knew how it felt to hit the pavement when she was done with him.

But before all of that happened, Rosalie and her father made a deal by uniting Lilith and Simon. There had been a grand wedding with friends and family. There was the intense training that Rosalie took over from her father. Even Lilith was impressed with her growing abilities. Rosalie had shown kindness to her, however brief, but now that was all gone. Now, Rosalie was an icicle ready to drop upon Lilith's head as soon as she was finished with her. She would use Lilith to get what she wanted and she wanted Serena.

With thoughts of Serena, Lilith was pulled to the present and then the future. She could not wait for this day to be over with. She deliberately turned her thoughts away from her daughter. She couldn't go there, she wouldn't go there. The day would be torturous enough.

She glanced at the clock to find it was three o'clock. A sudden and cold draft of air puffed underneath her door. Simon was back to his room. That had been fast. Usually he took his time with his wanderings. Her thought continued to circle her head like the cartoon drawing of birds chasing each other around. Simon, Rosalie, Stormy, Serena. Simon, Rosalie, Stormy, Serena. Simon, Rosalie, Stormy, Serena. The names blurred into one long word as she finally fell into an uneasy doze.

Chapter 25--Early Saturday Morning

Still unable to sleep, Simon padded into the bathroom. The heated tiles warmed his feet as he turned on the fan and started the shower. It only took a few seconds for the water to heat up and when it did he stepped in, letting the water stream over his body. He closed his eyes, taking a deep breath in then letting it out slowly. He always loved a good hot shower. His thoughts traveled back to his grandparent's house. He never got to have hot showers there, or even a hot bath. It had always been cold, just like them.

It was his grandfather who had named him Simon; his mother wanted nothing to do with him and he never knew his biological father, though he finally found out the man's identity when he was a teenager.

His grandparents raised him as an only child. He both loved and detested attention. His grandmother had been nicer than his grandfather, but not by much.

He turned off the water, grabbed his towel and began to dry off. When he was finished he wrapped the towel around the waist and took a look at himself in the mirror. His mother's eyes stared back at him. He shared the same shape, same mixed shades of green, accented by the black ring around it, and the same long, black lashes. They were the same eyes that had been passed down from his grandfather, then to his mother, her two sons and eventually two granddaughters. Yay for genetics, he mused.

He shifted his gaze to his square jaw, one of the few gifts from his biological father, because Jonathan and their grandfather didn't have it. He was always looking for something he inherited from his sperm donor. Eh, what did he care now? He had found him. Eventually. And he did share some things with the man. But not the things he was looking for.

Simon shook his head to clear it. Back to his face, did he need a shave? Yes, he did. He took out his shave lotion and razor, filled the sink with warm water and began the process.

As he stared into the mirror, his mother's face came to mind. She had been, and still was, absolutely beautiful. And she knew it. She was very vain. She had the hourglass figure every woman wished for. Her dark auburn hair was thick and wavy, her cheekbones high and defined, and her oval face attracted men of every age. But it was her green eyes that held their gazes. It was also because of her eyes that she was often accused of being a witch given how she easily captivated men. She never denied the accusations. In actuality, she just used it to her advantage.

She had Simon when she was a teenager, back when doing such a thing was not accepted, and in fact, was a disgrace. She had always been ahead of her time. When she was seventeen she gave birth to him and her parents took him home. While she was still in the hospital recovering, his grandfather had her committed to an insane asylum. Most people would think that was a drastic measure to take for a rebellious teenager, but she was a bit crazy. A few hours after Simon's birth a nurse caught her trying to suffocate him with a pillow. So the baby was sent home with his loveless grandparents, and his loveless mother was hospitalized.

Done with shaving Simon unplugged the sink to let the water out and wiped his face with a towel. His visage was smooth now, no nicks or any other imperfections. Glancing at the digital clock on the counter beside him he found it to be only four in the morning. He yawned and stretched. Maybe he could catch a couple hours of sleep before his mother arrived. He hung the towel on the hook, flipped off the light switch, and climbed between the sheets. Thoughts of his mother persisted, in spite of his drowsiness.

Simon never even knew about her until she was released a few months after his fifth birthday. They declared her satisfactorily sane. When she arrived home, he thought she was an older sister he never knew about. He didn't care much for her and the feelings were mutual on her end. She never hugged him, smiled at him, or spoke to him for the first month she lived at home.

Soon, Simon fell into a fitful sleep. His memories continued on within his dreams.

One day she broke her silence and addressed him with a voice velvet and sultry, "Boy, come to me." She sat in her favorite chair, reading a book. She wore a short skirt and low cut blouse. She looked him over just as closely as he looked at her. Small for his age and skinny too, his thick black hair was one of his best features, next to the green eyes he had inherited from her.

"Hmph," she glared at him. "You look like your father."

"So," he said. "He's your father too." He stuck his tongue out at her.

She held his gaze, playing a staring contest, showing him who was in charge. Her eyes narrowed before she ripped open his world. "No, he's my father. Not yours." Then she went back to reading.

He ran into the kitchen crying and told his "mother" what she had said. That's when he found out the truth. Simon's grandfather had yelled at Rosalie, slapped her a few times, and threw her in her room. Simon enjoyed watching through the crack in the door. After that day she didn't talk to him for another six months.

It wasn't until she caught him torturing the neighbor girl's cat that she began talking to him again. She sat in her bikini on the back porch, smoking and drinking a beer, as she watched him drown the kitten. Suddenly she took an interest in him. She told him she wouldn't tell anyone what he had done. She even helped him bury the cat. He didn't so much like her as he respected her after that incident. He stole cigarettes from "dad" for her, liquor from the wet bar, whatever she wanted. He was her errand boy and he loved her attention.

His grandparents saw how their relationship was growing and didn't like it. They had it out with her one night, telling her she had to leave the house because she was a bad influence on him. When she said no, Grandpa yanked her around and started whipping her. She refused to cry out. She told them their "secret" about the cat and how Simon was evil without her help. They didn't believe her until she dug up the animal and showed them. That was the first time he was beaten hard enough that he couldn't sleep on his back for a few days. She didn't seem to care about the beating, nor did she stick around to watch or defend him. She went out to party with some friends.

Early the next morning, Simon got up to pee and noticed her door was open a crack. He peeked in and saw a man in bed with her, his naked body sprawled out beside her. He was sleeping while she sat, wearing only a bra, her back against the headboard, smoking a cigarette and reading a book. She noticed him peeping and put a finger up to her lips to shush him, a slow smile stretching wide on her pretty face. He was so angry she had betrayed him that he ran into his grandparents' room to tell on her.

He shook his grandfather's hand that hung off the side of the bed. He didn't wake up. He ran around to his grandma's side and yanked on her shoulder, she slowly rolled over on her back, eyes open but not seeing. He stood still, waiting for either of them to do something, but they never moved. He slumped down to the floor and sat there for a long time. Finally Rosalie, his actual mother, joined him. She had changed into more appropriate pajamas and braided her hair. She looked innocent and quite young, except for the cigarette she had between her left forefinger and thumb. She slid down the wall next to him and spoke quietly.

"They had to die," she said, matter of factly. She took another drag on her cigarette and then put it out in the purple shag carpet, grinding the ash in as far as she could. "They were going to send me away again and there was no way I was going to go back." She leaned in closer, the scent of tobacco flowing over him, and whispered conspiratorially, "Besides, I heard them talk about sending you to an asylum too."

He was scared. "You killed them?"

"Yes," she winked at him.

"Now you're really gonna get in trouble," he warned her, his eyes wide with fright. "And then what's going to happen to me?"

"I'm not going to go away," she said, determined. "I poisoned them. I wrote a suicide letter for my father on his typewriter that he never let me use. How ironic is that? Ha."

"What does it say?"

"How unhappy they were with how things turned out, us kids, and how they were done with this life." She shrugged. "It was true for the most part. Come on, let's go call the police."

They walked down the hall, past her bedroom, the door closed now. "Is he still in there?" he asked.

"He left already."

"Why? You aren't going to get in trouble now."

"I know that, you know that, but he didn't and I didn't want him to figure that out. I woke him and made him leave as soon as you came in here."

"Oh."

She made the call, voice broken, crying over the phone even though there were no tears. As they waited for the police to show up, she coached him on how to cry inconsolably, which wasn't that hard since there was a part of him that really was sad. They were the only parents he had known for the first five years of his life. Mother and son stuck around for the funeral and the reading of the will. She was named guardian, but Simon was the beneficiary of everything. Once they received the inheritance money, they sold the house and left for the west coast.

It wasn't until they settled in California that he watched her perform a seance. That was fun, just the two of them, communing with the dead. Actually, it was terrifying, but every time she did one, and with each added person included, he became more intrigued.

Then she met Bruce and everything changed. She was working in a lawyer's office as a secretary, and though he had a wife and a couple of daughters already, Rosalie didn't care. She wanted him, and what she wanted she always got. Bruce was bored with the suburban lifestyle and her wildness attracted him. Simon would wake to the banging of the headboard against their shared wall.

At some point he fell for her too, but he wasn't going to leave his wife so Rosalie decided to do something about it. She got pregnant. When he found out what she did, he was livid until he learned she'd had a baby boy. He packed the four of them up and they headed north to a small town on the border of Washington and Idaho. Simon never knew what happened to his two little girls and wife.

They settled down in the little town, bought a piece of land and built a cabin. Bruce expected Rosalie to stay home with the kids as his first wife had, but she wasn't happy with that. She was okay for a little while, but once Jonathan was ready for kindergarten, she was itching to do something outside of the house. She felt confined, alone on the property surrounded by trees and mountains and no city life. Once she got antsy, things started getting rough between them. Then one day his mother found Bruce having sex with the secretary in his office when they had closed for lunch. He didn't know she had found out, so he was unaware that anything was wrong when he got home that night.

Jonathan and Simon hid out in the woodshed while they screamed at each other. The boys fell asleep in that old shed, not waking until after the cabin was engulfed in flames. She had already packed their clothes in the family station wagon and they hightailed it out of there. His little brother screamed as he and Simon watched out the back window as the house exploded.

The explosion in his dream startled him awake. He sat up, trying to catch his breath. The darkness outside was beginning to lighten to a gray, the snow giving it more light than there actually was. It reminded him of a stormy ocean with white caps upon the waves. A glance at the clock told him it was six o'clock. Time to get up. Another thud and the clattering of metal told him Lilith was already awake. He rolled out of bed, pulled on loose fitting lounge pants. He sighed. Countdown to Rosalie's arrival.

Those four murders, maybe five since his own father had been missing for twenty-five years, seemed to have made Rosalie more and more powerful, as if each victim's life had been added to her soul, making his mother stronger than before. Even if she was tied to any of those murders, she could not be touched legally. Coupling with Aza had been smart and that partnership had added to her dominance that she had been looking for all these years. They had now built a dynasty that would change the world and bring it to its knees in reverence of them. At least, that was what was she had schemed.

Simon had other plans.

Chapter 26--Saturday Morning

Serena woke feeling chilled, disoriented, and groggy. When the doorknob had stopped wiggling she had sprung up and jumped into bed. The music seemed to follow her and no matter how many blankets she put over her head she could still hear it. At one point during the night she had dreamed that Simon was watching her. Just as she had registered that he was there, he was gone and she fell back to sleep.

Sleep. That was what she wanted to go back to right now, but a faint light peeked through the window, revealing the sky brightening behind dark clouds. It was still very early, but her mind was already working.

A knock on the door pulled Serena from her rabbit trail of thoughts.

"I'm awake," she said.

"Good," Simon said. "Get up and get ready. My mother will be here in a couple of hours."

"Yes, sir." She pushed back the heavy down comforter covering her and she felt the cold even more intensely. She was freezing from the inside out. Any remnants of sleep faded, leaving her wide-awake. The light outside her window lightened as each second ticked by. The light gave her courage to go to the bathroom.

The tiles were icy cold on her toes. She hopped from one foot to the next as she turned on the water in the claw-foot tub. While the water warmed she flipped on the fan to cut down on the condensation, brushed her teeth, and ran a comb through her tangled hair.

When the water was hot enough she switched the lever for the showerhead and then climbed in under the spray. She closed her eyes as streams of water poured over her head and down her back. She felt her tension slowly release. Soaping up her limbs and washing her hair didn't take long, but she took her time with it. The Ivory bar and Almond scented shampoo relaxed her, recalling memories of her Pleasant Hill home. After her hair was rinsed, she stood under the water a little longer, wishing she didn't have to get out. As long as her eyes were closed she could pretend she was still at home.

Click

Her eyes flew open. A shadow on the other side of the shower curtain moved. She gasped. Despite the heavy steam from the hot water, her breath came out in a white plume as if she were standing outside in the cold.

"Who's there?" she whispered. She could have sworn she had locked the door.

No answer. Trembling, she peeked around the curtain, but no one was in the bathroom. She turned off the water. Silence filled the room.

She grabbed her towel. It wasn't warm or fluffy like it had been when she'd hung it there a few minutes ago. Instead, it hung damp and cold as if someone had already used it. She threw it on the floor and rummaged in the cupboard above the towel rack for another towel.

The next towel was cold, but at least it was dry. Her hands shook as she dried her body, wanting to get out of that room as soon as possible. Gooseflesh popped up along her arms and legs, partially from the cold, but mostly because she was so scared. When her body was dry enough not to drip down the hallway, she wrapped the towel around her head like a turban and then pulled on her robe. She was about to reach for the knob when a loud rap sounded on the door.

"Serena!" Simon's voice called. She jumped.

"What?" She swallowed the fear to keep her voice firm, her tone matching his.

"Did your father not teach you to use the fan when showering?"

"I did turn it on," but as she answered she realized the fan was silent. She remembered specifically turning it on. No wonder it was so quiet in here.

"Sorry." She switched the fan back on, effectively drowning out whatever else Simon said. She thought he'd walked away, but he startled her again when he spoke close to the crack of the door.

"And Serena, don't ever speak to me in that tone again. Do you understand?"

"Yes, sir."

After that, he was gone. Her heart was still in her throat, and she wanted to run out of there, but she forced herself to wait until she knew he was no longer hovering by the bathroom in the hall.

The light over the mirror flickered. Great. Simon was probably going to turn off the lights if she lingered there too much longer. She took the towel off her head and used it to wipe down the condensation from the mirror. At least there wasn't another message written on it this morning. She fumbled in the drawer for the comb she had just used. Where did that stupid thing go? Out of the corner of her eye something moved and when she looked back up her heart plummeted to her stomach.

There was another girl staring back at her from the mirror. Her stringy blonde hair hung in her gaunt face, and mud and grime were streaked across her forehead and cheeks, scrapes mingled with blood. A film of white, like cataracts, covered her hazel eyes.

Serena. A guttural voice spoke, too deep to belong to the girl in the mirror. *Serena. Serena. Serena.* More voices whispered from behind her, below her, above her, all of them calling her name, all of them whispering in the same deep voice, while the girl in the mirror continued to glare.

"No," Serena whimpered, and then she reached for the doorknob. It wouldn't turn. She jiggled harder, wrenching the knob one way and then the other. All but one voice stopped. It was the girl in the mirror. Soon her cackle turned into a horrific shriek. As she laughed pieces of her face began to crumble and fall off. Her jaw unhinged, but she kept on laughing, her voice growing darker and deeper with every limb that crumbled into ash.

Serena continued twisting the doorknob, terrified but unable to look away from the ashy remains. Finally, the image disappeared and the laughing stopped. In the mirror was her face again, skin white and eyes wide.

She knew the girl who had appeared in the mirror. Even with the face practically falling off, she recognized the eye shape and facial structure. Had the girl been Stormy's friend who had disappeared. She wondered if it had been Haley who had written, "Help me," on the mirror the other day. Serena wasn't sure. What she did know was that she wanted out of that room. She tried the doorknob again.

Serena, a soft whisper. With the knob turned halfway, she turned back to the mirror. A dark-haired girl in a long white gown stared at her with wide green eyes. The girl appeared before her as real as any human being, though Serena knew she could not really be there.

"Stormy," Serena said.

Help me. Stormy's mouth did not move but the words were still audible.

Stormy held her gaze captive. Serena watched, unable to help, as her cousin's green eyes darkened to a fathomless black. Blood dripped from the lengthwise cuts in each arm. Smoke began drifting up from the tips of her hair, and Serena could smell the distinct scent of the burning strands. An ember lit in Stormy's eyes, growing stronger as flames ate at the rest of her hair. Her eyes glowed red. Stormy opened her mouth to scream, but the raging fire inside her shot out in flames. Sparks and pieces of melting skin fell off her body, catching the floor beneath them on fire.

The doorknob was hot and seared Serena's flesh. Ignoring the pain she yanked open the door and raced down the hallway to her room. Her shaking legs couldn't seem to go fast enough.

Help me, Serena.

Stormy's voice chased after her. Chills ran up Serena's legs and something grabbed the hem of her robe just as she ran across the threshold of her room. As she reached for the door, a fiery hand stretched toward her. She tumbled inside and the door slammed shut.

Chapter 27--Saturday Morning

Both Simon and Lilith were tightly wound with anxiety. She stood in the kitchen, stirring a cap full of brandy into her coffee and nibbling a small bite of muffin. Unable to drink or eat, Simon stood beside the fireplace, attempting to draw warmth from it. He looked out the massive window to the white terrain. A yard was somewhere beneath several feet of heavy snow and bordered by spruces, pines, and firs.

Further down the mountain the trees were joined with Quaker aspens along with maples and alders. Their beauty distracted him as he waited for his mother and their business associate to arrive. He had hoped the heavy snowfall would deter his mother from coming, but it hadn't. Unfortunately, Rosalie loved the mountain lodge, she just didn't come up as often. This house and land held special meaning. It wasn't just the beauty of the terrain or the memories of his brother. It was the sacrifice made for this land that made the place so significant to them both.

Lilith offered him a muffin.

"No thanks."

She nodded but kept the plate in front of him. He looked into her eyes as he took the plate. "You need it. It's going to be a long day," she said.

He took a bite and swallowed as he went back to his watching post. Rosalie was a descendant from European witches who escaped the witch hunts of the 1600's by keeping their practices secret. Rosalie's aunt was a witch and taught her divination through lithomancy, telling the future using jewels and crystals. Her aunt also taught her how to conjure up the dead through private seances she and her friends would perform. There was a long held belief in her family that a familiar spirit passed through all the women in the bloodline and that Rosalie would be the embodiment of all of the Luciferian witches. All of their power would coalesce in this one person, making her powerful enough that she could build an empire or bring destruction upon the world around them. Rosalie believed that woman was herself. Simon believed it too.

It would be a long day. Simon knew that Rosalie had several reasons to be there. One, she wanted to observe Lilith. Was she stable enough to use again?

The second reason was to introduce her business partner to Serena. Azazel, a demonologist and sorcerer in his own right, would determine if Serena had potential to further their plans and if she possessed the object they were all looking for. Unfortunately, no one knew exactly what Jonathan had attached that power to or how involved Serena was to that plan. Azazel had been investigating over the last few months.

The third, and likely in Rosalie's opinion the most important, was to see how much of a threat Serena was to her. There was a prediction that a female descendent of Rosalie's could inherit the same power and bring the other down with the entire empire. Or she could make it more powerful. Either way, Rosalie would die at the hand of this woman. The only way to preserve her creation was to kill the descendant after her.

She was on the fence regarding Serena: she could be an amazing asset or a danger. The trick was to use her and then dispose of her before she gained that power. Azazel would be the one to decide which she would be: Powerful or dangerous.

Of course, he and Simon had already determined she would be an asset but he was a little bit nervous. What if Aza saw Serena as a potential threat after all? Ever since he had caught Simon's vision of mind control and Serena being the perfect specimen, they had plotted to find her and put her to good use, their use. Rosalie just didn't know how involved their plan was and how much she wasn't included in it.

The hood of the black Excursion peaked the top of the driveway. Ready or not, they were here. Simon turned and walked across the massive living room. The rest of the guests would be arriving soon as well. He used his adrenaline to propel him forward and give him the strength he needed.

He opened the door just as Rosalie was climbing out of the SUV. Azazel stepped down from the backseat. Unlike Rosalie and Simon, he did not like the mountain home. In fact, for reasons unknown to them, he hated it. A sharp, biting wind whipped through the courtyard.

"Welcome," Simon said.

"Simon," Rosalie said as she approached the front doors. She bent forward and they exchanged emotionless kisses, one on each cheek before she entered the house. Azazel shook Simon's hand. They only nodded, as if reaffirming their plans, Azazel's black eyes drilling into Simon's green ones. Yes, they were still in agreement. Simon stepped aside to allow the other man to enter the house. The SUV started up again, catching Simon's attention. He and Henry glared at each other, each one knowing what the other was doing up on that mountain. Henry geared down into four-wheel drive and continued around the circular driveway. Simon entered the house.

The living room was quiet, Lilith having already gone to her room to change and Rosalie in the guest room. She needed to change into the dress she wore only for special occasions. A group leader in Wales had given her the gown. It had been handed down through generations since the turn of the nineteenth century, worn only by the women who possessed the dominance in their world of magic. In fact, the dress wasn't so much given as it was taken. Upon threat, it had been presented to her, reaffirming her authority over all of the continents as the leader. The dress always stayed at the mountain house.

Both Rosalie and Lilith appeared at the same time. Lilith wore a black straight skirt that reached her knees and hugged her narrow hips, a black cashmere turtleneck, and her mother's necklace, a long chain with an emblem at the end of it. Her ensemble was completed with black silk nylons, black wedge heeled velvet ankle boots, and her long hair was parted down the middle, hanging on each side of her face. Most of the women in their group wore dresses similar to Rosalie's, but Lilith chose to be different, for which he was always thankful for. He hated the Victorian age style the older women wore; Lilith chose to look updated, classy and sexy all at the same time.

Standing ten feet away from Lilith, Rosalie wore the black taffeta and lace floor length dress that the former owners had most likely used as a mourning dress. Where some women might look sickly or fragile in such a dress, his mother only looked more powerful.

She glared at Lilith for taking away her spotlight by entering the room at the same time. Azazel, who had taken over Simon's room for the day, entered wearing an all black Louis Vuitton suit, with a black shirt and black tie.

Rosalie walked into the living room, establishing her position as the true leader. This was a matriarchal family. "Is she ready to be seen?"

"Not yet."

"Why not? I told you I wanted to see her before the others arrived."

"I know, but.."

Rosalie stood in front of the fireplace, looking up into the mirror. "She should have been ready and now we won't have the time to discuss how she is expected to act in a meeting such as this." She glowered at him before looking at Lilith. "Go get her ready."

Lilith set her jaw, then walked back to her room. A few moments later she emerged with a makeup bag, hair dryer and curling iron and marched up the stairs.

"Are you ready, Simon?"

"Yes."

"Good. Azazel will observe Serena from my right hand and will decide if she is usable. You will walk her into the living room and guide her to me. Lilith will be used if Serena is not forthcoming with the needed information."

"And what if she doesn't know what that object is?" Azazel asked, his tempered, but still strong, middle eastern accent coming through.

"Then we'll definitely use Lilith. She can find anything, even if she is weak at the moment. If she isn't up for it then we'll have no other choice but to be rid of her. Do you understand?"

"Yes," Simon's words were clipped. "I believe she is slowly coming out of her mourning period and will be usable soon."

"Good. I'm testing her today."

"I gathered that."

"You haven't lost your head over this girl, correct?"

He shook his head.

"I'm glad. We'll be talking about how she can be of use to us. Azazel has been discussing his ideas with me and they're very interesting indeed. I'm anxious to see if they will actually work."

The black SUV appeared once again, bringing the first set of guests.

Here we go, thought Simon. He adjusted his cufflinks and buttoned the one button in the middle of his suit jacket as he walked to the entryway. Rosalie stepped in front of him. "Go get Serena ready." Then she opened the front double doors.

"Welcome."

Chapter 28--Saturday Late Morning

A hard knock startled Serena.

"Serena," Simon said through the closed door.

She sat up in her bed and pushed her wet, snarled hair out of her face. It felt as if she had been in a trance, lulled into a stupor by terror.

"Serena," Simon called again, agitated.

"Yeah." she rose slowly. Disoriented, she walked to the door and opened it.

"Good, you're awake." Simon was wearing expensive suit pants and a form fitting suit coat. The way his eyes fell over her body made her feel naked despite her bathrobe. She narrowed the opening to her room so he wouldn't think she was inviting him in. Lilith stood behind him, arms full of hair tools and makeup.

"You need to get dressed. My mother is downstairs."

His words and tonal inflection brought on a serious case of déjà vu. Hadn't he said that before?

"What's going on?" He crossed his arms and planted his legs apart. He wasn't moving until she told him something.

"Sorry. I just had a bad dream."

"Tell me about it." He seemed genuinely interested.

"Um, you know, I don't exactly remember," she lied. Simon studied her a moment longer, his eyes clouding with suspicion. "Well, it looks like you already took a shower so start combing your hair."

"Okay."

The last place she wanted to go was that bathroom. Simon stepped aside and watched her walk down the hall, inching past Lilith. She locked the door, turned on the fan, and ignored the mirror. No shadows lingered around her.

She towel dried her hair and then began to comb out the rat's nest. A scratching froze her. Intuitively she knew it was Simon before he spoke. She could hear his breathing on the other side. His face had to be planted against the crack of the doorjamb.

"Yes?" she said.

There was a pause before he replied. His voice held an odd note to it. "I set out the clothes I want you to wear today."

"Okay," she pressed her ear to the door, listening for his exit. When she no longer heard him breathing, she opened the door and looked both ways before stepping out. Just then Stormy's door clicked shut.

Had Simon gone into Stormy's room? His voice carried from down the hall answering her question. He must be talking with Lilith so there wasn't anyone on the second floor with her, except Claudia.

Serena.

The quiet voice called to her.

I need you.

She was scared to death, but she was drawn to that door by the broken, tearful voice calling to her. She crept down the hall and tried the knob but it was locked. There had to be a key somewhere. She felt the ledge above the door, finding nothing but dust. Then she looked at the portrait of her cousin and froze.

The original picture was gone. In its place was another painting. In the dim light of the bathroom behind her she could tell it was of Stormy smiling at the artist. Serena turned on the light below the frame. In the painting Stormy was standing in the meadow from Serena's dreams. It was behind the detached garage across from the main house. Low lying fog covered brown grass. As if the picture were alive a breeze ruffled the white dress Stormy was wearing.

Trembling, Serena leaned closer to get a better view of the dress. It was the same white gown she was wearing in Serena's dreams. A sweetheart neckline ended in a bow at the fitted bodice, ruffled sleeves were at her elbows, and the skirt hung to her feet.

Her dark hair fell in loose curls, much like Serena's when she didn't straighten it. She looked more Bohemian belle rather than an Edwardian lady. It seemed as if she stared directly through the painting at Serena, locking her in a gaze. For a moment, it was as if the grass waved as some wisps of her hair caught on the breeze, and then the image froze in place again.

The haunted look in her green eyes beckoned Serena to find a way into the room.

A creak from the hallway startled her just before Lilith came around the corner. She followed Serena back to her room without speaking. As soon as Serena opened the bedroom door Lilith spoke quietly, but did not enter.

"Hurry," she said. "They are waiting."

"Who are 'they'?"

"I'll be back to help you with your hair."

Serena watched Lilith disappear around the corner before entering her room. On her bed sat an assortment of underclothes. White nylons, a white slip, white lace panties and a white corset were laid out on the bed for her. She was confused about all of the undergarments until she turned around.

Hanging on the opened wardrobe door was the same white Victorian gown, complete with ruffles and bows, as she had just seen Stormy wearing.

Chapter 29--Saturday Late Morning/Evening

Lilith found Serena sitting on the bed staring at the wardrobe, her face white. She was dressed in the slip and everything else that had been laid out on the bed, except the dress. The dress still hung on the closet door. Lilith placed her makeup bag on the counter. Then she went to the closet and took down the dress. Once she had it off the hanger, she turned and motioned for Serena to come.

The girl shook her head.

"Come now," Lilith said.

Serena stayed on the bed, both frightened but headstrong.

"Fine." Lilith slung the dress over her arm and headed for the door. "I'll just ask Simon to help you get dressed."

Serena jumped up. "No, I'll put it on."

"That's what I thought."

She raised her arms and Lilith slid the dress over her head. It was a near perfect fit. Next, she led Serena to the chair in front of the mirror and dresser. The headstrong gaze of just a few moments ago faded as soon as Serena saw herself in the mirror.

"I can do my own hair."

"Not to Rosalie and Simon's specifications." Lilith saw only fear in her eyes now. This girl was smart, she knew something was happening. The unknown could be far more terrifying than knowing. She sat down for Lilith to do her hair.

Shock would be the word to describe Serena's reaction when she saw herself. Her eyes were vibrant, framed by dark colors and black lashes. She wore a soft rose-colored lipstick and her cheeks were lightly bronzed. Her hair was slightly pulled back at the crown, but like Stormy's picture, wispy tendrils framed her face.

Lilith had used the same colors on Stormy's face but they had made her look more like a little girl playing dress up whereas Serena looked five years older. Lilith had a feeling the soft look on her face was a facade that even Serena didn't realize was there. She sighed as she left Serena's room, shutting the door behind her.

Stormy's door stared at Lilith. She walked toward it, drawn to it, but also fearing it. She stopped just outside the bathroom, the hallway to her right, Stormy's door in front of her. Which way did she choose?

Not Stormy's door. She couldn't go there. She had to be strong if she was to face Rosalie downstairs. But as she stepped into the hallway she heard a soft whisper.

"Mama."

***

Serena felt like a doll. At the very thought of dolls she glanced over at the ever-growing collection in the corner and shivered. She also looked too much like Stormy. She unclipped her hair and let the curls tumble down around her shoulders and then finger-combed through the mass. Now she was beginning to look like herself. She looked up and saw that Simon stood on the threshold. The look in his eyes scared her more than anything else had this week.

At first his eyes were critical, looking for any imperfections as he circled her. She swallowed. Once he was satisfied, his gaze ran over the front of her, from her feet to her face. When his eyes met hers they softened.

He took her arm and led her out of the room. "Come along, Serena. Mother is waiting." His brows were still drawn together, and a frown darkened his face.

She followed him down the stairs, her heart hammering. There was a man she had never seen before, standing beside Rosalie, along with several strangers in the living room, all wearing black. As she entered the room each conversation fell silent and their eyes followed her. Among the group of twenty people three faces startled her. Mr. Dawson, the albino teacher from school, Ms. Harold, and Mrs. Flinch, the school secretary. How many members of the community were involved with Simon?

In the midst of that black encased horde, she felt conspicuous wearing a white dress. They parted to make a path between her and Rosalie. Lilith stood in the corner, watching. Serena wondered what was going on in her mind.

Rosalie was standing at the windows with her back toward Serena. She wore a floor-length black dress from another century.

"Here she is, Rosalie," Simon said.

The tall woman turned. Her beautiful auburn hair was pulled back from her face, much like Lilith's hair. Her face was porcelain white making her cheekbones and lips more prominent than ever. She reminded Serena of Maleficent, the witch in Walt Disney's *Sleeping Beauty*.

The clock ticked off the minutes. No one said a word. The longer Rosalie stared, the more exposed Serena felt, as if the woman was peeling away her skin. She trembled in her dress, hard enough to disturb the ruffles at her neckline. Gooseflesh ran along her chest.

Serena.

Yes. She answered silently. She didn't know why she answered, or whose voice it was, but it came naturally.

Relax your gaze and watch her.

She closed her eyes, took a deep breath, held it, and then slowly let it out. It steadied her, giving her the ability to lift her eyes to meet Rosalie's. They stared at each other, until something strange began to happen. Serena's vision blurred and she began to observe things she had never seen before.

Some people talk about seeing colors, auras that emanate from people's souls. Rosalie emanated blackness. A smoke-like substance, smelling like sulfur, rolled off her like a dense fog from a swamp, thick and slimy.

At first, Serena thought the ground was moving, but then she realized black creatures were crawling along the wood flooring, slithering across Rosalie's feet with their red, beady eyes looking up at Serena. When they realized she could see them, they snarled and bared sharp fangs that dripped green saliva. When they drew close and snapped at her shoes, she kicked at one of them, forgetting that only she could see them.

Her eyes jerked back to Rosalie whose red lips stretched into a thin smile.

"You see them, don't you child?" she said.

Serena didn't answer, but she didn't have to.

"Tell me what you saw exactly."

Serena shook her head.

"You want to do it the hard way? Lilith, come here." The woman came as beckoned and stood directly in front of Serena. Her gaze was blank as she placed her fingers along Serena's forehead. Lilith closed her eyes, and Serena could see her pupils move quickly behind her closed lids. She pressed harder until her fingers dug deeper into Serena's forehead and again she caught a whiff of sulfur, black smoke, and a brief vision of

Haley, the girl she had seen in the mirror, crouched below Rosalie, chained at the wrists. Serena gasped when she saw her. Haley looked at her and opened her mouth to scream but then she disappeared.

Serena looked back at Lilith, her aunt's eyes closed in concentration. She closed her eyes as well and tried to keep up a shield around her to prevent Lilith from coming in, but it weakened and then dropped. Lilith was much more powerful. It felt like someone had broken in through a back door and was prowling around her head, looking for something but unable to find whatever it was. Every time she hit a specific area, a memory of her father for instance, she would pause for a moment and then move on. Serena felt naked in front of the woman.

She knew what Lilith was doing. She had grown up with a father who analyzed the occult, psychics, mediums, and shamans--to the point of obsession. At the time, she didn't know why he cared so much. She did ask him why, as a religious scholar and professor, he would spend so much energy and focus on the occult. He told her it was good to know what he was up against. Now she understood why he so thoroughly investigated the subject.

Lilith's search stopped abruptly when she saw what Serena had seen in the bathroom that very morning. Serena could see her face pale and watched her swallow.

Lilith opened her eyes. She spoke to Rosalie, but her eyes were still on Serena. "She sees your pets. She sees ghosts. She has the ability to see much more, but I cannot find what you are looking for." Her voice was unfeeling, just like her eyes. She walked back to her corner of the room and melted deep into shadows.

Rosalie's eyes sparked with interest. She tapped her bottom lip with her finger. "Maybe you're right, Simon. We'll talk about this later."

"Yes, Rosalie." Simon bowed low to her.

"Take her upstairs. I'm done with her for now."

"That's it?" Serena asked, surprised.

"Yes," she said.

Serena followed Simon back through the kitchen to the stairs, more bewildered than ever. What was going on here? As she was about to climb the stairs she overheard Rosalie speak. Serena snuck a quick glance and saw her grandmother lean over to one of the men who had come with her. Above the murmuring voices she could hear Rosalie, which was odd since she was far enough away that she should not have been able to hear their words.

"Find us a substitute."

The man nodded in agreement and began walking toward her. She picked up her skirt and flew up the stairs, trying to catch up with Simon. They did not speak until they reached her door.

"What do you want me to do now?" she asked, emboldened by the subservience she had seen in him downstairs. He seemed to pick up on her change of attitude. His smile turned into an ice-cold stare. She shrank back, too late realizing her mistake.

"I'm sorry sir," she said. He lowered his face to hers so that they were nose to nose.

It was as if an animal was sniffing her, and she knew if she moved he'd attack. He ran a finger along her collarbone and up her neck to her earlobe. He bent his head to hers and her heart hammered against her ribs.

"I will see you later," he whispered. His warm breath flowed over her face, sealing the promise before he straightened. When he turned away and walked out of the room, she took three steps and slammed the door, locking it behind her. She ran to the bed and climbed under the covers. Shaking, she tried to think how to could get out of this nightmare. Who could she call? Not the Youngbloods. Not anymore. Rosalie was too powerful to mess with, and Serena didn't want them to get hurt. Whatever Serena did, she couldn't involve them.

Her grandmother confused her. What was this all about? Why the dress? Why the makeup? And for what? Rosalie had dismissed her, but it was clear her original plan had involved her, so what changed her mind?

"What did she want?" Serena she whispered. She didn't expect an audible answer.

"You don't want to know," the female voice said. Stormy appeared at the window. She wore the dress that looked identical to the one Serena was wearing, but Stormy's was muddy and torn. Her hair was tangled around her face, and mascara and dirt were streaked down her cheeks. She lifted a fleshless finger to her bloodied lips, gesturing for Serena to be quiet.

Just then the doorknob jiggled. She glanced at it and then turned back to Stormy, who was no longer there.

***

Simon, Lilith, Rosalie and Azazel congregated around the kitchen island after the crowd had dispersed. The business had been discussed, plans for the next world order had been organized, this meeting had been more of a formality than anything else. Why they had the meeting at all was beyond Simon, but then again, most of Rosalie's plans were convoluted.

"We need to talk," Rosalie started. "There's been a slight change of plans."

"What do you mean?" Simon looked from Azazel to Rosalie. "We had a plan to take over the government and merge all countries together, forcing them under our rule."

"Yes, that was the plan." Azazel's voice was velvety smooth with a thick middle eastern accent. "But Semjaza has been in communion with Lucifer."

"Wait," Lilith interrupted, "Who's Semjaza?"

Rosalie glared at Lilith. "If you hadn't checked out on us three years ago, you'd know."

"Oh, *I'm so sorry*, Excuse me for mourning my daughter." Lilith's eyes sparkled with anger and tears.

"You knew why you had Stormy, you were warned not to attach yourself to her but you did it anyway. It's no one's fault but your own." Rosalie said, matter of factly. Simon flinched. He had distanced himself from Stormy but it still bothered him to think about the child dying.

Lilith glared at Rosalie but didn't say a word. She'd never win a fight with Rosalie.

"Ladies," Azazel said. "As I was saying, Semjaza spoke with me and explained that the plan was to deconstruct this realm and merge both his and ours together."

"So basically we're destroying this world," Lilith said.

"Yes and no," Azazel said. Simon glared at his partner. Azazel stared back at him. "Semjaza takes precedence over all. You know this. If he says we are to change our plans then that's what we do."

"Why?" Lilith asked.

"Because, Semjaza is all-wise, all-knowing, and sees how we can better our world. He also supplies what we need, monetarily and spiritually."

"So," Simon said, "What are we going to do with Serena?"

"Ah, Serena." Azazel said. "Serena is truly important. She isn't just *a* key to the plans Semjaza has, she is *the* gateway. "When she holds the key and opens the box Jonathan has, then she can open the door between the two realms. If she has just one or the other then they are useless. And," Azazel paused for a moment. "She is the only one who can do it. It won't work if I do it or Simon or Rosalie. It has to be Serena."

"What? Why her?" This time it was Rosalie. Obviously she didn't know about this plan either.

"Semjaza believes Jonathan tied a spell to Serena and the music box to keep her alive. He also believes that Jonathan gifted her in other areas as well, but we don't know what they are. The good news is that she doesn't know anything so she can't use them against us. Her ignorance may not aid us in our quest, but it may protect us from whatever she could do."

The foursome stood silently, each pondering on their own issue with this plan. At least Serena was safe, Simon thought. How this was going to affect his personal plans with her he didn't know, but he'd ask Azazel later.

As if Azazel could read Simon's mind he said, "You are to follow through with our plans concerning Serena. She still needs to be malleable in order to do these things."

Simon nodded. At least he had that going for him.

"Now," Azazel brought his hands together in a prayer stance, "We shall thank the almighty Semjaza." He spoke in a different language that only he knew while the rest of them bowed their heads in solemnity. When he was finished he spoke. "Semjaza is pleased with us. We shall go now, Rosalie."

"I need to change first." She stalked to the room, her frustration with the need to keep Serena alive evident.

"She will get over it. She has no choice."

"It doesn't seem that any of us have a choice," Lilith said. She sighed. "I'm going to change too."

Once she was out of earshot Simon confronted Azazel. "I thought we had a deal."

"No, Semjaza and I have a deal. That deal involves Rosalie remaining the matriarch of this family, not you. You are subservient to her as she is to me and I am to Semjaza. According to the plans, the biggest goal is to get that music box and use Serena. Whatever we do with her after that is entirely up to us."

"I want her then."

"She is yours." Azazel gave Simon a firm handshake and a slight bow of his head as Rosalie came out of her room. He leaned in close to Simon and whispered, "if Rosalie doesn't get to her first."

Chapter 30--Sunday Morning

Sunday morning all was quiet. It was a deep silence as if Serena was truly alone. She crept downstairs for something to eat. No one was in the living room or kitchen. Her backpack was still in the corner where she'd dropped it when she'd gotten home on Friday, so she grabbed it and a banana on her way back up the stairs. When she reached the top, Stormy's door opened down the hall.

For a moment she thought it must be Stormy inside, but it was Lilith who came out. She was dressed in a nightgown and her ever-present afghan was wrapped around her shoulders. Her shoulders were drooped forward, her face pale and gaunt, and her eyes red-rimmed. She locked the door behind her and stuck the key in the hiding place before she saw Serena.

They locked gazes, and again Serena felt compassion for her. She was a very broken woman. She said nothing about Simon. In fact, Lilith said nothing at all. It seemed as if her resentment toward Serena had faded.

As Lilith drew closer, she glanced down at the banana Serena held. Lilith reached for it, and Serena handed it over. Then Lilith put out her other hand and Serena grasped it.

"Come, dear," she spoke barely above a whisper. "I'll make you a real breakfast."

Serena followed her down the stairs and into the kitchen where Lilith scrambled a few eggs and toasted bread. The rest of the day was spent downstairs, which was a nice break from her room. They didn't talk much. Serena did her homework while Lilith watched old television shows. It was quiet but as evening approached, Serena's anxiety grew. As she climbed the stairs for bed, she wondered what she'd wake up to the following morning.

Nothing happened that night. No creaking floorboards, no feeling of being watched, no nightmares. No ghouls behind the shower curtain or messages written in a steamy mirror. After a week of spooks and hauntings, she was wary but relieved that it all seemed to have dissipated.

Lilith even made her a pancake breakfast and a sack lunch. Henry drove her down the driveway, and for the first time since arriving Serena felt a glimmer of happiness. As they sat in the silent car, Saturday's events began to unravel in her mind. What had happened two days ago felt like a bad dream. So much so, in fact, that she questioned whether it ever happened. But she knew she had seen a deep evil in Rosalie, Simon, and the rest of the group. She shuddered at the memory. What did they want with her?

Chapter 31--Monday Morning

As Henry drove them down the hill, Serena lost herself in thought. Why hadn't her father told her about all these things? Both guilt and anger warred inside. She shoved both feelings aside as she made a mental to-do list. First, she needed to research this insane family. Second on the list, was to figure out how to get away.

Henry sighed, interrupting her thoughts. It occurred to her then that he was not at the meeting. She wished she could get some answers from him.

The lights of the school bus came around the corner before the actual bus did. She gave Henry a quick goodbye, hopped out of the SUV and clambered onto the bus.

As the bus wound its way to school, she began to formulate a plan. She would turn eighteen on May first and graduate in June. She needed a place to go as soon as graduation passed. Lilith was sweet this morning and made the home more welcoming, but how long would that last? Besides, Serena needed to put as much space between herself and Simon as possible. He still posed a danger, especially if Rosalie wasn't around. Her grandmother hadn't been protecting Serena; she had been protecting Simon. Both mother and son were super creepy. How did her father come out so normal?

She had six months to get her plan together, if she could last that long. One thing was for sure; she wanted to return to Oregon. By the time she got to school, Serena had figured out an outline for her master plan. At lunch she ate a sandwich on her way to the computer lab.

The room was quiet and a relief from the constant noise in the cafeteria. She found a laptop in the furthest corner and logged on. Google was a girl's best friend. She word searched Simon Robertson. Immediately a long list of articles popped up. There was a business called Monarch Inc. attached to his name, and the articles ranged from accolades of his business to blogs blasting him and his business partner. She perused the top two sites that popped up. One was about how amazing the company was, their "Commitment to Excellency," the number of congressmen and government officials who couldn't say enough good things about the company, blah blah, blah. There were photos of Simon with various celebrities at red carpet events.

Another picture popped up of a woman tagged as Angel James who was cozied up to Simon. She had long platinum blonde hair that hung down her back, big blue eyes, and a heart-shaped face. Another picture showed Simon and his business partner. According to the picture his name was simply Azazel. Both men were wearing suits and ties. Simon looked dashing with his thick black hair and penetrating green eyes while Azazel was . . . intense. He stared into the camera as if he could see her on the other side of the screen. His eyes were such a dark brown they almost looked black and were deep set under thick, dark eyebrows. His skin was a dusky olive, and he had closely cut black hair.

She closed that window and looked at the next website that had been heavily visited. Whoever had started it was an obvious conspiracy theorist. The author wouldn't identify himself but accused Monarch Inc., Simon, and Azazel of mind control, hypnotism, MK-Ultra, and deals done under the table with the government. The list went on. She scanned through the articles looking for proof behind the guy's allegations but couldn't find any. He said a lot of the things he experienced himself, but out of concern for his family and friends chose to keep anonymous. He had several guest bloggers sharing what they'd learned. None of it was good.

She searched for the Monarch website. A picture came up of a butterfly in the background. All it said was that it was under construction and momentarily down. The date was from five years ago. She looked up any addresses or maps to the main building that housed the company but only found a San Diego post office box.

The bell rang for the next class, but she barely heard it. There was still so much to learn. She hadn't even googled Rosalie's name. Just then a teacher walked in with a cup of coffee.

"If you're not in my next class you better move it." He busied himself at his desk as she packed up her books. She could feel his eyes on her, drilling holes into her head. When their eyes met, he made no excuse or apology for staring her down.

"You're Stormy's cousin aren't you?" he said.

"Yes." She slid between chairs, trying to get out of the lab as fast as possible. He looked familiar. Ah yes, he had been at the house on Saturday.

For the first time since Saturday she heard the voice. *Clear the history,*

Serena.

She stopped and turned back to the computer and noticed the teacher was eyeing it as well. "I think I forgot something."

"What is it? I can grab it for you." He was on his feet and inching toward the computer.

"It's okay, let me do it." She reached the laptop first and sat down. She went directly to the history tab and cleared it for the last hour. Once that was done she fished through her backpack. "Oh well, I must've left it in another class." She leaped up and made her way to the door. She felt the teacher studying her until she left the room.

The second bell rang and she glanced up to see Jesse watching her.

"Serena, wait," he whispered. His warm voice flowed over her, making her skin pop up in gooseflesh. He gently grabbed ahold of her arm.

She paused but didn't look up. Instead, she pulled away from him just as gently as he had pulled her close and walked to her next class.

The rest of the day flew by, and she was back on the bus before she knew it. When the bus pulled up to her stop she was exhausted. Henry sat waiting for her like he had on the other days. She climbed in the SUV and let the heat warm her as he began their drive up the hill.

Lilith stood at the window, watching for them. When she saw the SUV crest the hill she put her hand up in a slight wave and Serena returned it. Her eyes drifted up to her window above the living room. Once again, Stormy stood there, her hand going up in a small wave as she disappeared. Out of habit, Serena waved back and then felt silly for doing so. Really? Waving at a ghost?

That night was nice; Lilith maintained her kindness, which was pleasant. At nine o'clock, Serena made her way up the stairs, steeling herself for an evening confrontation. It never came and again, she slept through the night.

The following day she skipped lunch altogether and headed for the computer lab. She was alone. She settled back into her spot from the day before and quickly typed in Rosalie's name. There were nearly 140,000 hits. But after looking through the first ten or so screens she could tell that there was nothing at all about her grandmother on the Internet.

No address, no nothing. That was odd and deflating. She typed in Simon's name with Rosalie. Nothing showed up again. In all of the World Wide Web, there was nothing on her grandmother. She finally gave up and was about to start another search when the teacher from yesterday entered the room. She glanced at the clock. He was early today. She could feel his eyes on her, watching, waiting to jump on her if she moved too quickly.

She cleared the history and typed in colleges in the Midwest. Whenever she glanced up, the teacher would move his eyes, pretending to read his book or check the time. It still bugged her that she couldn't remember for certain if he had been at the party. She thought so, but there were several new faces and they all dressed alike.

Students began drifting in and, soon after, the bell rang. She got up, grabbed her bag, and started for the door. The teacher turned to his class, giving her his profile. Suddenly she was positive that he had been at the house on Saturday. He had been standing close to Ms. Harold. He most definitely belonged to Rosalie. Damn. As if he knew where she finally placed him, his face stretched into a devilish grin. He winked. She ran out the door and straight into Jesse.

He grabbed her arm, steadying her. "Are you okay?" he asked.

"No," she gasped. "I've gotta go!" She ran down the hall to her next class.

On Wednesday, things changed. Passing by each other in the hall, Jesse slipped her a note.

Library at lunch.

Serena read it again just before her fourth period ended. When class was over, students flowed through the hallway and she moved along with them, crossing in front of some kids to get to the library. When she entered, a vacuum of noise was sucked out of the room leaving her ears ringing. The woman at the front desk glanced up, did a double take, then shrugged and went back to her task. Serena didn't feel the sense of being watched like she had with the other teachers. The deeper she walked into the rows the more silent and comforted she became. Her head began to clear; her muscles relaxed. One row led to another and then to another. How big was this library?

"Serena," Jesse's whispered voice sounded from her left between the shelves. She turned to find him peeking through a gap of books. She hurried down the row and stepped into his. Jittery anxiety from the last two days dissipated in his presence. She swallowed and noticed he did too. He broke the stare first.

"Come on, I have a place where we can do some research."

Jesse brought her to a back table, his laptop already on and ready for use. She followed him to the desk, sitting where he pointed, which was in front of the computer, then he sat beside her.

"We won't be bothered here since no one comes back this far."

"Not even the librarian?"

"Nah, she doesn't care. She's the newest to the school and hasn't been inducted into the creepy teacher society just yet." As he spoke he swiped the mouse pad on the laptop and entered a word in Google. "Rosalie Robertson, monarch, Simon Robertson, Azazel" His word search brought up far less hits, but they were pertaining directly to the ones she needed.

"So," Jesse began quietly. "Your uncle, his partner, his mother and your aunt are all part of a business called 'Monarch,' or at least they used to be." He pulled up the web page Serena had found that was no longer in use, then he typed in another word. Immediately the website popped up. It looked like a legitimate business. Jesse moved the mouse to the bio tab. Simon's name came up first, along with his picture. He was handsome and professional in his suit. His bio was short. According to this small snippet, he and his mother put together the business to serve both important government officials and even celebrities in their search for a more successful life, professionally as well as spiritually. Backed by their business partner, Azazel, who carried the same vision as theirs, they had changed many lives of the men and women who consulted with them.

"Wow," Serena whispered. "How did you know where to look?"

"I've been studying them for awhile, especially after Stormy disappeared." He scrolled down a bit more. "They don't mention her on this page, but on a previous one from a couple years ago Lilith's name was mentioned as one of the partners." He clicked on a separate tab, this one of Lilith, her background and a couple of newspaper articles. "She's actually more interesting than Simon, if you want to know the truth."

Serena took over the mouse and clicked on a headline. "Marriage announcement of Simon Robertson and Lilith McCay." The story stated they were to be married, who their parents were, and their wedding announcement. Of course, there was information on Simon but Serena wasn't as interested in him as she was Lilith.

'Lilith Adalaide McCay, daughter of Alistair and Adalaide McCay, is to be married to Simon Robertson on the 1st of May, Nineteen hundred and ninety-five in New York, at the bride's family home.'

Along with a picture of a young Lilith and Simon was a picture of Lilith's childhood home. It wasn't a home. It was a mansion that looked like it had been there for at least a hundred years. A brick wall surrounded it, giving it the sense of a fortress, not a home. All it needed was a moat and drawbridge. The picture that had been taken was from an aerial view.

Jesse clicked on another tab and another story popped up. "Prominent wife, Adalaide McCay, wife to Alistair McCay, jumps to her death from penthouse suite." The headline was dated to 2000, five years after Lilith and Simon's marriage. Jesse clicked on still another story, dated from 2005, of Lilith's father's death. The picture of the house showed one side burned while the rest of the house remained untouched. The building had been made of stone so it would have been difficult for the house to burn all the way down to the ground. According to the story, Lilith's father had jumped from the fifth story window to get away from the roaring flames and broke his neck when he hit the pavement. The lunch bell rang, startling Serena. "Is lunch already over?"

"Yep." He began picking up his computer and bag. "This time tomorrow?" He paused to look at her. "You go first."

"Okay, see you then." She turned to leave, then stopped and looked back. "Thank you," she said.

He looked up, his face soft and voice serious, "I know it feels like it, but you're not alone."

She nodded and then left. Somehow she found her way through the bookshelf maze. The librarian was at her desk still, a stack of books in front of her. She didn't look up, but that did not mean she hadn't noticed Serena. Friend or foe? she wondered. She pushed through the door and ran into Mr. Gordon.

"Hello, Serena. Nice to see you again." His eyes drilled into hers. "Running a bit late, are we?"

"Yes, sir." She inched away, walking in the direction of her classroom. At least, she hoped it was the right direction. He fell into step with her.

"Enjoying our library?"

"Yes."

"A little research for class?"

"Yes."

"Which class?"

Think Serena. "History. We're studying the Druids." Her classroom door was still open with students filing in; she hurried to catch up. "See ya," she said to the albino teacher. She felt his eyes on her until she stepped out of sight. She wondered if Jesse made it to his classroom

Sitting in class, as her teacher rambled on about the very subject she had told Mr. Dawson she was studying, she thought about Lilith. She was far more important than Serena would have guessed. Was she a pawn in Simon and Rosalie's plans? No, she thought, she wasn't anybody's pawn. She was a smart woman. Serena couldn't see Lilith allowing herself to be manipulated, but that didn't mean it wasn't happening. Serena had to do more research. Would Lilith ever allow her to go to the town library by herself? Was there even a town library?

The bell rang again. Just before the last class ended she was called to the front office. "You can take your things, Serena," Ms. Harold said. Serena gathered her books and hurried to the office.

Henry stood waiting for her. The little old secretary addressed her. "You're being picked up today. Also, we have a new locker for you. She handed a lock with the directions to the combination on it and the locker number. "He'll show you the way."

"How would he know?" Serena asked.

"Because, dear, it is Stormy's old locker."

The locker was strategically placed so that she could easily be watched. They must have considered her a moron if they really assumed she would use a lock for which they knew the combination. On the other hand, if they thought she was that stupid then maybe she could play them. She opened the locker door. It had a mirror inside but that was it. The girl in the mirror stared at Serena. Their eyes met before Serena slammed the door extra hard. She didn't want her reflection to watch her. What was she doing? She must be going crazy if she was actually growing fearful of her own face in the mirror.

Serena glanced at Henry. He wasn't watching her. Instead, he was acting like her bodyguard. No one would dare speak to her without his permission. He began walking for the school's front doors. With no other option, she followed.

Chapter 32--Monday

Watching the snowfall, Lilith stood at the window, lost in thought. Saturday afternoon continued to play back in her memory. Rosalie had told her to read Serena's mind, and she did. Her old self had been making its way back to her, strengthening her physically, but more importantly, spiritually. To rebel against Rosalie would take a far stronger being than she was just yet; so she did what was expected. Besides, she wanted to know what Serena was thinking too.

However, what she found in her niece's head was not what she expected. The girl could do so much more than Simon imagined. Reading Serena had been difficult which was a surprise. She could read nearly everyone, even from far away. Frightened that she had lost her most valuable power, she searched the other minds in the room and read every single one of them, so it hadn't been Lilith. It had been Serena's ability to shut her out. Snippets of her thoughts still emerged though and she had told Rosalie about most of them. Not for the first time, she was relieved Rosalie could not reach into other minds.

Serena could see Rosalie's "pets" and she could see ghosts, but it was only Haley's form that presented itself to Lilith. She searched more, or attempted to, but a sudden wall of darkness blocked her way. Frustrated, she moved on. The next area she reached into was Serena's memory. She saw faint pictures of Crystal and Anna, playing like a silent home movie. Running on the beach, racing her sister, rocking in a chair on her mother's lap, hanging upside down in a car, arms reaching through a window to gently pull her out. A graveside. Jonathan crying. Flowers. A church. Strangers giving their condolences. Surprisingly, Simon was there, watching Serena. Serena had seen him, but had not realized who he was. The memory was tucked back enough that one little movement could bring it up to the forefront, which Lilith could do if she needed to.

Loneliness. Grief. Weeping. Was that Serena? No, it was Serena watching her father in his home office. Watching him through the crack of the door, his head bent, shoulders shaking, collapsed on the floor.

Serena backs away so she doesn't bother her father. She begins to roam her mom and dad's room, lightly touching the dresser, a film of dust on her fingers, running her fingers over the same pictures she had brought with her. A hope chest at the foot of the bed, a musical jewelry box far back in dark closet corner, an old doll sitting in the corner of their room. A memory within a memory of her parents playfully bantering.

And then sudden darkness again. Lilith had been so close. She could feel the presence of the object, but couldn't see it and still didn't know what it was.

Suddenly Jonathan rose up, blocking her further entrance.

"No," he said. "OUT!"

Lilith was shoved out of Serena's head. Usually she chose when to leave, but not this time.

The ringing phone pulled her out of her thoughts. It was Simon. He was next to the last person she wanted to talk with, the ringing stopped and then thirty seconds later started up again. He would go like this all day if he had to and then when she did answer she would be in for a tongue-lashing. She might as well get it over with.

On the fourth ring she picked up. "Hello Simon." She sat on the couch, still gazing at the falling snow.

"Where were you?" He was already piqued.

"What do you want?"

"Since you failed to read Serena you need to search her room again."

"Don't you think we would've found it by now if she had it?"

"Go upstairs and search. Also, you need to become her friend."

"Are you serious? That's the oldest and most obvious plan in the playbook. She'll see right through it!"

"Not if you use the tincture Rosalie gave you."

"She's not five. She's old enough to realize that I'm drugging her if she doesn't see me eating the same food I make for her. "

"Can you think of a better way? Get upstairs and start looking!" Their line disconnected.

Sighing, she tossed the phone on the couch. Whether she wanted to or not, investigating was necessary, besides what better time than when Serena was at school.

Curiosity drove her, along with the idea that if she found the item first then she could use Serena to bring down Rosalie's empire and all of those who worshiped her. It was that thought that pushed Lilith up the stairs regardless of her anxiety of who, or what, she could run into while up there.

As soon as she entered Serena's room she noticed the accumulation of dolls piled into the corner. Instead of the three dolls that had once sat on the window seat, there were six dolls. They all faced her, eyeless stares as if they really could see her without the need for eyes. Lilith shook her head out of the spell she had fallen under. Glancing at her watch she swore when she saw two hours had already passed. Damn the hex of time that resided in the room. It didn't seem to affect the hall leading up to the room, just the room itself. Did it affect Stormy's room too? She didn't remember it ever happening when she and Stormy played in there on rainy days.

Lilith searched hurriedly, trying to make up for lost time. Not under the pillow, not in the vanity where her makeup and hair dryer sat. She looked on the dresser. A necklace lay beside her mother's picture. On the necklace was an oval locket. She picked it up, clutching it inside her fist and closed her eyes. Unfortunately she did not feel any vibration from it, only flashes of Crystal wearing it. She set it back down and continued her search.

Next she looked at Jonathan's picture. His eyes were kind in the photo not fiery like they had been when guarding Serena's mind. In her brain she knew he couldn't touch her, but she still picked up the frame with apprehension. She turned it over to look on the back for anything that would clue her into Serena's secret. There was nothing. The drawers didn't reveal anything either. She looked on the fireside hearth; nothing but dust and a small rag doll with buttons for eyes and a sewn on smile. Serena must have brought it with her from home. Lilith was in the third drawer down in the vanity when she looked at her watch. It was already four o'clock. The vanity wasn't giving up any secrets. The dolls? Would Serena have placed it there? It seemed unlikely, but Lilith couldn't leave it untouched. She had just arrived at the dreaded corner when the doorknob turned and the door swung open.

Serena jumped when she saw Lilith. Her immediate surprise turned into fierce anger, "What the hell are you doing in here?"

The dolls gave her the alibi she needed. "When I was up here on Saturday I noticed the accumulation of dolls in your corner. I didn't think you had brought this many."

The anger began to melt away from Serena's face. "No, I hadn't." She joined Lilith in the corner. "They just keep popping up, a new one every day."

Lie forgotten, replaced by genuine concern, Lilith asked, "Is there a new doll now?" She watched Serena's face as the girl looked over the pile. She shook her head.

"No, not yet, but honestly I try not to look anymore."

"How do you sleep with all of them in here?" Now she really was curious.

"I throw a blanket over them. The blanket is usually on the floor when I wake up though.

"Hmmm. Okay." Lilith wandered the room a little more carefully this time, no longer concerned with being caught searching. Her eyes caught the small doll sitting on the mantle.

Serena turned to her, "I take it you weren't doing this."

"No."

"Claudia?"

"That's what I'm thinking."

Footsteps sounded on the ceiling. Serena blew a hair strand out of her face. "So, what's her story?"

Lilith set the doll down carefully. "Come downstairs and I'll tell you."

As they made their way down to the kitchen it occurred to her that even though she hadn't found anything, she had still succeeded with making a connection with her niece. Maybe, if Serena thought Lilith was on her side, she would begin to open up. Maybe.

Lilith ushered Serena to the large marbled island and then put water on the stovetop. In the cupboard were the teacups, the set her mother had given her before she had died. It was one of the few things she took when moving out of her house.

"Mint? Earl Gray or chamomile?"

"Chamomile."

She put a tea bag in each delicate teacup; her thoughts ruminated as she pulled out a box of buttery cookies she only ate with her tea. She arranged them on dainty flowered dessert plate that matched the cups.

Simon needed to know what Claudia was doing. Lilith had tried to tell him for a few years, since before Stormy had died, but he wouldn't believe her. After Haley's disappearance the housekeeper's presence had grown. Both she and her daughter could feel the woman joining them in every conversation so they had stopped talking altogether, conversing only in Henry's small apartment up the hill, away from the garage and the house, or hand signing their conversations, unsure if Claudia could see or understand the language, but willing to try anything.

A whistle blowing interrupted her thoughts. She grabbed the teakettle to quiet it and poured the water into each cup, pushing one to Serena, along with the plate of cookies.

"So," Serena started the conversation when Lilith sat on her stool. "What's the deal with Claudia?"

Lilith looked at Simon's niece. In some ways she reminded her of

Stormy or Crystal, her mother, but her no-nonsense, intelligent questions and quick-witted answers were all Jonathan. She wondered if Simon would have taken more interest in his daughter if she had been more like Serena.

"Claudia basically raised Simon."

"Where was my dad? Did she raise him too?"

"No. Rosalie had very little interest in Simon, she treated him more like a younger brother than anything else."

"Which explains why he sometimes refers to her as Rosalie."

"Exactly. Anyway, your father was truly her son and even though she killed his father, it had been a murder borne out of passionate fury. She still loved the man. She was a completely different mother with Jonathan and kept him close to her as much as possible, except on her trips. She couldn't bring him with her then.

"Anyway, Simon's care was given to the woman upstairs." Lilith raised her eyes to the top of the stairs. "She saw Simon was neglected so she adopted him in a way. She taught him her family's trade and built him up for power as well."

"Okay, that explains why Simon allows her to stay here, but what I want to know is where exactly did she come from? What's her story? Where did Rosalie find her? And what's this 'family business'? Simon mentioned it when I first got here."

Lilith sighed. Regardless of her fear of the housekeeper she had to tell Serena about the woman. If she didn't the girl would look for herself and that would be disastrous. "I'll tell you, but this is a topic I don't want to discuss out loud. Would you let me try a different way?"

"Um, okaaay."

"Hold still, relax." She scooted her stool closer to Serena's until they were six inches apart. With her hands up she leaned in to touch Serena's temples. Immediately Lilith was transported into Serena's head Serena pulled back, breaking the connection.

"Just trust me, please."

Serena nodded, still apprehensive, but Lilith could see the curiosity in her eyes. If Serena allowed her entrance, inviting her inside, then Lilith could gain access to her anytime she wanted.

They drew close again. The same scene popped up: they sat on stools, facing each other against a black backdrop, as if on an empty stage. She let Serena get used to the feeling of Lilith being inside of her head. Lilith cleared her mind of all thoughts and focused solely on Claudia's story.

"Are you ready?" she asked.

Serena's head bobbed up and down physically as she did mentally.

"Did you do this with Stormy?"

"No, she didn't have this gift, unfortunately. We communicated in different ways when it came to the subject of Claudia."

"Oh. How did you know I had this ability?"

"I took a wild guess. I figured if you were anything like your father, then you could do this too."

"What? My dad could do this?" Serena's mental eyes widened, her shock sent a wave through them both, almost breaking the connection again.

"Yes, he could, but I can tell you about that later, when I'm outside of your head. Let me tell you about Claudia."

"Okay."

"No one knows how Claudia and Rosalie know each other, nor for how long. What we do know is that it's a relationship that has lasted several decades. Claudia was born and raised just outside New Orleans. Her mother was from Morocco and practiced Voodoo. She passed her gifts to her daughter, raising her to be just as powerful as she, and when she died Claudia took over title of Voodoo Queen."

"There's an actual title or position named that?"

"Yes. A Voodoo Queen can hold séances, perform divination, and create dolls . . . Among other things. That's why you aren't supposed to go up to her apartment. Who knows what she'd do to you if she caught you."

"How come I never see her?"

"You should be glad you don't, it means she doesn't consider you as a concern although the dolls are worrisome. She seems to have noticed you but doesn't care about you. Yet."

"Why would she even be interested in me?"

"If she sees you as a threat to Simon or sees even an interest Simon might have in you, she will make your life miserable."

"A little jealous, I take it."

"Like I said, she raised Simon. She sees him as a son and won't let go of him. Why do you think I stay down here as much as possible? Until you showed up I hadn't been up there since . . ." She let the sentence drop off. The memory of brushing Stormy's hair that last day froze her in place.

The connection broke so suddenly Serena fell forward. "Are you okay? Why did you stop?"

"The story was over." She stood, shook her arms and stretched her legs. The outside world had turned dark; night had come upon them. She glanced at Serena. Had she seen anything before they disconnected? No.

She wouldn't have been able to see that deeply nor that quickly into Lilith's head. That gift took years to perfect. She shook the fog out of her mind. That was another side effect she could do without: a sluggish mind and body.

Lilith went to the refrigerator for some deli meat. "Sandwich?"

"Sure." Serena stood and stretched too. "You must miss her quite a bit. I saw your memory of brushing Stormy's hair before you stopped the whole mind meld thing."

Lilith froze, knife in mustard jar, "You did?"

"Yeah."

"Did you see anything else?"

"No, just you brushing her hair and a flutter of white ribbon. That was it."

Lilith spoke quickly before Serena could connect any dots. "It was the same kind I used in your hair Saturday morning. That is how Rosalie will expect you to dress every time she comes to see you. That's how it was with Stormy too."

Lilith could tell that Serena was not completely convinced. The wheels were turning as evidenced by the faraway look, a slight tilt of her head. Serena was forcing another connection.

What had Lilith done? What Pandora's box had she blasted wide open?

"No," she sternly shook her head at Serena. "This can't happen without the other person's consent. That's not the way this works," she lied.

"You mean it can't or it won't?"

"Both."

"Okay," Serena pulled away, thoughts and body. "I have another question: what's with all those people being here on Saturday morning? Who are they?"

"They are Rosalie's local coven."

"As in witch's coven? That kind?"

"Is there a different kind?" Lilith answered sarcastically. She watched Serena's hairs along her arms stand up on end.

"Are there more people like them?"

"Do you really want to know?" Lilith watched Serena's head bob up and down even though there was fear in her eyes.

"Yes. Like I said, this was the local coven, just one of many across the states and other countries. Now, let's watch something on TV." Serena took the sandwich Lilith had just offered her. She watched the girl sit on the couch and turn on the TV with the remote. Was Serena going to let this go or was she strong enough already to push past the barriers?

Time would tell. What Lilitlh did know was that Simon, Azazael and Rosalie had no idea they had grabbed a snake by the tail. And here they thought they were in control.

Chapter 33--Monday Night

That night Serena was lost in thought after her experience with Lilith. What happened there? It was the most terrifying thing to have someone able to reach, speak to her, while in her head. What was also very odd was Serena's ability to search through Lilith's mind, her memories, without Lilith knowing. As they had talked, Serena had the real sense of stepping over a threshold. She hadn't gone far but it was enough to see that sliver of memory before their connection broke. One question rattling around her brain afterward was: could she do it again? If so, could Serena do it without that connection and without being found out? And how in the world did she have this gift? Obviously her father had it.

It had been a strange night indeed. Not only had she learned about the crazy lady upstairs, Lilith's mind trick had really rocked her. How did she do that? And what was that comment about her father? Just who was this man she had known only as her scholarly professor dad? The dad who read her books, sat by the fire with her, who had kissed her goodnight and prayed protection over her from the evil in this world? Just who was Jonathan Kelly? Wait, Kelly wasn't even his last name, but it was hers, it was on her birth certificate. She felt like she had been shaken out of a tree and dumped on the ground, all the air pushed out of her. She no longer knew who she was or who her father was.

Deep in thought, Serena walked into her bedroom and instantly saw there was a change. As was her habit now, she scanned the room, searching for anything different. Another doll had appeared. What really frightened her though was that each doll had begun to look familiar to her. They each looked like a real person.

Frozen in place, she debated whether she should carefully investigate them, which she hadn't done before. Maybe looking at them, picking them up might dispel the mysterious aura around them. She crossed her room to set her backpack down in the corner. It was odd that each of the eyes were closed, even on the dolls that were posed in the standing position, as if they were sleepwalking.

She walked over to one of the dolls that sat on the window seat. One in particular actually looked familiar to her. The doll wore a pink pinafore with a white apron over it, her legs and feet stuck straight out in front of her, little black booties finishing the ensemble. Her black hair was in ringlets and pulled back into a pink satin ribbon that matched her dress. Serena picked her up and the lids opened, revealing empty, hollow holes where her eyes should have been.

Serena instinctively threw the doll back on the seat, far away from her. The doll fell and landed on the hardwood floor. The face cracked at the forehead and down the left side of the face, her eyelids opened again to vacant black holes. Revulsion twisted Serena's insides, and she bit her lower lip to keep from crying out.

Serena had seen this face before. Where though? Memories ran through her head like a slideshow, scene to scene to scene, and as she did so she turned to her dresser where her family's portraits watched over her. Without a word she asked her father's picture, her mother's picture, and then her sister's picture. And therein laid her answer.

She looked at the doll again and finally her sight registered with her brain as to why the face looked so familiar.

Even with no eyes at all, the doll was a dead ringer for her sister Anna.

Chapter 34--Monday Night/
Tuesday Morning

Serena lay down, shaking from the image of the doll. It sat in the corner with the rest of the dolls. Her mind swirled around her. Sleep came slowly, even stealthily.

She was completely aware of her dream world, aware of herself within each disjointed scene. In every one of them her name was being called but she could never find the source. She pleaded with the dream maker to release her but the answer was always no. Instead the world around her shifted constantly: a hall would turn into a sandy beach, and the beach would turn into a lagoon. The lagoon turned into a forest, where she climbed a tree to see where she was from the top branches. Higher and higher she climbed, the bark digging into her skin and needles scraping against her face. She was almost to the top, her hand grasping the last branch when it snapped, sending her into a free fall that picked up speed, plunging her into the dark fathomless pool below it. A hand from below grabbed her ankle and began to pull.

"Serena!" Stormy's voice yelled to her.

She tried to respond but could not. She knew it was a dream and she wouldn't drown but she still couldn't open her mouth.

"Serena, hold on to my hand!" Another hand broke through to clutch her arms, pulling her upward, while the hand yanked even harder below until she felt that she would be torn in two. Her left leg began to ache as the tug of war continued, her lungs burning from lack of oxygen. Finally the hand around her ankle let go. She swam upward to the surface of sleep and finally broke through.

Damp from sweat, no it was actually water, and lungs aching from holding her breath for so long, she pulled in a ragged breath. What had happened? No dream like that had occurred before. She had experienced lucid dreams before but it was nothing compared to the reality of this experience.

Serena sat up, trying to shake off her fear. Stormy appeared suddenly at the foot of her bed.

Serena pulled her feet in close as she bumped up against the wall behind her.

Fear robbed her voice as she watched her dead cousin sit and stare back at her. Stormy wasn't wearing the white dress as when she first appeared. Instead, she wore a red sweater with a white collar at the neckline. It stopped two inches above the red and black plaid skirt, leaving the white-buttoned shirt to show underneath. It was tucked into a black pleated skirt, black tights, and black Mary Jane's. Her dark hair was pulled back at the crown with a thin red ribbon. Wisps of black tendrils had escaped and lay at her temple, framing her face. She looked like the first picture Jesse had shown Serena, her face angelic and sweet. She was even dressed in the same outfit.

"Boo," Stormy said, as if they were playing the peek-a-boo game. She giggled, a silvery bell-like sound. "Don't worry, I don't want to hurt you."

"Are you . . ." Serena couldn't form the last word.

"Dead?" her voice soft, resigned.

Serena nodded.

"Yes." Stormy's gaze was kind with curiosity illuminating the green in her eyes. Serena tried to swallow, but her throat was too dry. Her voice barely above a whisper, she asked, "Why are you here?"

"In this house or in your room?"

"Both?"

"Well, this is my home so I can roam anywhere I want to. The reason I'm in your room is because I've always wanted to meet you."

"You've always wanted to meet me? How would you have known me when I just got here?"

Stormy shrugged as she got up from the bed and crossed the room to the cold fireplace. "I've always known about you, but evidently you had no idea we existed." She ran a finger along the mantel, not quite touching it. Serena watched, scared to death, but curious as to how solid Stormy was. She always thought ghosts were transparent.

"How come you're not see-through?" she asked.

Stormy turned with the same half-smile of her father, "I am sometimes but right now, with you, I feel more alive. Besides, I'm not ready to leave yet."

"Oh." Dream or reality, Serena couldn't tell. She would hope it was a dream. The conversation they were having would be far less terrifying if it was a dream.

"Do you need help moving onto the other side?'"

The ghost laughed that time, still singsong, but strong too. "You're funny." She came back to the bed and sat down again. Serena saw her sit, wrinkling the bedcovers but didn't feel the weight of a live person. Closer up, Stormy was less solid, but she was in color.

"I always hoped we'd meet and become best friends." Her smile faded. "Your dad kept you well hidden."

"From what I know of your father, I can imagine why. No offense." Serena hugged her knees, still apprehensive about the ghost at the foot of her bed, but not as scared as she was at first. The longer she watched Stormy, the more she relaxed.

"No offense taken." Stormy's gaze dropped to the floor. "I understand." She raised her eyes and looked around the room, her eyes never landing on anything for longer than a moment. "Are you looking for something?"

"Sort of, but more like someone." Apparently satisfied with the empty room, she turned back to Serena. "You need to be careful of him, Serena."

"I picked up on that a couple days ago, but thanks."

"Not my father, although he isn't good either. No, the one you need to stay away from is Aza. And Rosalie. She is evil and with Aza around, she's even more so. And she doesn't like you."

"That's what your mother said."

"She's right." Sadness swept over Stormy's face. "Be wary of my mother too. I love her, but she's on my dad's side, sort of."

"I kinda figured that one out too."

Stormy nodded.

"And Claudia too?"

A light flashed in Stormy's eyes. "Believe me, you don't want to go near that woman. I wouldn't speak her name."

A movement among the dolls caught Serena's eye. The air dropped several degrees. A very transparent girl appeared, weeping uncontrollably, her hands over her face. She disappeared just as quickly as she appeared. The air remained freezing. Serena began to shake as her lips turned blue.

She didn't need to ask, but she did anyway. "Was that Haley?" The apparition startled Serena far more than Stormy's appearance had. She wasn't sure if it was because the vision looked like a traditional ghost or if it was her weeping, but Serena was much more frightened.

"Yes, that's Haley."

"Can she talk like you can?"

"No, and you mustn't call her either." Stormy's gaze became furtive.

"Also, don't play with those dolls. They aren't what they seem."

"I got that. "

Down the hall the music box began to play and Stormy jumped and spun around to the door. "I need to go."

Serena glanced at her door and then back again.

Her cousin was gone.

"Stormy?"

No answer.

The temperature warmed.

The music stopped playing,

The alarm clock rang.

Serena didn't need to wake up; it hadn't been a dream.

***

Panting, sweat rolling down her forehead and into her eyes, Lilith sat up. The room was quiet, the house still and silent. Claudia stepped out of the shadowed corner. Her face pale, a black glaze trickled down her rigid cheeks, past her cracked lips, and dripped off her chin.

"She's MINE!"

Chapter 35--Tuesday

Breathless, Serena rounded the last bookshelf that stood between her and Jesse. He glanced up at her sudden arrival, then down, then back up. The pent up terror from earlier that morning finally hit her. Suddenly all of the feelings of horror she felt when Stormy spoke and Haley appeared, then disappeared, overcame her, melting her legs like wax.

Jesse jumped up from the table and caught her before she fell to the floor. "What's going on?" he whispered.

Unable to speak, still in the grip of terror, she merely held on tight. He didn't say anything more. Instead, he relieved her of her backpack and then pulled her even closer. Her head leaned against his chest where she could hear his heart beat steadily, the sound calming her, bringing feeling back to her legs. She began to breathe normally again but didn't want to let go. He was solid both in body and spirit. By the feel of how tightly he held her, he didn't want to let go either. His lips brushed her temple. She knew if she looked up he'd kiss her. She wanted him to; she almost needed it. But what then? If she opened that door now, nothing would ever get done, because the feel of his lips on hers would chase every thought away. She swallowed.

He squeezed her, his arms tight around her waist, and then let go. The moment was lost and she immediately regretted the kiss that could have been. Running his hands through his hair and looking away told her he felt the same way but he wouldn't, or couldn't, walk that road toward her. With a gentle hand he led her to the table where his laptop sat. "What's going on?"

Sucking in her breath, then blowing it out again, she told him everything that had happened since she moved into the house. His face paled as she ended with her morning.

"I don't know what to say," he said.

"I don't know what to do."

He dropped his head into his hands. Disheartened by his response, she stared down at the table. Would he continue to help her or decide the water was too deep and swim back to shore? She knew what her only option was, swim for the other shore. Not only was she was too far into this to escape; it was her family inheritance. Thanks to her dad, she had to go forward. And didn't she want to? Yes, she actually did. She just didn't want to do it alone. With a deep breath, she looked up to find Jesse watching her.

"I understand if you don--," she didn't get a chance to finish her sentence.

"I didn't say that. In fact, you need more help than I thought. I just don't know if I'm powerful enough, but I'll help anyway I can." He leaned in. "I have connections that can get you out of there too. I'm thinking we'll need to do that soon."

She nodded her head, relieved.

"So, what do you want to do next?" he asked.

"Research my dad. There's a whole side of him that I don't know about, but whatever it is, it seems to be the key."

"That's what I was thinking too. Let's get to it."

They both glanced at the clock and then at each other. Lunch was almost over and they had so much to do. They couldn't both leave campus either; it would give them away.

"Do you trust me?" he asked her.

"Yeah."

"I'll go to class. You stay here and get what you can on your dad. Next period I come back and we'll switch. Hopefully, they won't notice for a while. What do you think?"

"I'm in."

The bell rang. He pushed his computer to her. "I'll see you in an hour."

"Take good notes for me."

He winked. "I was about to say the same thing."

***

The library was void of sound. So much so that silence had sound itself. Fingers poised over the keyboard, Serena quickly typed her father's name in the search engine. His obituary was the first thing that popped up. She thought about skipping it but stopped. Maybe there was a clue in it. His death was still so surreal it actually helped her to read without connecting to it. Nothing new. On to the next thing. Not much else on a Jonathan Kelly that pertained to her father. Wouldn't his last name actually be Robertson like his brother's? She typed in that moniker. Names popped up but nothing stood out to her. Would Rosalie's name be in the papers in connection to her father? It seemed like a long shot, but she had to try. She put together the names Rosalie Robertson, Jonathan Robertson and hit enter. Ninety-eight hits popped upped. Serena groaned. This would take forever. A quick glance at the clock told her she was nearly out of time. She typed Jonathan Robertson, Simon Robertson, Monarch Inc. Only a few stories popped up and they were all conspiracy theories, but there seemed to be a running theme. She clicked on the first one:

"According to some stories Simon Robertson did have a younger brother, Harrison Robertson. He disappeared in 1990 and hasn't been heard of since. It is difficult to hide in this day and age of technology but somehow he managed to do so. His sudden disappearance leads one to believe he died but there is no way to determine so since there was no death notice in the papers. What we can prove is that Harrison Robertsons was a founding member of the company Monarch, Inc., now known as Aleahil, Inc. The name changed when new partner, Azazel, stepped into the vacant spot Mr. Robertsons left open. Whether he died or not, he still remains to be found. Maybe he really did vanish into thin air. We may never know."

Harrison? A long ago memory, bits and pieces of a conversation from when she was little, tried to surface but quickly disappeared. Regardless of the name change it seemed that her father was a stranger to her. Who was he? Not Jonathan, that was for sure. She sighed heavily.

She entered Harrison Robertson, Monarch to see what would show up. Only a few websites appeared with the three names connected. She clicked on images and Bingo. There stood her father, a very young version of him at least. He stood on one side of Rosalie, his brother on the other. All three pairs of eyes the same. Rosalie was stunning with her long, thick auburn hair and green dress, and Simon striking with his thick, black hair. His face was serious, more to the point of scowling. Then there was her father. His face was rounder in its pre-pubescent age, his body stockier, his hair a deep black like his older brother. He was the only one who had a genuine smile, whereas Simon's was a scowl and Rosalie had only a hint of one. In Jonathan's face Serena saw her sister, Anna. She had never noticed it before. Of course, she had never seen a photo of her dad at a young age. It wasn't until just then that she realized he never had shown her pictures of his family. He had told her his mother and father had died in a fire that engulfed everything and everyone except him because he had been playing with a friend.

Everything her father told her about his past was being called into question now. It was weird to think of her father as anything other than her father. A kind man, intelligent and well read in all things of a religious nature, especially that of the occult. Now it made sense. He knew so much from personal experience

And what about her mother? Did she know any of this or even been a part of it? Who were her parents? Who was she? She wasn't sure whether she wanted to throw up or cry or laugh in hysteria. Her whole life had been one big facade.

She sat back in the chair, despondent. Numb. That was the word for it. A large, gentle hand rested on her shoulder.

"Did you find anything?" his deep voice echoed within her.

"Yeah. I think I found out too much, but not nearly enough."

He was silent.

"I don't know who I am. I don't know my dad, not even myself." She swallowed the growing lump in her throat. Her voice cracked as she went on. "I don't think I can go on with this research, or maybe I just don't want to."

He was still silent but he squeezed her shoulder.

"What do I do?"

"You let me do the rest."

She finally lifted her head to find a kind face, the rigid jaw softened, the hard look in his eyes now warm.

"Okay." Her sagging shoulders would have drooped further if that were possible.

"Give your brain a rest and go to class."

She nodded her head, then stood and grabbed her books.

"I'll see you on the bus."

"Okay."

Her heavy legs managed to walk her out of the library and down the hall to her next class. She heard the teacher without actually listening. It wasn't until the end of her last class that she began to pull out of her fugue.

She sat next to Jesse on the bus and he gave her the quick highlights of what he had read, all of which were ones she already knew.

"I was thinking," he began. "What if you started looking into your mom's history"?

She shrugged. "I guess I could try that. I've been puzzling about my dad though. Sure, he vanished in the 90's but the internet was still there, even if it was just barely up and running. How did he stay out of the public eye and keep him and me from being found by Rosalie and Simon, especially with their resources? Why not go to Europe or another place faraway?"

"That's a good question."

"Yeah. It's too bad the only person I could ask is gone." She bit back the tears. "Oh Dad," she whispered. "Why didn't you tell me?"

Jesse had no answer but he reached out and took her hand. He gently pulled her closer. "One thing is for sure, we have to get you out of there. I'll start looking around to get you out of here."

"How? I just said it was hard to disappear with the internet and everything."

"Yeah, it would be hard but not impossible. I have a good friend who can relocate people and give them new identities. Why don't I talk to him?"

"Sure. Whatever." She fell silent and leaned against his shoulder. When they arrived at her stop he stood to let her her scoot off the seat. She didn't look back.

***

Same silent ride up the mountain. Same sense of being watched but not finding the culprit spying on her. She could almost feel the house breathe in and out, steady as if it was asleep. She could feel it shifting and stirring, ready to wake.

The silence around her was loud. Lilith was nowhere in sight which was odd since she had greeted Serena at the door. She purposely dropped her bag on the floor to make noise but the sound didn't register. It was as if headphones had been placed over her ears and she couldn't hear anything except a distant sound that cut in and out.

She walked further into the living room, looking around the space, up into the exposed wood rafters, back down the walls and windows. Her eyes stopped at the large mirror hanging above the fireplace. In it was her reflection, watching, waiting? Her image walked closer toward the pane while she stood rooted to the floor.

Come here, Serena, the other 'her' whispered. *I have to tell you something.* Her green eyes lit with a color Serena didn't recognize.

The other her placed her hand on the glass between them, as if she could push her way through to Serena's side of reality.

"Look away," Stormy's voice echoed through her mind. Serena pulled her gaze away, which was more difficult than she thought it should be. When she glanced back, it was just her again, the same frail, pale, hollow-eyed girl she had now become. She hung her head. She was losing, she could feel it. Eyes cast down; she turned and trudged up the stairs.

167

Chapter 36--Early Wednesday

Whispers all around the room pulled Serena from a deep sleep.

"Serena," a voice said quietly. "Serena wake up."

Was that Stormy again?

"Serena, wake up."

"Yeah wake up, come play with us."

Us?

Slowly Serena lifted her head from the pillow and searched the room. Her eyes landed on the dolls. They stood, their lips animated, calling out her name. Every eyeless socket turned toward her. Except one pair. One pair had eyes. One face was not a doll. It was Haley. As Serena stared at her, she faded away and the dolls went back to normal.

Shaking uncontrollably, Serena pulled the blankets over her head and whimpered. Why was this happening? How could she possibly stop it?

A few moments later she heard Stormy's voice. "Serena."

She was beginning to hate the sound of her own name.

"What?"

"Haley's gone. You can come out now."

Afraid of what she might see, she peeked out over the blanket. Stormy, dressed in flannel pajamas, her hair tumbling around her, sat at the foot of her bed again. "What's happening?" Serena asked.

"Don't worry, I'm here to protect you. You're why I'm still here."

For the first time since arriving, Serena felt peace envelop her. If her cousin had been sent to keep watch over her, chasing away Haley and shielding her from Claudia, then she would somehow be ok. Gradually her teeth stopped clacking against each other, her clenched jaw loosened, her rigid body relaxed.

When she finally took a deep breath Stormy spoke.

"I need to tell you why I've been sent to help you."

"What is it?" Serena sat up.

"My dad, mom and Rosalie are searching through your room for something, and you need to find it first."

"What in the world do they want from me?"

"When your dad left the family, he took an object with him that gave him amazing abilities. This object, whatever it is, is dangerous to you as well as to them, but they want it anyway."

"What are you talking about?"

"I'm sorry. Let me start at the beginning. Before your dad left he was next in line to take over Rosalie's place as a powerful leader that would infiltrate our government, and then our nation. With the right people in place they could set up a new world order that they could control everything and everyone. She had trained your father to rule with her and they were close, so very close, but then he met your mother, and your sister came along and then you. Rosalie would have killed all of you if she could've except that your father had been granted a lot of abilities over the years and knew how to fight her and how to hide himself and his family. Unfortunately, he realized too late how dangerous Rosalie had become and that her rage would kill anything or anyone who got in her way."

Anyway, when your dad left, he had bound whatever power he had into a specific object and he took it with him. The problem is that they don't know what object he bound it to or where it is and they need to find it before you do."

"But I don't know what it is." Anger and betrayal pierced Serena's heart. There were so many secrets her dad kept from her, secrets that could have protected her had she known what was happening, why she was so important.

"Regardless, you must find it first. It will protect you; give you the abilities you need to fight them and win. If they find it first then you're definitely dead. "

"What does this thing look like?"

"That's the one important detail everyone needs and no one knows. They were hoping you had it, that you might even know what it was."

"I have absolutely no clue what it could be. Do you have any idea?"

Stormy shrugged. "Usually things like this are bound to something important to the person. The problem is that if you don't know, then I don't know. The only good thing is that Dad, Mom and Rosalie don't know either."

Stormy got up from the bed and began to pace. She stopped at the mantle and looked at the hand stitched doll staring at her. "When did you get this doll?

"What doll?"

"This one." Stormy pointed at the ugly thing that seemed to move its eyes to look at Serena.

"That's not my doll." Serena began to tremble.

"You need to get rid of it! It's a VooDoo doll!" Stormy said.

"What?"

"Claudia made them for years. Throw it away as soon as possible. Take it to school and leave it there. She uses these kinds of dolls to curse people."

"What about these other dolls?"

"I'm not quite sure." When Stormy spoke again, her words rushed at Serena. "Time's running out and I have to tell you something else."

"More?"

"Yes. You have to get in my room.."

"Okay." Serena slowly slid her legs from under the covers.

"You can't right now. The door's locked."

"Where's the key?"

"Claudia. You have to go up to her apartment."

"Are you kidding me?" Serena frantically whispered.

"No. You have to do it. I can help you by keeping an eye out for her."

"When am I supposed to go in there?"

"The next time she leaves the house."

"I can't."

"You have to. That key, my room, it's too important not to do so."

"This is too much."

"I need your help, Serena. Please."

Down the hall the barely audible notes of a music box began to play, growing ever louder. This time Serena kept watching Stormy as she disappeared.

Chapter 37--Wednesday Morning

Simon spent the night tossing and turning, never still and never resting. He finally gave up at four am. Careful not to wake Angel, he eased off the bed, grabbed his pants and his phone.

The cool winter sun had not yet risen, but the promise of its coming was on the horizon. Pink clouds against light blue sky reflected off the ocean beyond their property. This was why he loved the West Coast.

He made a cup of coffee before walking out to the patio. As soon as he sat on one of the deck chairs, his mind went back to Colorado and Serena. He suspected something was going on there but was unable to see anything, which alarmed him. Typically he could "see" all, or most of, what happened inside the house, but over the last several days, his vision had clouded to the point that he felt like he was looking through scratched lenses. Everything was distorted, their voices, their actions.

Of all five people on that mountain, Serena, Lilith, Claudia and her husband Frank, and Henry, the groundskeeper, the two that concerned him the most were his niece and his 'second' mother.

Each one posed a threat to the other and in the end there would be no doubt who he would choose. He needed to return anyway. Azazel had the power to make the executive decision that the time had come to set their plan in motion. It excited Simon. His coffee gone, Simon rolled out his yoga mat on the deck, sat down and assumed the lotus position, once again attempting to see inside the winter retreat. He focused, his mental lens sharpening and then blurring, like a camera. When it sharpened again it was scratched in every room but Serena's. This was not a good sign. Lilith's ringtone sounded beside him. "Lilith," his tone was abrasive though he was relieved to hear from her.

"You need to come back."

"What's going on?"

"Claudia is," she paused, as if searching for the right word, "hunting Serena."

"What is she doing?"

"Those dolls she makes are showing up in Serena's room and one is her specially made voodoo doll."

The unease he felt a few moments ago was now alarm. No wonder he couldn't see into the house. Claudia was the one systematically blocking him from every room. "I'm on my way. Keep Serena safe."

"I will." She terminated the call first.

***

Ticket in hand, Simon followed the small group of passengers to the gate. The cup of coffee he held in his hand would be sure to wake him once he was on the plane.

By the time they took off, his stomach ached from the stress he held inside. He wished they were already there to deal with Claudia. She was just like his own mother, but instead of pushing him away, Claudia taught him how to do what she did. Her magic wasn't like his mother's; Claudia's was steeped in voodoo. He had learned a lot from her, including how cruel a person could be. She was a powerful woman.

He had three things to do on this trip. The first, obviously, was to deal with Claudia, but the second had to do with Serena. Where had his brother hidden their secret? The thought did occur to him that the object could still be at her house in Pleasant Hill and that she might not know what it was for. Wouldn't his brother tell her though? Maybe not. Maybe he figured that the less she knew the stronger or more protected she would be. *Bad move little brother.* Simon shook his head. Not enough information could be just as dangerous as too much.

The third reason was what interested him the most. He was to begin the transformation of Serena, molding her into what he knew she could be. That part of the weekend would be the most thrilling.

Deep in thought, Simon was one of the first people out of the plane. He found Henry waiting for him as Lilith said he would be. The man took Simon's carry-on. Once in the car Simon felt a sudden sickness come over him. Something was wrong at the house.

"Hurry," he said.

Henry must have felt it too because the man went white. He immediately shifted the four-wheel drive into gear and drove as fast as he dared. Simon opened the middle console, removed the false bottom and pulled out a nine millimeter gun. The phone rang. He answered.

"Where are you?" Lilith said.

"We're on our way."

172

Chapter 38--Wednesday Late Afternoon

Now, now's the time. Stormy's voice came through loud and clear. It was now or never. Serena swallowed and went back to the stairs. Where was Claudia? Where did she go when she wasn't in her living quarters? It didn't matter, except that she would come back, could come back and there was no telling what time that would be. By the time Serena reached the third floor her palms were slick from perspiration and her heart pounded so loud it echoed in her head. She gulped when she reached the last landing.

Instead of a hallway there was an ornate door with swirls carved into the wood. The swirls seemed random, but she had the feeling that if she stood far enough back she would see some kind of message in it, most likely a warning. Nerves clawed her stomach, twisting, turning it. Could she go through with this?

"You have to turn the knob to open the door." Stormy's sudden appearance startled Serena.

"What if it's locked?"

"I know where the key is. Just trust me on this."

Serena looked into her cousin's eyes. The girl was solid, almost as if she were alive and Serena half wondered if she was. Okay, trust her she would. Besides, if this search uncovered information she had to do it. She reached out her hand and twisted the knob only to find it locked. "See," she said.

With a small shake of her head and hint of a smile, Stormy pointed above to the doorframe. "Really?" Serena asked. "That's such an obvious place to look."

"I know, right? But it's not like she's trying to keep outside people from breaking in. The key is more for Dad to get in whenever he comes home."

"Does he come up here often?"

Stormy shook her head again. "Not so much anymore. I wonder if Claudia even remembers it's there. Come on," she urged. "We only have so much time."

"Okay." Serena reached up and took the key off the ledge. It shook in her fingers as she inserted it into the keyhole and turned the knob. She stopped and turned to Stormy. "Doesn't Claudia have a husband?"

"Yes, but the man follows her everywhere so if she's gone so is he. Besides, even if he was here he's so deaf he wouldn't hear us anyway. Now. Open. The. Door."

With a deep inhale and trembling hands, Serena swung open the door. Obviously it was kept well oiled, which made Serena wonder how many times Claudia might have come down the stairs without anyone hearing her. She shuddered.

"Put the key back on the frame." Stormy said.

Serena followed the directions, entered the room and then closed the door behind her. It suddenly felt as if she had shut the door to a tomb.

"Come on," Stormy whispered.

Serena turned to look around the room. The shades were all drawn and dust floated in the air. "She isn't much of a housekeeper of her own apartment, is she?"

"Ha," Stormy said sardonically. An old rocking chair made of logs stood in the corner, an old cushion on its seat matched the ancient, flowery upholstered couch that had been pushed against the wall. The cushions looked as dirt-grimed as the shades. An old couch sat across from the rocking chair, both facing the fireplace that looked exactly like Serena's downstairs. A small kitchenette stood to the right of them along with a back door with glass on the top and solid panels below.

"Where does that door even go? She's on the third floor."

"She has a small deck and stairs that lead to the ground, in case of a fire or something. Now hurry." Stormy pointed at the two doors facing them. One of them was open revealing a queen sized bed covered by a bedspread decorated with mustard yellow and brown flowers of the 1970's. A bedside table and ornate lamp stand with yet more flowers stood to the side. Pictures of faded flowers hung on the walls. "Good grief. Has this woman been off the mountain since the 70's? It looks so outdated in here. And gross." There was at least an inch of dust on the table that Serena could see.

Stormy stood in front of the other door; it was closed. Anxiety was written on her face. "You're wasting time."

Spurred on by her cousin's urgency Serena opened the door. The room was filled with dolls, and each one, standing or sitting, faced her, as if they had been waiting for her. "I can't go in there."

"You must. The key is inside."

"They look like they could attack me."

"I know, but they're just dolls."

Serena took a tentative step inside the room. "Where did they all come from?"

"She makes them, now come on."

Serena noticed a corner filled with paint brushes, paint and porcelain figures and heads. So this was where the dolls were coming from. The sense of time passing by prompted her to move as Stormy came alongside. "Come on, Serena. We really have to get that key and leave."

She nodded in agreement, "Okay, where do we start?"

"Over here." Stormy led the way to another corner with an old desk and lamp and pointed to the top drawer. Inside sat a thickly padded envelope and several keys with different colored ribbons. "The powder blue one." Serena reached and grabbed it, then shut it just as the back door closed. "She's here," Stormy's frightened voice said right before she disappeared, leaving Serena to fend for herself.

The sound of heavy footfalls got closer. Frozen, Serena scanned the small room for any kind of exit. She could hide in the pile of dolls but she knew it would be her death. The steps halted just outside the door. Serena gulped. There was nowhere to go. She had to face the woman. Maybe she wouldn't be as bad as everyone kept saying.

On the threshold stood a very small woman whose heavy footfalls didn't seem to match her appearance, until her husband, Frank, stepped around the corner and stood behind her. He looked skeletal with his sagging skin, worse than when she had met him at her Pleasant Hill house.

The woman's graying black hair was pulled back in a bun so tight that it stretched the skin on her forehead and jagged cheekbones. Despite her bird like bony arms and clavicle, she looked like a giant. Ebony eyes stared Serena down.

"What are you doing here?" Each word was a sentence in itself, and they carried a strong Colombian accent. However, her lips did not move.

Serena opened her dry mouth but no words could squeak out.

"I said: what are you doing here?" Again, the woman's lips did not move, but it felt like surround sound because Serena sensed the vibration and this time more than one voice spoke in unison. Scuffling behind her reinforced the sense that she was far outnumbered by whatever stood there.

Claudia walked into the small room, an odd smell following her. She began to circle Serena, each step methodical. Serena turned in the circle too. Once Serena faced the rows of dolls the woman stopped. The dolls' faces took on the same expression as Claudia's, threatening though their limbs couldn't move. Could they? In the middle of the dolls stood Haley's fading apparition, her arms and neck shackled, ghostly chains gripped by the four dolls surrounding her. Her face alternated between tearful grief and a glowering stare. Standing in front of her dolls and her captivated spirit, Claudia was even more threatening. She was like a General with her loyal troops behind her.

The room darkened, little spots of white appeared before Serena. She took a breath before she passed out. Her mind was jumbled, her thoughts scattered and disoriented. Breathe, she told herself. Just breathe. Her hands curled into fists, the left one curled around the ridges of the key she had stolen. Okay, now what? She couldn't stuff it into her pocket, that would immediately draw Claudia's attention, but she didn't want to risk losing it either. Her hands were slick with sweat, the ribbon damp.

"Did you know," Claudia's voice interrupted Serena's thoughts, "that the mind is much more powerful than people realize, that we only use perhaps a quarter of it?"

Serena nodded.

"No you didn't."

"Yes, I did. I'd read that we only use a portion of our brains."

"Not our brains, girl. Our minds. The two are different."

Suddenly she remembered she had this same conversation with her dad only a few weeks before he had died.

Claudia continued. "You are correct that we only use a portion of our brains, but that isn't what I care about, for it is the mind that is much more powerful. The mind," she tapped her temple with her finger tips, "is where our soul is, our actual being if you will. It is there that we are connected to the spiritual realm. It is with our minds that we can see more, we can do more, and we can even command and direct people and things at will."

Suddenly a bright, searing light invaded Serena's head, throbbing like someone's fist pounding on the door. "What are you doing?" she gasped, gripping her head with her hands, losing the key in the process. It fell with a heavy clunk and lay on the floor with the blue wrinkled ribbon attached to it.

"Aha, so you did find Stormy's key," Claudia said. Her attention diverted she released Serena from the intense pain.

Serena reached down for the key but the light seared through her again, and this time it was sharp, like the tip of a white-hot iron rod fresh from the furnace and sharp as a sword. It pierced through her eyes and began drilling a hole into her mind like a jackhammer. She screamed, this time dropping to her knees, and gripped her head. The light dug deeper and deeper, peeling away the outer layers of her mind that kept her soul protected.

"Did you know Lilith could do this?" Claudia's voice spoke into her head, as if the light in Serena's head lit the way for her to enter. "Before she was ruined by loving that child, your aunt was more powerful than even I am at this. Of course, I've taught myself over the years whereas Lilith came to it naturally, which made her all that more powerful."

The pounding increased, but instead of it drowning out Claudia's voice, it only got clearer. There was sense of someone or something invading Serena's sanity, attempting to pry open a bolted door she had placed there. There was no memory of putting a locked door to her mind. Her father's face immediately came to her. She didn't know when he did it, but instinctively she knew he had done so years ago. The steel door he had placed there to protect her was giving way though. Lilith had tried to penetrate the door at her grandmother's meeting, but not to this extent.

There was no way Claudia could get through, right? The pounding turned into a sharp drill and Serena screamed out both in her head as well as physically. The drill stopped for a moment and a solid shove moved the door an inch. Serena strained to close that small gap.

Through the crack a tentacle slithered, growing longer as if searching for something. Below the door another one slithered out. Sticky hairs grabbed on to her and wrapped tightly so she could not move and then the drill began again. The crack widened and Serena screamed out in fear and pain but she still kept her hands on the door to keep it from opening and allowing whatever was on the other side inside her head.

Legs weak, arms shaking she couldn't keep the door from opening further. It finally gave way and the thing that crawled in glowered at her with all of its eight eyes. The tentacle holding her brought her closer to its fangs.

"That's enough, put her down," Claudia told the spider as she moved into the room. The arm that held her dropped her immediately. She landed on her hands and knees, panting, finally able to speak.

"You don't belong here. This is my body, this is me."

"Of course I do. This is my domain now. You are my domain."

"No!" Serena struggled to her feet.

"Child, I am so much stronger than you."

Pounding began again but this time it was from outside her body, not in her head.

"Claudia!" Simon's deep voice yelled as he burst through her apartment door. "Release her!"

"She's already mine."

The woman's quiet voice scared Serena more than if she had yelled back at him. Simon and Henry's interruption pulled Claudia and her 'pet' out of her head but the door to her mind had been forced open, her sanity left hanging off its hinges, leaving her raw and vulnerable. She opened her physical eyes to find herself lying limp on the rough hardwood flooring. Her surroundings blurred except for the sight of Stormy's key mere inches away. Simon stood in the doorway with Henry just behind.

"You cannot beat me, Simon," the woman hissed.

"Oh yes I can," his voice dropped another octave. "I'm much stronger than you'll ever be."

Serena watched the old woman shuffle away. "Henry," Simon said, "Take Serena to her room."

Henry came to her side and lifted her gently off the ground. With the last bit of strength Serena grasped the key. The room grew dark and splotchy again, but she held the key close though the dull edges bit her palm. Simon's voice sounded as if he were talking in a tin can.

"I bind you to this apartment, Claudia. I will be back for you."

Serena no longer cared what else he said as she let the darkness pull her down.

Chapter 39--Wednesday Night

Henry's back prevented Simon from seeing Serena's face as they left the apartment. With Claudia bound to her apartment he didn't need to worry about her escaping. Before he did anything with the old woman he wanted to speak with Lilith.

He stepped out onto the landing. The small platform gave the perfect view of the downstairs living quarters. His mother wanted to do away with Claudia after Stormy's friend disappeared, but he couldn't bring himself to do it. Now, he realized how wrong he truly was concerning his second mother.

Lilith stood on the small balcony. Not wanting to look weak, he kept his eyes locked on his wife.

"What happened?" he asked .

"I don't know. She's been slowly gaining more power, which you'd know if you actually listened to me."

"How long ago did you notice it?"

"A year."

"Hm, okay. Go downstairs." He turned back to Claudia's door.

"You're ordering me around too?"

Turning back he saw venom in her eyes. "No, I'm trying to keep you away from Claudia. You know what she is capable of."

"Don't you think I know? I can do the same things she can and I'm better."

"Correction. You *could* do it. You're too weak to protect yourself or be any good here."

His words made her flinch. He was right, he knew it, and deep inside she knew it too. It still hurt to hear someone else say it. However, it might jerk her out of this endless grieving process. There were things he needed her to do and the longer she waited to get back in the game the weaker she became and the less useful to him or his mother.

Shoulders sagging, she began her long descent.

"Lilith."

She paused but did not look back.

"You have waited for too long to come back to us. If you don't get it together Rosalie will exterminate you, no matter hard I beg her not to."

She nodded and kept moving down the stairs, gripping the railing as she went.

He shook his head as he pulled out his gun and checked it to make sure it was loaded.

Simon stepped back through Claudia's door into the dark living room. The clouds outside prevented any light from coming through the windows, so the room was even darker and seemed to close in on him. Claudia's cold eyes met him. She sat on the couch next to Frank who was pale and holding his side. A fire sparked in the fireplace and was the only source of light for the living room. One doll, looking like Serena, stood in the corner. Her dark hair hung around her face, she wore ripped blue jeans and a University of Oregon sweatshirt, and her eyes were wide open, showing green marbles instead of hollow sockets.

"You gave the Serena doll eyes," he mentioned.

"Of course," she responded. "She's still alive."

"What do you mean by that?"

Claudia sighed heavily. "I only remove the eyes if they're dead."

Simon looked at the woman, incredulous. He knew what he had to do. She was too much of a risk now, especially since she had tried to kill Serena. She knew how important Serena was to him and she still attacked her.

"You're sick, Claudia."

"Ha! I'm the only sane one here!" She sneered at him. "You're running around calling the shots, trying to save that girl when you should be getting rid of her!"

"You have no idea what you're talking about!" he shouted at her. "She is important in more ways than you know!"

"Why?" Claudia got up and moved around the couch. "Why is she so important? Is it because of how much you loved her mother? Maybe it's because you're getting her mixed up with her mother! You couldn't have Crystal so you take Serena instead!"

"What are you talking about?" He didn't move, blood draining from his face.

Frank moaned from the couch.

"Shut up, Frank!" She turned back to Simon. "You think I didn't know?" Claudia's voice dropped to a whisper as she crept closer. "The very first night you brought her home you crept into her room and watched her sleep, dreaming of the day you'd take her."

"As if you really care!"

"You're right! I don't care about her!" Her voice was hard. "But I do care about you. Serena will kill you. Your obsession with her will kill you." She walked closer to him until they stood a few inches away from each other. "You think you will live with her forever, that she will be yours and you'll make her love you, but that will never happen. You have to kill her or she will be the death of you."

"You don't understand what Azazel and I are doing. It's not about love anymore. It's about the fact that Serena can see into other people's minds, form their thoughts for them and so much more. Things that even she isn't aware of."

Claudia stomped her foot. "You are such a liar! Maybe that's what Azazel wants to do with her, use her to reach into the unknown, but I know you Simon. You want her for yourself!" Spittle flew from her lips as she spoke.

The room was silent except for the occasional crackle and pop from the fire. Frank didn't turn or move. When Claudia turned around for a moment and when she turned back she had a plate of cookies for Simon. Her smile was crooked, and there was a vacancy in her eyes. She opened her mouth to speak, but instead of her usual contralto, a man's deep voice emerged. "Here son, have something to eat." She began laughing hysterically.

Simon glanced again at Frank who was still unmoving. He flash-backed to when he had run into his grandfather's room and tried to wake him up, lifting up the lifeless arm that hung off the bed. Frank was every bit as dead as his grandfather had been twenty years ago. He looked at Claudia. Her mouth opened and the deep voice of a demon spoke. "Go ahead, and shoot her. She's no good to us anymore."

Simon didn't think about it, he simply pulled the trigger and shot her three times in the chest. Claudia dropped the plate and looked down at the blood seeping through her blouse. She touched the wetness that was spreading across her body and looked up at him. "Why?" she asked.

"Why not?" he asked as he holstered his gun. Claudia dropped to her knees, her face in shock.

"Why?" she asked again, but her voice was weak and she wasn't looking at him any longer. She stared into the fire as she fell down on the floor. "I thought you loved me." Tears ran down her cheeks. Simon stood over and watched her eyes widen in fear and horror as she shook her head back and forth. She tried to scream but only a hollow whisper came out with her last breath.

Behind him was a creak down the hall. What was that? Great, now he'd have to search before he left the apartment. Entering the room he had found Serena in there were dolls all over the place. Now that he knew the eyeless sockets meant the person was dead, he was more creeped out than usual. Did each doll represent someone his mother had killed? He shuddered to think if any soul was attached to the doll made in their image.

Another creak startled him and he whipped around but no one was there. Simon pulled out his gun and cocked it. More footfalls sounded down the hall back to the living room. He quickly checked an extra room. Nothing in there. He turned and nearly tripped over a doll that hadn't been there a moment ago.

The doll looked up at him, head lolling to one side like it had been broken at the neck and black hair like Lilith's, but eyeless like the rest. He shoved it aside, and moved onto the next room. This one had more dolls, a bed and a table. He turned for the bathroom and tripped over another doll. Again, one that hadn't been there before. This one had brown hair and was a boy doll, he looked like he had been in mid step, as if walking when Simon turned around. The doll had a heavy rope and noose around its neck. Simon shuddered this time. He had to get out of here. Another foot fall. He pulled open a door. How many doors were in this apartment? He didn't remember there being this many.

Behind the last door there was the sound of scraping behind it. Simon wiped the sweat away, checked the gun again, and then pushed his way into the room.

It was completely empty except for two things. A pentagram was drawn on the floor and a red headed doll lay in the middle of it, it's eyes rolling around on the floor a few feet away from three other dolls. Suddenly the doll burst into flames and he heard Claudia's screams of terror. He ran down the hall. He knew had killed the woman! How was she screaming? Claudia still lay in a pool of blood. Her eyes were open, but nobody was there.

It was time to leave this apartment from Hell. He holstered his gun as he left the apartment, locking the deadbolt behind him.

Chapter 40--Wednesday Night

Deep grooves ran along the hardwood floor. Disconnected thoughts came and went. Serena tried to grasp any one of the random thoughts, hoping it would bring her out of the cage she seemed to be in. She needed to sit up.

The room began to spin when she moved, forcing her to stop and put her head between her knees. Her neck hurt. Actually, everything hurt. She saw Simon's legs in front of her She looked up to find him watching her.

He means you harm.

She shook off the voices and allowed him to reach down and pull her up. The pretense of strength had seeped out of her, leaving her hollow.

Don't trust him.

Her tongue was dry and it felt like she had chewed on a cotton ball. "I don't feel so good,"

Her bones ached and so did her head. Her left knee throbbed under her jeans.

"Come on," Simon purred gently in her ear.

Don't listen to him.

"Let's get you on the bed."

As soon as she sat on the bed, Simon handed her a glass of juice. After a few sips she gave it back. She gazed up at him, thankful he had come home to take care of her, protect her from Claudia. "Drink some more," he whispered. She swallowed the rest of the liquid, and her body relaxed, leaving her with a sense of calm. He set the glass down on the bedside table. What was difficult before was nearly impossible to do now. She grasped for anything to stay alert, but her brain was letting go, the surreal taking over as he bent over and began unbuttoning the front of her shirt. She pushed his hands away, though it was in slow motion.

"No," she whispered. She couldn't tell if she said the word or thought it. He shrugged.

"Have it your way."

Slowly he laid her back and swung her feet up onto the bed. The fight to stay awake was seeping out of her; she only wanted to sleep. Even with the light on and the covers off she was letting herself go. There was a weight on her ankle and a metal clink. Her eyes began to adjust to the darkness though she still felt dazed. She moved her foot, but it couldn't go very far. Her eyes flew open but she saw two of everything, so she closed them again. A click. Her eyes opened to a dark room. Was she asleep? Awake?

A raspy breath blew the hair by her ear.

"Serena.,"

WAKE UP! The deeper part of her screamed. She tried to push away the black fog that pulled her down. She kicked, but couldn't move her feet, so she squirmed, trying to sit back up, only to feel the weight of Simon on top of her.

"No." Her grunt was barely audible. "No please."

His hand went over her mouth and he hissed in her ear, "Be quiet. Now."

She tried to move one more time and then another voice spoke clearly into her ear. "Let me help you Serena," said the girl from the mirror. Serena could see her faint outline in the vanity mirror. She stood strong and stable, not weak like Serena had become. "Trust in me. Sleep."

An ocean of blackness tugged at her and Serena didn't want to fight it anymore. Like a tide going out, she let herself float away from her bed, then her room, and then the house. Everything disappeared and she found herself drifting along a calm river. She closed her eyes and listened to the water swish and swoosh beneath her raft. She no longer cared how she got there, nor cared where the little boat would take her. Somewhere in the distance she heard a girl crying, but what could she do? She closed her mind to it and continued to sail away.

Chapter 41--Thursday Morning

From the comfortable couch Lilith watched the snow fall outside. Serena had been sleeping for over twelve hours; regardless of her curiosity and small bit of concern, she let her niece be. Claudia was dead. Finally. As soon as the shot rang through the house Lilith was relieved; it left her with some semblance of peace. When Henry took her and Frank's bodies outside and buried them that morning she breathed a sigh of relief.

But she had a much larger concern. Simon had been right the night before. She had lost her edge, her ability to see into people's innermost thoughts and use their own weakness against them. That realization had kept her up all night.

She sat huddled under her large, heavy blanket holding a cup of coffee. The fire put off heat that should have warmed her, but she still trembled from the chill that came from within. She sighed.

She took another sip but it was cold now. She set the cup down on the coaster, and then lay down. Her eyelids were suddenly heavy from the sleepless night and Serena would be out for another twelve hours, if Simon was correct. And he was always right.

As soon as sleep came her astral self woke up, ready to 'walk' through the house. The first place she would go to was Serena's room to check on the girl. Lilith floated to just outside her room, ready to enter but the room was barred to her. No matter how much she pushed she wasn't strong enough to break through. It was as if Simon was taunting her, reminding her that there was a time when she could have done it, she would have been strong enough to do it, and now he was bent on showing just how weak she had become. The two things she wanted the least were Simon being right and her being as weak as she was.

She prepared for the return back to her body when her daughter's voice stopped her.

"Mama," Stormy whispered.

Lilith moved down the hall to Stormy's door. It had been a long, long time since she heard her daughter's voice. The door was solid wood, but that meant nothing to her.

On the other side sat her daughter on her white, ruffled bed, looking out the window. They couldn't actually touch, she knew, but the desire was so strong she rushed for her only to find her spirit pass through Stormy's, neither of them feeling the other. They gazed at each other.

"Oh mama," her girl said. "I need your help."

"What do you need?"

"I need you strong. I need you strong enough to save Serena."

"Why? Why is she so damn important to everyone? Why you too? You're gone."

"I know, but I've been appointed guardian of Serena's soul and I need your help to do it. She is of great importance to us all and I need her to be on our side, not Rosalie's. But in order to do it I need you back to who you were before."

"Before . . .?" Lilith prompted her daughter to finish the thought she already knew the answer to.

"Before I was born." Stormy's voice broke. Her green eyes shone with unshed tears as she raised her translucent chin. She was beginning to fade. "Please help me, mama."

Stormy's favorite tune began to play on the music box as her daughter's frame began to disappear. "Please, please help."

The music box lid slapped shut as soon as she was gone. Lilith allowed herself to be pulled back to her body like a heavy magnet.

Her body inhaled sharply when she reentered her shell. Stormy's words came back to her, and Lilith sat up, her head pounding relentlessly. The noise of someone standing near her grabbed her attention. She spun around to find green eyes watching her.

"Simon!"

"Where were you wandering as you slept?" he questioned, his voice patronizing.

"I thought you left." She got off the couch, picked up her teacup, now filled with cold coffee, and walked to the kitchen.

"We need to talk about Serena."

Lilith sighed. She rinsed her cup in the sink and then walked to the coffee maker for another cup. Maybe she'd finish this one while it was still hot. Of course, with Simon there she'd need more than coffee. In the cupboard on the second shelf was her other chosen alcohol for her morning coffee, Sambuca. She poured in a bit more than a splash. There would be more needed as the day went on she was sure.

He left her in the kitchen as she mixed her concoction. Settling into the overstuffed chair closest to the fire, he crossed one leg over the other and watched the snowfall. He was still waiting for her to ask him what it was he wanted. Fine. He could wait. She felt like a petulant child but she didn't really care. That's what alcohol did for you. It made you no longer care. After a few sips, she finally joined him in the living room. She sat gingerly so as not to disrupt her drink, pulled the heavy blanket on herself and took another sip, and watched the snow fall and fall and fall some more. It took them forty-five minutes before Lilith caved, hating herself for it. "What about Serena?" she refused to look at him but she could feel the smirk.

"It's time to put our plans in action."

Stormy's words rang through Lilith's mind. In order to save Serena she would have to play along, She'd do anything for her daughter. "And what does that look like?" She asked before taking another drink. The liquid warmth filled her belly and made her head float. "You don't even know what you're looking for, do you?"

"No, but I believe Serena does," Simon said, " It may be in the far recesses of her mind but I think she knows what it is we're looking for and I'll get it out of her. I've already started the process."

The pleasant warmth a minute before turned sour at the thought of what he may have done to the girl. If there was one thing she couldn't stand it was Simon's way of pushing a person over the edge. How did he do it this time? Beat her? Or . . .

She couldn't go to the other possibility because if he had raped Serena then what had he done to Stormy? That thought froze her. Her stomach turned and her coffee threatened to come back up. Did she really want to know? She would kill him if he did.

As if he knew her question, he answered. "No, I didn't do that to Stormy."

Lilith breathed a sigh of relief.

"Aza did."

That did it. She gripped the being, the dormant spirit within and used it to push through Simon's walls, but he pushed back, with a smile on his face.

"You're not strong anymore, remember? You let yourself go, while I built myself up."

She pushed again, but his mental defenses were as strong as ever. She stood, screaming in frustration.

"Ahhhhhhhh!"

He jumped up at the same time.

"How dare you!" She flung the cup at his face, striking his forehead, immediately shattering the china and drawing blood.

"Damn you!" He stomped to the kitchen for a towel. "You know how this works, Lilith!" He pressed the towel against his head. "In order to get what we need we have to break people down. Your father did it to you, but in the end you were too strong for him."

"And what makes you think Serena isn't too strong for you, huh? And if Aza broke Stormy what kind of handler is he? A weak one!"

"No! He is much stronger than even me. She was the weak one!" His voice cracked at the last word. He regained his control, "When he realized how weak her spirit was he broke her down completely. There was only one other way she was usable to us afterward."

Simon was silent. He dropped the towel to the counter. The bleeding had stopped. He pressed his knuckles against the hard marble. The seconds ticked by. He lifted his head finally and locked his gaze with hers.

In a quiet voice, he said, "You have lost sight of the end game. You need to get yourself together before my mother breaks you too."

"I'm not a horse and neither was Stormy," Lilith croaked, her throat ached from unshed tears. She began pacing. "You killed my little girl."

"I didn't kill her. Aza did."

"What's the difference? You stood by while he had his way with Stormy and then tossed her aside. Is that what you're planning to do with Serena?"

"We are dedicated to the greater good. And the greater good depends on Serena and my brother's secret for now. We can't move on without them. Now it's time to use Serena to find what we need. After that we will use Serena for another project Aza and I have been working on for a few years now."

"And what if you still can't find this magical totem? Will you kill your precious niece too?"

"My precious niece," he sneered, "will be used regardless of what she finds because I am her handler; she belongs to me. I control her and my mother can no longer touch her."

"What is it about that girl? Is it because she is Crystal's daughter?"

"Yes." His one word answer halted the conversation.

Lilith stopped moving. She could hardly stand to look at him, but she lifted her head and her eyes met his. She would not let him see her broken. "It's always been her."

He rapped his knuckles twice on the hard surface and then left the kitchen, walking behind Lilith. He paused to whisper in her ear, "Not always. It used to be you."

He continued to his room saying, "I'm leaving in an hour. I'll be checking in often. Be ready every time I call or I will come back before the allotted time. We both know you don't want that."

"Okay."

"Everything should be ready sometime this spring. That will give you two months to work with her."

"Fine, just don't bring Angel."

He gave a derisive laugh. "Even I don't want that." He disappeared into his bedroom and shut the door quietly.

Lilith went back into the kitchen to find the Tylenol. She shook out two pills and downed it with what were a few drops of the now bitter coffee. A creak sounded on the stairs and she turned, knowing Serena was there.

The girl looked down at her, holding Lilith's eyes with her own. Whatever Serena was, she didn't look broken.

Chapter 42--Monday Morning, Four Days Later

Jesse was the first one to notice the difference in Serena's manner. Surprisingly, Kendra noticed it as well. He heard her sigh as he was pulling his first period's book out from his locker.

"What is it?"

"Serena is acting weird, have you noticed?"

"Yeah, I have. What do you care?"

"What's going on?"

"How the hell should I know?" He bent in search of a pen or pencil.

"You're dating her, aren't you?"

"No."

"Oh come on, everyone knows it. Obviously, you guys are into each other."

"No, we're actually not dating. What made you think that?"

"Nobody thinks that now. Now everyone assumes you guys have broken up."

"Okay."

"You guys were always disappearing during lunch and then there are the subtle glances, which, by the way, weren't all that subtle. But suddenly, she's back in the cafeteria, eating by herself, all glassy-eyed."

Jesse slammed his locker door.

"You can talk to me, Jesse. We're friends. Whatever you need to say, you can say it to me."

"Really? Well, how about you tell me why you threw her into the janitor's closet a few months ago?"

She stood in front of him, mouth open to speak but he wasn't waiting for her response. He turned away and began walking to his class; she fell into step with him. "Why couldn't you just leave Stormy in the past?"

"I was trying to do just that, but then I saw Serena with Lilith that one day. I want to make up for failing Stormy." His voice trailed off.

Logan appeared at their sides, his face serious, and his hazel eyes intense.

"Have you guys seen Serena?"

Kendra beat Jesse to the question. "No, why?"

"Man, she's, I don't know. I don't know how to describe her, except that she looks different and everyone is scared of her. Hell, even I'm scared of her."

Jesse scanned the hall. "Where is she?"

"Not here. Someone said they saw her go to the front office. Maybe her aunt picked her up." He shook his head. "Something is seriously cracked in that family." He turned to Jesse. "Dude, you gotta stay away from her, far away. She's not just mysterious or weird. She's creepy. She's something--," he fumbled for a word, and then gave up when he glanced behind them. "I gotta go. Just promise me you'll stay away from her." He didn't wait to see Jesse's response. He jogged to the door, calling for one of his other friends.

Jesse and Kendra looked at each other, alarmed.

"Hello kids," Mr. Dawson said behind them. They turned.

"You two have been enjoying a nice little chat."

To get away from the teacher's gaze Jesse looked in his backpack, pretending to search for something. His heart stopped when he saw he really had lost something. He had accidentally switched out the wrong notebook. The excuse to get out of there wasn't just made up. "I need to go back to my locker. I left something in there. See ya Kendra."

Before the teacher replied Jesse turned and jogged to his locker. He rounded the corner and skid to a stop. His locker door hung slightly ajar. Pages were scattered on the floor below it. He thought of his notes he and Serena had been making. "No no no no," he prayed silently. He ran to the papers and gathered everything up, flipping through the pages for the research notes but not finding them. Those notes weren't in the pile. He looked through his locker for the only other notebook it could be in. It too had pages ripped out. Who would've done this? He tried to breathe deeply but he couldn't. Those notes could be the death of him, or her. Most likely both of them.

As if on cue, the clacking square heeled shoes of the school secretary echoed against the linoleum floors and metal lockers. Mrs. Flinch appeared around the corner.

"Jesse," she called out. "What are you doing outside of class?"

He continued to shuffle the papers, finally catching the breath that had been alluding him and centered his being. His voice steadied as he answered.

"Nothing, Mrs. Flinch. I dropped my notebook out of my locker and my homework fell out."

"Did you find what you were looking for?" she was getting closer.

"Yes, ma'am. I just did."

"Good, then. I'll finish cleaning up for you." She was standing a couple feet away from him.

"No, but thank you though."

He grabbed his history book and math and slammed the locker door shut. He glanced to find her shrewd eyes staring at him. "See ya."

He ran to his next class. What was Serena going to say when she found out about their notes? When he reached the door he paused. The teacher saw him through the door window.

"In or out, Jesse," the teacher called. He opened the door. Everyone looked at him, fear in his or her eyes. Oddly, all of the students were sitting close to the front of the room instead of the back, like they normally were, then he saw why.

Serena sat in the back row with several empty desks around her. She didn't acknowledge him, no brightening of her eyes, no smile on her face. It was if a stranger had taken residence in her body. Her hair wasn't pulled back into a messy bun or straight and smooth down her back. Instead, the girl in front of him wore her hair soft and curly, with tendrils around her temples and the top half loosely pulled back with a red ribbon. She wore a burgundy blouse with transparent sleeves, a bow at the scooped neckline, and the ruffles at the hem above black plaid, pleated skirt and black Mary Jane's. He took in her entire appearance, realizing with a jolt that Serena was wearing one of Stormy's favorite blouses.

Dressed like this Serena looked like Stormy's twin. Even her facial expressions seemed to take on Stormy's. Her hands were folded on top of a closed book exactly like Stormy used to do. He gulped.

Serena turned to him. He dropped his gaze and when his eyes caught on the book her hands were resting on he froze in terror. Several frayed notebook papers peeked out between the pages.

Chapter 43--Monday Afternoon

The yoga mat was placed directly in front of the hot fireplace. Sitting in the lotus position, her arms and hands relaxed, Lilith looked like the picture of centered peace. But she wasn't.

Claudia's presence in the room could be felt regardless of her being dead. Lilith had been sensing it for a while now, but hoped it was all just her imagination. Rookie move. Had she been on top of her game she would have been aware of what the old woman was doing. She wasn't on top of her game anymore though, which was why she was here, trying to conjure up the old her who knew how to control these things. Unfortunately, it was taking more time than she had expected to get back to her old self. All the while, Serena seemed to be growing in her power, albeit unaware of just how much power she actually did possess.

It had been three months since Simon had visited the mountain house, but he had maintained contact with Lilith at all times. He called her once a day to get a report. It was the same questions every time with only slightly different answers.

She actually hadn't been up to Serena's room for a month now. The presence she was feeling at that very moment had originated in the girl's room and every time Lilith entered, it seemed as if it let out a little more evil. The last time she had been up there she was met by Stormy, eyes wild with fear, who warned her mother not to come back to the room. Out of self-preservation she needed to leave the girl and the room to Stormy. Instead of worrying about Serena as much, she focused on her own person. She was on a deadline to be ready for Simon and Rosalie. She was getting closer, feeling her strength coming back. Her spirit guide was once again with her as she performed her noonday relaxation stretches.

She was making so much progress, in fact, that she didn't hear the door open and close, or the sound of Serena's shoes tap across the hardwood floors until she was standing a few feet away from her. Lilith jumped, her guide fled, taking with it her peace. Shoulders sagging, she stood to greet the girl. She had been so close.

Serena stood watching, her lips pursed. There had been a growing difference in her over the last couple of months. Instead of her usual ripped jeans and boots, she was dressed in a pleated, plaid skirt, white tights, and black patent leather Mary Jane's. Oversized tunics and the jacket Lilith had bought her had been replaced by a red sweater and white collared blouse beneath it, and with the top half of her hair pulled back into a bow, she looked almost like Stormy. Lilith had been watching her morph into this new person with curiosity and concern. Today she felt the tremor inside her swell into fear. Simon would be proud of his creation. As she took in Serena's clothing she knew why she looked so much like Stormy.

"Where did you get that outfit?"

Serena tilted her head to the side. "This? I thought you had put it in my room."

"No, I wouldn't have. That's Stormy's favorite outfit. Did you go into her room?"

"No. Like I said, it was in my room this morning. I thought you put it there." Her voice lowered to a loud whisper, "Do you think Claudia put it there?"

"Shhhhh," Lilith stopped her. As soon as the woman's name was said the feeling of being watched suddenly came over her.

"What?" Serena whispered. "What is it?"

"Claudia is listening again."

"Isn't she dead?"

"Yes, she is in body, but never in spirit. The spirit doesn't die. I can still feel her."

Serena looked up in an effort to find Claudia, "Serena!" Serena's eyes dropped to meet Lilith's. "Don't look for her." Serena rolled her eyes, but she stopped looking around.

"What do we do then?" she asked.

"We wait." Lilith went silent. She could feel the spirit's eyes roaming. Serena thought only she knew about Stormy, Haley and this house. But that wasn't true. Insanity roamed this land and viciousness ruled it.

Of course, there was always a chance that Lilith herself had gone crazy up here on this mountain. This wasn't the only time she had thought this. Her great-grandmother, grandmother and mother were all diagnosed clinically insane. Her great-grandmother had a frontal lobotomy, her grandmother, having given birth to her third baby and suffering from paranoia, coupled with the belief that demons were after her, slit her own wrists. And then there was her mother, the third baby that drove her own mother to suicide, who had become so deranged, that she was heavily medicated to the point of catatonia. The only time she was brought out of her drug induced stupor was when Lilith's father needed her clairvoyance. That was the one link each woman had to each other: all three of them, now four with Lilith, were powerful psychics, mediums or fortune tellers. Lilith inherited all three gifts, which led her to believe she was insane too.

"Lilith?" Serena waved a hand in front of Lilith. "Are you there?"

"Yes." She ran fingers through her hair and found strands damp with sweat. It was coming again, this ancestral curse, and she could not stop it. Her psychosis was her power and she had to harness it otherwise it would consume her too.

Serena's hand waved in front of her again. "Lilith. Wake up."

Lilith's eyes snapped back to Serena, but she immediately wished she hadn't. Serena's face distorted as an ever-growing wolf spider crawled its way up her body. By the time it reached her head its cephalothorax was the same size. It was a hallucination; she knew it was. Wasn't it?

The eight-legged monster combed through Serena's hair with hairy legs, searching, searching for something. It paused for a moment, as if it had found what it was looking for. Without warning it sank its fangs deep into her skull as its front legs stretched out, down the sides of her head until they reached Serena's ears. Little claws crawled into her ears, deeper and deeper. The rest of the legs began to wrap herself around her neck, squeezing harder, blue imprints beginning to grow from the lack of oxygen. Serena's face grew steadily bluer, but she did not look like she was being choked. She continued to stare at Lilith with a look of horror, as if she were beginning to feel the body on top of her. Legs continued to grow until they found her eyes and pushed through the inner corner of her eye. The spider grew faster, the beady black eyes daring Lilith to try to remove it. Its exoskeleton began to crack under the intense growth. Serena's face shrank as the spider grew, as if the spider was draining her life. Blood from the puncture wounds, where the fangs were still lodged deep in her scalp, began bubbling out and pour down her face.

Lilith searched frantically for something to kill the spider. She had to get it off Serena before it took over her body. It was fragile right now, as the skeleton was breaking apart. She could get it off; she could slam a book over its head. She finally pulled her eyes off the horrific scene in front of her in search of a large book. She found something better. A fire poker. She ran for it, tripped over the coffee table, banging her knees, but she ignored the pain. She had to get the spider off Serena. It was killing her and when it was done it would consume Lilith too. Grabbing the heavy iron she swung it around, lifting it high above her head, ready to squash the eight-legged demon. She jumped on top of the table, shrieking and swinging. Serena ducked and screamed.

Lilith went after Serena again. The spider was still growing. The girl was scrambling up the stairs as fast as she could, still screaming. In her peripheral vision Lilith saw a huge spider after her too. It jumped on top of her, pinning her to the floor. She felt a hard slap on her face. Another one.

"Lilith!" Serena's voice was a hoarse cry. "Oh God, what are you doing?" She was crying high above Lilith.

Lilith craned her head to see if Serena was dead yet, only to find her spider-free and in tears at the top of the stairs. A heavy weight held her body down and stopped her arms from moving. Henry straddled her, keeping her pinned. In her left hand was a fire poker. It had happened again. Just like three years ago. Her stomach twisted, bringing up bile. She rolled as far as she could and threw up. Serena's terrified sobs quieted.

Lilith wiped her mouth as she struggled to stand. Henry stood before she could and helped her up. Her arms and legs shook uncontrollably as she looked at the fire poker on the floor. It wasn't usually this bad. Bad dreams and nightmares, yes, but not hallucinations.

"I'm so sorry, Serena," she whispered so quietly she wasn't sure if the girl heard her. She stumbled to her room to clean herself off. Henry followed her, reaching to hold her steady when she lost her footing and fell against her bedroom door. He opened it for her, flipped on the light, dispelling the shadows in the corners, and led her to the bathroom. He helped her undress and climb into the shower where the cool water woke her to the horrible reality that she was coming unglued. Tears welled up and flowed down her cheeks, mixing with the water. What was she going to do? The question circled her head like those little cartoon birds. She was lost.

The water turned off, the frosted glass door was pushed aside, and Henry was there again. He gently helped her out and wrapped her in a towel, and then he picked her up and carried her to her bed where he sat with her on his lap, rocking her gently.

"I'm s-s-so s-s-scared," she stuttered.

He didn't say anything; he just held her and rocked from side to side, lulling her into a deep sleep. She knew she was already damned, so it didn't matter what happened to her, but she did wonder if Serena would live through all of this or whether she would die in the same horrific way that Stormy did, at the hands of those who should have protected her.

***

From her perch up on the stairs Serena watched Henry walk Lilith to her room. She smiled.

Chapter 44--Monday, Two Weeks Later

Serena's fingers dragged through the cool water, making small waves of their own. It was peaceful in this place, wherever she was. Slow, gentle waves rising and falling beneath her, water whirling and whispering its secrets in words she couldn't understand. And warmth. When was the last time she felt this warm?

The small wooden raft gently came to a stop. Soft, grainy sand brushed her fingertips. It was beautiful. It was calming. It was still. Only bird song and leaves rustling in the slight breeze filled the air. A tree stood on the bank where the sand came up against the grass through which dainty daisies, yellow buttercups and daffodils were scattered. She stood up and walked through the refreshing water that was not too cold and not too hot. The tree branches were heavy with both oranges and apples. She had never seen a tree like that. Her stomach growled in response to the sight and she walked to the large tree where she picked an orange.

Flopping to the ground she began peeling the rind, the citrus scent filled the air. She couldn't get the peel off fast enough. As soon as she was done she began eating. Nothing tasted better. Serena was so engrossed with her fruit she didn't hear the footsteps behind her until the person sat beside her. Serena jumped and turned to find Stormy sitting there. This was the closest to her cousin she had gotten and for once she wasn't transparent.

If Stormy was real did that mean she was . . .

"No, you're not dead," Stormy answered her unasked question.

"Oh." She was a little disappointed. "Where am I then?"

"I don't know. This is your special place, not mine." Stormy surveyed the water beyond them. "I do love it here though. I don't blame you for not wanting to leave here."

"Am I imagining you?"

"No." She turned to Serena, her green eyes so clear that Serena could see herself inside of them. "I'm a spirit. I can go where I want to go and where I need to go."

Serena broke the connection and looked out to the sea again. The tide must be going out, she thought, as she watched the water recede from the grassy knoll she sat upon. Stormy's last words came back to her.

"Did you want to come here or did you need to come here?" she asked her cousin. She snapped a daisy off its stem and then another, beginning a daisy chain. She had always loved them. There was a picture of her mother and sister with daisy chains. She wondered what had happened to the photo. She snapped off another stem.

"I needed to come here."

"Why?"

"I need your help. Things are falling apart at home and you have been gone way too long." Stormy's voice was strained. She was attempting to remain calm, but the cold hand she placed on Serena's arm trembled slightly.

She looked at Stormy. Fear was written in her face as she very slowly began to fade, her solid frame becoming transparent once again.

"How long have I been gone?" Her heartbeat picked up.

"Four months." Stormy whispered frantically.

It couldn't be. She had been sitting here only for just a little while, right? Deep inside her soul she knew Stormy was correct and with that acknowledgment came an urgency to go back. She looked to her raft. It had floated away with the receding water. In fact, the water was receding all over, as if someone had pulled the bathtub plug. She gulped. "My raft is gone. How do I get back?"

The sun overhead began its descent; the shadows of trees and flowers grew longer, wilting as they did so, their petals dropping to the dead grass.

Stormy scrambled up and grabbed Serena's arm, yanking her to stand and then pulling her into a run. Her grip was strong even though she seemed to be disappearing. "Hurry." Her frantic tone pushed Serena into a dead run.

That grassy knoll she thought had gently sloped upward was in fact, a jagged, rocky hill. She scrambled up a couple of feet, her foot slipped and she felt a deep slice across the sole of her foot. Warmblood immediately began to bubble out. Was she dreaming? Can people hurt themselves like this if they're dreaming?

Abrasive rocks bit at her fingertips, making the climb so much more difficult, so much more painful. But still, she climbed. At the top was barren land with a layer of fog drifting through and around the scrub brush, and even more rocks. It looked like the landscape of her dreams when she first arrived at the mountain home. In the distance was a half-burned house.

"Hurry Serena," Stormy's voice sounded faint. "You have to get to the house or you'll be trapped here forever."

She had questions and was about to ask them when she glanced back to find the scenery behind her was literally disappearing. She broke out into a run. The scrub brush reached out and scratched her legs, causing blood to well up at each wound. Soon the rough ground she ran on gave way to frozen ground and then snow. The cold felt good on her aching feet until her feet grew numb,

Lungs burning, muscles straining, eyes stinging. She looked up to find the house looming before her.

So close. So close, breathe, just like dad taught her on the track.

The snow melted and gave way to grass; the house rebuilt itself until it looked the way it had when she had first arrived. Stormy appeared again, but this time she levitated at the second-floor window outside her bedroom.

"Come, come here," she called quietly, the light wind carrying her voice.

"How!"

"Take a step up like you're climbing stairs."

Puzzled and shaking, Serena took a step up, and to her surprise, her foot fell on something solid, though still invisible.

"Hurry!" Stormy called.

Serena glanced back again and saw the land beyond them was fading, as if an invisible child was erasing a picture he didn't like. She pushed herself harder up that invisible staircase until she stood beside Stormy looking into her room, watching herself.

The 'other' her danced to the tune of the music box. The body shape was hers, no doubt, but the clothing was too prim and proper. Her hair was pulled back into a bow that Serena would never wear. She watched as her other self turned slowly to face them. Stormy yanked Serena out of view. She put her finger to her lips and began to inch around the wall to the stairs that Claudia had always used and ran up them to Claudia's door.

"I can't go in there." Serena felt the blood rush out of her head.

"She's dead and you don't have a choice. " Stormy pointed down at Serena's feet and the tips of her toes had begun to fade, making her transparent like Stormy. Without another word Stormy pushed Serena through the closed door. Serena felt the thick wood pierce through her and then she came out on the other side.

"Why am I still fading?" Serena cried out.

"Follow me."

Serena moved behind her cousin to Claudia's bedroom. The room was still, nobody there, no soul to be felt. Stormy ripped off a cover that hung on the wall covering a mirror. "Why was that covered?"

"Because that girl knows that you can push your way through the glass and send her back to this world."

"Won't she be able to just come back through?"

"No, not on her own. She can only come back if you or someone else much stronger summons her. You are stronger than she is and now that you know what she is up to you can prevent her from coming back again. Next time she looks in the mirror, preferably the one in your room, simply push through the pane and she will have to go away. You have to do it now though. She has done too much damage to your world, to you while you've been 'away.'

"Why? Why is this happening? Why does she want to replace me?"

"Because she is looking for the same thing my mother and father are looking for. If she finds it first she can keep you here in this hell and live your life for you.

"Now, will you please trust me? I can coach you through this but in order for me to help you we both have to go into that mirror and I can't go without you taking me." Her voice became more faint. Her frame was disappearing. Serena held onto her cousin's hand and pulled her into the mirror just as the room beyond them disappeared.

Once inside both girls were once again solid. They hugged each other with relief and then stepped back.

Serena stepped back from her. "Now what?"

"Come on." Stormy led Serena back through Claudia's apartment, though everything was backward. Serena felt evil lingering in the air.

They went out the door and rushed down the stairs to her floor. It was like wading through cotton balls until they reached a picture frame or mirror that quickened their speed. There were no mirrors down the last hallway to her room. "There used to be pictures here," Serena said.

"I know. She put them away. The other you is no dummy."

Serena nodded. Together they moved to her room. It was an odd feeling to be on the other side of a mirror. "Can she see me if I were to walk in on her without a mirror? Could she do the same thing to me?"

"No. You are the true YOU. She is only the reflection."

"How come I could see her through different mirrors and windows?"

"Claudia gave that power to your reflection. With her gone, I don't know what will happen. Now, stop talking and let's get in there."

Stormy grabbed her hand and pulled her to the full-length stand-alone mirror. "I never use that mirror," Serena whispered.

"I know, but the other you does."

Serena nodded and looked into the mirror. Suddenly she could think better, see better, and hear better. The things and people she had forgotten while on that peaceful beach came back to her. Her dad, Jesse, Simon and Lilith. She had her compass in the right direction. She had a job to do and that was to get the hell out of there, find whatever Lilith and Simon wanted before they did, and help set Stormy free.

Footsteps in the hall.

"Now listen, Serena," Stormy said in a rush. "When the other you looks in the mirror and you two lock gazes, push your hands through the glass and step out like you're getting out of the shower, okay? As soon as you do she'll disappear. Ignore the screaming, crying and objects that will get thrown at you, just keep pushing."

As soon as the words were out, Stormy disappeared and the other Serena stepped into the room. Serena watched her other self go through her jewelry box but take nothing. She picked up her brush and ran it through her hair, set it down and finally looked in the mirror. She started from the bottom to top. Serena thought she'd never look all the way up but when she finally did their eyes locked and Serena felt a rush of power and strength. She began to push. It was much easier than she had expected although Stormy was right. Her other self roared with fury. She threw the dolls at her, the jewelry case, books, but Serena still pushed her way through until she was out.

She stood there, looking at the other her who had twisted her face into an ugly sneer. "You don't know how to send me back, do you? You're so dumb, standing there with your thumb up your a--"

"GO!" Serena pointed her finger to the mirror she had just climbed out. The pane reached out as if it had hands and grabbed onto the other girl, dragging her, literally kicking and screaming back to her own world.

"NO! NO! NO!"

And suddenly the screams were gone, but the girl was not. She stood, pressed up against her side of the reflection. "You can't keep me here forever. You know that, don't you?"

Serena whispered back. "I'm done with you. You are not to speak to me again. You are only my reflection, nothing more." With those words came another burst of power that seemed to pop the air around her. Her reflection snarled and glared, opening her mouth one more time but didn't finish what she was about to say. Her facial expression changed from hatred to exhaustion, her hair long and scraggly with actual branches sticking out of it, her prim school girl outfit now shredded jeans, complete with ripped fingernails and bloody footprints. Serena sagged down to the floor and her reflection did the same.

Chapter 45--Monday Morning

Serena woke achy and stiff and barely able to move up from the floor. She looked up at the vaulted ceiling above her waiting, as her body and mind melded together. Had it all been a crazy dream? Or was it real? She wasn't sure. One thing she was certain of was that she was fully herself.

She had no idea what day it was. The morning sun shone brightly through the window. The window was open, allowing a cold breeze to flow in. It ruffled the curtains and filled the room with the scent of fresh rain and grass. She finally sat up. The room spun but quickly came to a stop. A dark ring of dried blood and bruises and scratches covered her legs where her jeans hung tattered. That answered her first question. It had really happened. She looked in the mirror, afraid of what she might find. The 'other' Serena was gone. The girl gazing back was really her. She could tell by the clear look in her eyes, that girl was gone. With relief, she took another deep breath and blew it back out. She stood up, unsteady and lightheaded and in pain. The soles of her feet were so scratched she could hardly stand.

Heart beating erratically, she searched the rest of her body and found more wounds, some deep and some superficial. She knew she had to talk to Lilith. She hobbled down the hall and down the stairs to find Lilith in the kitchen making coffee.

"Good morning sleepyhead," she said with a smile.

"Hi." It was all surreal.

"Are you okay?" Lilith's voice seemed to come from within a tunnel. Serena scanned the living room and found it bright, cheery. Beyond the windows she took in the view of mountains and trees in the distance, clumps of snow melting and dripping to the ground. The more she looked, the more she realized how much time had passed. Snippets and fleeting memories raced through her mind, but none of it made sense.

 Lilith followed behind as Serena walked closer to the window, her voice sickeningly sweet, "Honey?"

Serena looked back at her and noticed her aunt had changed too. Lilith

"

was no longer dressed all in black. She wore a powder blue blouse and black trousers, her hair had been brushed, and she was wearing makeup, which made her look healthier and much younger.

"What's going on?" Serena asked. The last clear memory she had was of a frozen dinner on yet another cold, stormy night. The news had called for snow the following day. "What day is it?"

"Monday."

"What month?" she hoped it was still February.

"April." Lilith cocked her head to the side and stepped forward. "Honey, are you okay?"

"No!" Serena stepped back. "No. I'm not. I don't remember the last couple of months."

It occurred to her that Lilith didn't seem surprised at her response. "Why are my feet like this?"

Lilith looked down at Serena's legs and feet, which looked worse in the bright light. "Hmmm, obviously you were sleepwalking."

"I have never sleepwalked in my life."

"Are you sure?" one eyebrow arched up. "Obviously you got out again. The wilderness can be a dangerous place if you're not careful." She sauntered back into the kitchen. "I can get you some ointment if you'd like."

"No thank you."

Serena hobbled up the stairs to change, desperate to flee the house. She stopped at the bathroom. She couldn't think of changing clothes without a shower. Ignoring the trepidation, and the mirror, she turned on the faucet. Her legs stung as the water flowed over her body. When she was finished she left the shredded clothing in a pile on the floor and wrapped herself in a towel. Back in her room she searched for her favorite pair of jeans and t-shirt. They had been shoved in the very back of the drawer behind a bunch of clothing she didn't remember owning. Had she worn those things? They weren't her style at all. Frustrated, she pulled on socks and shoes and then had to search for a sweatshirt. Again, it had been pushed to the back of the drawer. Something was different about the room too, but it wasn't until Serena was looking for the brush that was normally on the dresser that she realized what it was. All of her pictures were gone.

"No," she whispered. That word brought a memory with it. Darkness. Struggling. Tears. Pain. Suffocating. She swallowed the bile that crept up her throat as tears threatened to flow.

Gulping for air, the sense of being smothered was so strong that she could see black dots float in front of her eyes.

"Breathe," she told herself. By the time she was again aware of her surroundings, she had curled up in the corner by her open window. Time was lost, but according to the clock, it had only been three or four minutes.

"Serena!" Lilith called from downstairs. "You need to get going."

"I'm coming," she called out weakly. Disoriented by her missing pictures and dark flashback, she grabbed a green and tan flannel shirt off the floor. She pulled it on as she walked down the stairs. Lilith stood at the door, a fake smile plastered on her face, and held out a lunch sack for Serena. As she took it Lilith leaned over and kissed her cheek.

"It will be okay, Stormy," she murmured.

Serena limped to the car, confused and shaky. Her feet ached with each step. The bus doors were just closing when she slid out of the SUV and staggered up to the doors. They opened to let her climb on. No one spoke to her as she made her way to the back row, her eyes scanning for Jesse.

"Serena!" the bus driver yelled.

She jumped then turned to face him. "I told you two weeks ago that you were no longer allowed to sit in the back."

She nodded obediently and moved to the seat directly behind the driver. What had she done to deserve that?

"Don't try that again!" He stuck his pudgy finger in her face. "Do you understand me?"

"Yes sir," she mumbled. About a mile down the road, it finally dawned on her what Lilith had called her.

Stormy.

Chills rippled over her scalp and down her arms and legs. What was going on? Where was Jesse? She needed to see him, to ask him what had happened. By the time the bus parked she was a nervous wreck. Being behind the driver had its perks: one of them, maybe the only one, was getting off the bus first. Backpack slung over her shoulder, she rushed up the sidewalk, brushing past the other students. Where was Jesse? She ran to his locker, but he wasn't there. She turned around; everything seemed to be moving in slow motion. Tears ran down her cheeks. She tried to push them away before anyone saw. She had to find him. Where would he be? As soon as she asked the question, she answered it: the library. With an effort, she slowed her walk down as she moved through the halls. The others gave her wide berth. On their faces was not just surprise; it was fear.

As soon as she stepped inside the library, the rest of the school seemed to disappear, the silence drowning out the noise outside. The girl behind the counter eyed Serena with suspicion. She ignored her and started for the maze of books.

"Serena?" Jesse said as she came to their alcove. He stood and came close; his eyes searched her face, her eyes. "Is it actually you? The real one?" She realized what he was asking.

"I think so. Who else would I be?" she looked into his blue eyes, stepping closer. "Seriously, who else would I be?" Had the girl in the mirror gone to school in her place? A sinking feeling settled in her stomach. "What's happened?"

"Not much, but you haven't been . . . you. I don't know how else to describe it."

"Well, try. Please. I'm scared. I woke up this morning with no memory of the last couple of months. The bus driver yelled at me for sitting in the back seat. Hell, the other kids look at me more scared now than they were on my first day of school!" She angrily swiped at the tears that wouldn't stop flowing.

His brows knitted together over fearful eyes. "It's okay," he said stepping closer. "You haven't been yourself. It's as if someone had taken over you. You went from being a curiosity to, to . . . . I don't know how to describe it."

"Okay. Just tell me when it started."

He turned and went back to the table. "You started dressing differently. Your clothing changed from what you're wearing now to skirts, tights and blouses. Your hair even changed. That was the freaky part."

"Why? Why was it freaky?"

"Because a lot of the clothing you wore belonged to Stormy and your hair was exactly like hers. And then you started acting weird. That's how you got in trouble on the bus. The driver kicked you off and your uncle had to work hard at getting you back on."

"Oh my gosh, what did I do?"

"You attacked Kendra. She was mouthing off but when she started saying horrible stuff about Stormy you really lost it. You hit her and used your nails in the process and left deep scratches on her face. That's when the bus driver threw you off the bus."

"No wonder the driver was so mad at me." She followed him and sat down slowly, absorbing the information.

"Yeah, no wonder. Even I was pissed at you for that one." He sighed. "The only reason I didn't do anything about it is because you had this odd, faraway look to your eyes all the time, like you weren't really with us. You would go to class, but you didn't speak to anyone about anything.

You just stared at the wall.

"But you look different today, and it's not just the clothes. Your eyes are clear and you're actually looking at me and not through me."

Her ears were ringing with the news about what she'd done. "What do I do now?" she put her head in her hands.

There was a sound of a book clapping shut a few aisles down from them. They both stilled. Two low voices spoke quietly and then moved further away. Once they were gone they both exhaled.

Jesse raked his fingers through his hair. "You've gotta get out of there, Serena." His voice was quiet but emphatic.

"I was making plans to do just that before all this happened. I was just waiting for my birthday and graduation."

"You can't." He leaned forward with his arms braced on his knees. His long, tapered fingers were laced together. "You can't wait that long. You've gotta leave now."

"And where would I go? I don't have any money, and I can't get my inheritance until I turn eighteen. That's why I was waiting."

"Look, I know you may not like this, but you might want to skip the inheritance. You need to get away from them. I'll help you as much as I can, but you have to get out of that house."

"What will I do for money?"

"Simon is not going to let you just leave without a fight. He'll go after you and if you show up for your inheritance, you'll leave a paper trail. You have to go somewhere new, make up a new life, stay away from any social media or he'll track you down. Can you do that?"

"Yes, I can do that." She thought for a moment. The gravity of what she was about to do hit her full force.

" How can I make it on my own? Who am I supposed to be? I can't just make a new identity.". She was terrified. She was supposed to venture out on her own without a job, a place to live? But wasn't living in a haunted house, with a woman who thought she was her daughter and a man who had something evil planned for her, just as terrifying? The thought of Simon made her stomach roll. She clenched her jaw. So which terror could she live with?

"Calm down." Jesse put his hand on hers, covering it completely. "I'd already started working on your escape a little while ago. My friend, Frank, is an expert on this sort of thing. He is working on your papers and background so if anyone does research on you, or, I should say, Ava, they'll get a "real" identity. He's making you twenty-one so it will be easier for you to find a good job. He's also friends with a guy who has an apartment complex in Portland, Oregon. It's a walk-up studio on the fourth floor, and the guy is willing to work with people if they've come highly recommended. I've given you a glowing report, but they think we met at some of my college classes, not from high school. What do you think?"

Serena sat back in complete amazement. "Okay, let's do this," she said, sounding more confident than she felt. He seemed to pick up on the waiver in her voice because he moved around the table to sit next to her. Putting his arm around her shoulders, he pulled her into a hug.

"I'm gonna get you out of here, Serena. I won't fail you like I did Stormy."

"Okay." She leaned into him; thankful she had someone on her side.

Chapter 46--Monday Afternoon

After school, Lilith met Serena at the door with a vacant smile. Was she faking too? Serena asked herself.

"Welcome back. Ready to eat?"

"Isn't is a little early for dinner?"

"Oh no, it's never too early for dinner." Lilith gave a soft laugh that would have sounded sweet if it had been someone else. "Come on in. I felt like I just needed to cook something today. Tomorrow I might do some baking too. You never know."

Simon stood in the kitchen with a carving knife. Serena trembled.

"It's okay Serena, I'm not going to kill you."

"What are you doing here?"

"I said I would be coming back to check on you once in a while."

"You told me, not Serena. Now honey, take a seat and have some mashed potatoes." Lilith hadn't been lying when she said she knew how to cook. Lilith invited her to sit down at the counter and served her a healthy sized portion of every dish. Serena couldn't remember the last time she'd eaten a meal like this. When she was finally done she was exhausted. It was five thirty. She could barely keep her eyes open.

"Why don't you go upstairs and take a nap?" Lilith said.

"Okay." She clumped up the stairs, her feet feeling like stone bricks. She walked to her room, her head seeming to float as her body weighed her down. When she entered her bedroom she could feel Stormy's presence but couldn't see her. As soon as she turned on the bedside lamp Stormy was gone immediately. Serena lay down and fell instantly asleep.

She didn't know how long she was out. She heard feet scuff the wood floors at one point but was too weary to open her eyes. Sleep came over her again.

When she finally came awake, her room was dark. Something was different, but she couldn't figure out what it was. She fumbled for the lamp. Hadn't it been on ? Lilith must have come in and turned it off. With the light on, the cobwebs drifted away, leaving a pounding headache in its place. She needed water. Serena stood unsteadily and paused for a few seconds to regain her balance. She sat back down and put her head in her hands and closed her eyes. Was she sick or something?

Down the hall the chimes of a music box began to play. It was as if Stormy called to her through each note. Serena opened her eyes. A shiny object peeking out from beneath the table caught her gaze. She pulled it out. It was a key with a silky ribbon tied to it. Memories of how she got the key came back to her. This was what she was looking for that night. Stormy's room. She could get in there now.

It was now or never if she was going to investigate. Her heart hammered against her ribcage as she opened the bedroom door. Even though there was a dormer window in the hall, there was never enough light, and tonight was no exception. Clouds were moving outside, and a full moon shined intermittently through them, casting shadows along the wall. When Serena finally reached Stormy's door, she was out of breath.

With trembling hands, she put the key in the lock. As she turned the knob the haunting notes of the music box stopped.

The clouds broke apart in the night sky, allowing moonlight to spill into the room. The bed had the same eyelet duvet and matching pillows as in her room. It sat under the eaves to her left. An antique dresser with a connected mirror stood near the opposite wall. On the dresser sat a lamp and the open music box that had been playing the same tune over and over. Serena closed the lid. A curtained bay window seat was directly across from the door. It looked inviting, and she imagined this was Stormy's favorite place in the house. Sheer curtains hung on either side of the window. Serena envisioned Stormy using them to enclose herself from the world. Two books still lay on the seat, as if she'd just left the room and would be back any moment.

Serena shuffled closer to the window seat, curious as to the view. Across from her room, a two-story garage that looked more like a barn faced the house with the upstairs window directly across from her. She was tempted to hide, but the room was dark. There wasn't anyone watching. Past the garage, she recognized the field from the painting in the hall. Tall grass waved at her in the moonlight, as did the trees, and in the distance was smoke as if someone was sharing a bonfire. It was a spooky night, and she shuddered at the memory of Stormy appearing to her. Would she come back if Serena said her name? The sense of being watched washed over her as if her thoughts had beckoned her cousin.

Serena. A warm, soft breeze blew across her face.

A movement in the fields grabbed her attention. Two people in long cloaks and hooded faces were slowly making their way through the meadow. Serena took several steps back in case they could see her. As she did, she bumped into the vanity, knocking over the lamp. She grabbed for it, catching the lamp just before it hit the floor. Would they hear the crash if it had fallen? She didn't know, and she didn't want to find out. She set the lamp back on the dresser, and the music box began to play, only this time the tune quickened. She was about to close it again when something caught her eye.

There was only one thing in the box. A photograph. A photograph that seemed to mirror the painting in the hall but was different. In the painting, Stormy leaned against a fence post with a soft smile on her face and the breeze lifting her hair. Not so in the photograph; the scene depicted a nightmare.

Serena pulled the photo out of the box and moved so that she could see it better in the moonlight. Instead of standing next to the post, Stormy was tied to the post. Her face was stretched in horror as flames leaped up, catching her dress on fire. A group of cloaked men and women circled her as she screamed. Serena could hear faint murmurs as if the scene was currently being reenacted in front of her.

Noooooo!!!

Chanting incantations; words that made no sense. Fire roaring, a louder scream, a voice wailing. Serena!

She jumped, as if someone had tapped her on the shoulder.

She found herself sitting on the floor. She didn't think she had passed out but was dazed by what she was hearing. Had they really burned her cousin alive? On the back of the photo was a hand-written date. It had been taken on October 31.

Hurry Serena!

She felt rather than heard the sound of the door opening downstairs. She had to get out of Stormy's room before she was caught. She dropped the picture back in the music box and the lid clapped shut on its own, silencing the music. Then she silently ran out and closed the door behind her, hands trembling so badly she couldn't get the lock to turn. Finally it worked. She was too far away from the front door to know if they had come in but Simon gave himself away. His voice was getting louder and closer, bringing a rancid smoky smell. He was coming to check on her.

She ran for her bedroom. The hall seemed to have gotten longer since leaving Stormy's room. Lilith's voice drifted down through the hall. Had she followed him up the stairs?

"Simon, leave her alone. Please." Her pleading did nothing to stop him.

"Go back to your room, Lilith."

Serena crossed the threshold to her room and quietly turned the doorknob so it wouldn't make a sound when it clicked shut.

Simon's footfalls came closer.

She scrambled under the covers, closing her eyes and pretending to be asleep. The next moment, the door opened. She could feel Simon's scrutiny, and she prayed he wouldn't notice she was awake.

He came near. "You are so beautiful," he whispered as he stroked her cheek before he turned and left. She could barely breathe. She risked getting caught and slit one eye open as Simon walked to the door. With the hall lights behind him she could see the cloak he wore. When she was sure he was gone, she rose and locked the door. Then she climbed back in bed, curled up in a ball and wept.

Chapter 47--Tuesday

Simon was gone the following morning before Serena woke up. Once she arrived at school she met Trevor, one of Jesse's friends, at the entrance gate. He drove her to the little diner. Serena was itching to meet up with Jesse anyway, but even more so now since she found the photo. Anxiety gnawed at her stomach. Could Stormy have really been burned alive? This had to have been another dream. What would Jesse say when she told him? The word "if" never entered her mind. He had to know what they were dealing with.

Trevor drove her around to the back of the little restaurant. Serena opened the car door and was barely out of it when the wheels started to roll. He had been antsy to even have her in the car with him. She went to the back door and was about to knock when it flew open. Jesse stood in front of her, eyes clear and blue. She took a deep breath and let it out. She felt anchored to an unmoving rock that would keep the waves from washing her out to sea.

His brows drew together as he looked her over. It was no wonder. Her hair pulled back in a loose bun that was falling apart. Her eyes were cloudy and distressed and exhausted. With no makeup on she must look like a ghost herself.

"Are you okay," he asked, voice soft and low. He opened the door wider for her to come in.

Shaking her head, she said, "No. We need to talk."

He ushered her to the last booth in the back corner of the restaurant where they'd sat before.

She described what she saw. He grew quieter and whiter as she came to the end of the vision. He didn't even excuse himself when he ran for the bathroom. She could hear the retching loud and clear.

When he finally exited the bathroom he was still pale, his eyes were steel instead of the refuge they had presented to her at first. Had she just pushed him away?

"I'm sorry. Maybe I shouldn't have told you."

"No, I'm glad you did. I just feel sick at the idea of her . . ." His voice cracked. He clamped his jaw shut to keep the nausea and tears at bay. "We have to get you out of that house NOW."

With that last word he began to set in motion what they needed for her escape.

"For starters, I think it's best if you kept that vacant look in your eyes so they won't suspect anything. I would go back to wearing Stormy's clothing too."

Serena cringed at the idea of being her mirror self again. Jesse typed out an email to a friend who specialized in creating assumed names. His friend, Frank, was a computer genius who would provide a fake ID with a new name on it, Ava Celeste Williams. He made up names for her parents and their backgrounds just in case anyone began looking into her past. Because changing her name wasn't enough, Frank also gave her a new social security card. He said the card would be done in a couple of weeks, just in time for her to leave.

Next, Jesse, using his own money since she had no way of accessing hers, bought a bus ticket under another name given to him by Frank so her new name wouldn't be connected to Colorado in any way.

"Okay, the next thing you need to do is start packing what you want and smuggle it to school for me to hang onto. I would bring anything you don't want to lose forever, like family pictures, because you can never go back. I'll pack a bag for you and have it ready when your new ID arrives." He glanced at the time and realized how late it was. "School will be out soon. We only have a few minutes until we need to leave, we better hurry."

They were in the middle of planning the next step after her arrival in Portland when Jesse froze.

"Go to the bathroom, Serena."

"Why?" She glanced behind her to see what Jesse's eyes were focused on.

"Mr. Dawson is here. Go. Now."

Jesse's grandmother approached the teacher, keeping his gaze from roaming in their direction. While Mr. Dawson was occupied, Serena ducked into the bathroom and locked the door behind her. Just outside the door she heard the teacher's voice.

"What are you doing out of class, young man?"

"Well, if you must know, I'm finishing my class project and it was less distracting here than school.

"Are you alone?"

"What else would I be?"

"Are you with Serena?"

"No. She's changed so much recently that I kind of don't know who she is anymore."

"I've noticed," Mr. Dawson said.

"Listen, if you see Serena, tell me. She seems to have disappeared at the same time you did."

"I'll let you know."

By the creak of the wooden floor outside the door, Serena knew Mr. Dawson was leaving but she stayed in the small bathroom. A few minutes later, Jesse's voice came through the door.

"Serena?" Jesse said, his voice muffled.

She cracked open the door.

"You can come out now."

"Do you think he's been following me around?" She sat in the booth, her nerves bound.

"You already know that answer."

She did. She watched Jesse's face as his eyes scanned the small diner. His square jaw was set, his wide shoulders tensed, ready for action, and his light blue eyes, roamed before dropping to meet her gaze. He didn't say anything, nor did he blush or pretend he wasn't attracted to her. In his eyes there was wildness, a passion, which seemed ready to engulf her. For the first time she felt his attraction was for her and not the residual feelings he had for Stormy like he had when they first met.

Her heart came to a screeching halt. She wanted to stay with him or bring him with her wherever she went. She felt safe with him by her side, not to mention alive in every part of her being. If they were alone right then she was sure he would have kissed her and she would have let him. She dropped her gaze as she reached for her water. She needed something to cool the rush of fire that ignited inside of her. When she glanced back at him she saw he was finishing his email to his friend. He hit one last button before he shut the computer and began putting it into his backpack. She would've thought the moment of attraction on his behalf had all been a daydream, a wish, but the rapid pulse in his neck gave him away. He seemed to want her just as much as she wanted him.

"Come on, let's get you back to school."

"How?" she stood up too. "If they're watching us."

"Have you ever seen the inside of my trunk?" he winked.

"Are you serious?"

"It's the only way."

"Let's go then."

They ducked out the back door where an old Land Rover with tinted windows sat. Clouds covered the sun that had been out earlier and the slightly warm breeze had now cooled. "Trust me, it'll be a warm ride back since the heater will be on you. I also have blankets back there if you want them." She nodded. He started the vehicle and then opened the hatchback door for her. She slid past him to climb inside when he grabbed her waist and pulled her close. His lips covered hers for a brief moment. He pulled back. She leaned in and he took the invitation. This time the kiss deepened.

His tongue ran along the seam of her lips. Her arms encircled his neck and held him close, urging him to stay in case he thought of pulling away.

It was the clearing of a throat that shattered the magic.

"Why don't you help your grandmother with the dishes. I'll take her back to school," Jesse's grandfather said. Jesse kept his eyes on her. He finally pulled away one of his arms, leaving her feeling colder than before. He placed one hand on her face, his thumb caressing her cheek with his thumb. She closed her eyes and leaned into the palm of his hand, breathing in his skin's scent.

"Jesse." His grandfather's voice was sharper.

He kissed her once more, softly this time. "I'll see you tomorrow," he whispered. He turned and walked toward his grandfather, back rigid and his hand in tight fists, ready for a fight. Instead of throwing a punch though, he brushed passed the older man and went inside. His grandfather's glare scared her. She half wondered if he would drop her off at school or in the middle of nowhere so she would freeze to death. Obviously, he hated her.

He walked up to her, shut the hatchback, gripped her forearm, and walked her to the passenger side door. "Get in," he ordered.

He was silent for the drive. Instead of dropping her off in the middle of nowhere though, he dropped her off at the back door of the school just in time for the last bell to ring, signaling classes were done for the day. All she had to do was blend in with the crowd. She ran for the bus, and this time sat behind the driver, careful to keep her gaze unfocused and empty. She went over and over in her head how she was going to act at home. Would Lilith notice something off about her? Probably not.

Lilith might be easier to fool, but not Simon. Was he going to return home anytime soon? She hoped not. When the bus stopped at her driveway, she slowly descended down the stairs. It was time to do some serious acting.

By the time the SUV made it up the hill, her palms were slick with sweat. Henry parked by the garage and waited for her to get out. Something about the structure jogged a shadowed memory, giving her the strange sensation of having been inside. The image of her walking through that side door flitted through her mind. She shook it off. Now wasn't the time to play Sherlock Holmes. Lilith was expecting a half-baked niece any moment.

As soon as she opened the front door, the scent of melted chocolate and warm cookies filled the air. Her stomach growled in response. She followed the smell to the kitchen to find Lilith making cookies and watching another television show. She looked like the picture of domestic bliss. She turned to give Serena a distracted smile.

"Hello sweetie," she purred. "I was wondering when you'd get here. I have a batch of cookies already on the plate. Here, take one." Lilith held the cookie up to her mouth for a bite.

"Sure," she tried to sound dull, hoping her aunt would buy it. With no plausible way out of eating it, she took a bite of the cookie. It was still warm, and the chocolate was melting on her fingers. As she ate she felt more relaxed, all of the worries shedding from her shoulders. She gazed outside as she chewed. Halfway through the third cookie her head began to feel fuzzy. The lights dimmed a bit and the voices on the sitcom sounded like they were coming through a tunnel. She tried to form words with her mouth, but they wouldn't come. She lay down on the couch and gave into the drowsiness.

Sereenaaaa. Sereeenaaaa. Sereenaa. The voice drew closer until she felt a nudge on her arm. She opened her eyes to find Stormy sitting next to her on a swing in the middle of the forest.

"Where are we?"

"We're in your dream." Stormy looked out into the distance as they swung over a cliff, their feet dangling above the steep drop below. Serena grabbed tightly to the rope on her side and could feel the blood draining from her face. Stormy laughed when she looked back at her. It sounded like wind chimes tinkling in the breeze.

"Don't worry, cousin. You can't die. If you fall you just wake up. I think." Stormy closed her eyes and seemed to enjoy the back and forth motion as they glided through the air.

"It was the cookies, wasn't it? They're drugging me?" Serena asked.

"Yes and no." Her eyes were still closed whereas Serena's were wide open.

"What do you mean? Yes and no?"

"Yes, they've been drugging you. Mom is putting something in your food that makes you sleep or stay awake, but Father has his own way to make you sleep. He can cast a sort of spell, for lack of better words. It'll make you unaware of what's going on around you so you're more . . .

how do I say it? Compliant? Malleable? It's more powerful when he's around. However, you're pretty strong so his spell doesn't last as long on you. That's why you "woke" up when he left this morning. When he's not around Mom drugs your food."

"Why didn't you tell me before?"

Stormy finally opened her eyes and looked at Serena; her green irises were nearly black. "I tried. I tried to tell you, but you were already being manipulated. There was nothing I could do except watch and plead with you to wake up."

Serena remembered Stormy begging her to wake up, to come back from her make believe world.

Stormy interrupted her thoughts. "Father has big plans for you, you know."

"How do I escape him?"

"Expose Simon for what he is, of course. It strips some of his power away when the truth comes out."

"How do I do that?"

"You remember the garage? Of course, you do. You noticed it as soon as you drove to the house today. All the other times you've walked past that building without even looking at it, even though you've been in there enough times."

"I have?"

"Yes. You need to go in there when you're wide-awake, not while under Simon's spell. Go see what he does in that room upstairs. I don't know why, but it will make you less sensitive to his sorcery. That's how I woke up."

"What happened?"

She closed her eyes again and smiled. "Just go, Serena. When you wake up just go."

She then launched herself off the swing, falling silently into the blackness below. Serena screamed and reached for her, losing her balance and plummeting after her.

Her eyes opened to a gloomy living room, her mouth gaping in a silent scream.

Sitting up at least allowed her to get her bearings. She was still on the couch. Moonlight streamed through the windows and tree shadows danced along the walls. She could hear the wind whistling through the gables, the same wind that blew in her dream as she swung with Stormy. Her words came back again. She wanted Serena to go to the garage; Stormy wanted Serena to expose Simon.

Once her eyes adjusted to the dark, the moonlight seemed brighter and illuminated the living room. She rose and walked to the kitchen for a glass of water. The clock on the oven read 3:30. She had gotten home around 3:30 yesterday afternoon and promptly fell asleep. Whatever they were using was some strong stuff.

Once her thirst was quenched, she grabbed a flannel jacket that had been flung on the back of a chair. Outside the breeze was cool, and the moon lit her way to the garage. The side door was cracked open, allowing for an easy entry. Inside, the air was stale, especially compared to the fresh wind outside. She fumbled around for a light switch but found a flashlight instead. She turned it on.

Directly in front of the door stood a steep staircase. She started up the stairs, but the further she got, the more her breathing labored. Flashes of disjointed memories hit her like shrapnel. Her heart raced and fear coursed through her veins. She'd definitely been here before. Her legs grew heavier, but she pushed on. Her time was running short; she could feel it in her soul. If she didn't break this spell, how would she escape whatever Simon had planned?

By the time she reached the door at the top of the stairs, sweat was trickling down her face and neck. She reached for the knob, expecting it to be locked. Instead, the knob turned and the door swung open. The smell of rot and something metallic flooded the air, making her gag and her eyes water. She covered her nose and mouth with her sleeve and shined the flashlight inside the room. The walls were painted black. This was the room directly across from Stormy's bedroom window. The window in here was covered with a blanket, so no light could penetrate. The flashlight beam swept over a rectangle table with seven chairs around it.

Serena moved closer to the table. On each corner were four metal shackles and in the middle was a pentagram, drawn in black charcoal and smeared with dark splotches. There was also a bowl of what looked like pudding. It took her a moment to realize it was the congealed blood she had smelled when she first opened the door. Her breath came in hard and fast as she tried to wrap her head around what she was seeing. She flashed the light, hitting the walls, ceiling, and corners. A ram's head, complete with horns, hung on the black wall directly in front of her. Red slashes of what seemed to be blood were painted on the other walls. She didn't know what they meant or what they were for but knew they couldn't be good.

In the far corner was a black armoire. On top of it stood a statue of a man with the head of a goat. She pulled open the top two doors. Skeletal heads of animals and rodents cluttered the top shelves.

She then knelt down and reached for the bottom two-cupboard doors. As soon as she tried to open them, frigid air blew in her face, and the chairs started knocking together before levitating and dropping to the floor. The cabinets above her head started shaking, clacking open and shut. Gusts of wind buffeted her so hard that she almost gave up. Then Stormy's words came back to her. She had to expose Simon in order to break his hold on her.

She leaned forward and grabbed the handle of the cabinet. It swung open with a blast of putrid smell, but the swirling air around her died down. She shined the light inside and gulped.

She had finally found her cousin and Haley. Staring at her were two human skulls, stacked on their individual bones. In front of the stack to her left was the name "Stormy" written in white chalk. In the stack to her right, "Haley" was written. Between them was a white circle where another person's remains ought to be. In front of that circle, with the pentagram crudely drawn inside of it, was her name, scrawled in white chalk, "Serena."

***

Lilith woke with a start. Serena had found the room!

Chapter 48--Wednesday, Early Morning

Shock smothered all sound and fear. In a way, knowing what they had planned was like finding the last puzzle piece. Serena closed the cupboard doors, straightened the chairs, and then closed the door to the room.

Her body began to tremble only when she was back in the house standing in the kitchen, unsure what to do next. Should she go to her room or back to the couch? Her legs were shaking so hard she didn't think she'd make it up the stairs. She collapsed on the couch and pulled the blanket over her head.

Her first reaction should have been to call the police, but the mind does funny things when it's in shock. It goes into survival mode. Emotions detach from the brain and fear takes over. She wasn't sure what she should do, so she did nothing. The blanket provided a cocoon as well as warmth, both of which she craved. Huddling beneath gave her a false, but welcome, sense of safety. At some point, she drifted asleep, only to be wakened by Lilith an hour later.

On autopilot, Serena readied herself for school, her mind still reeling from what she'd found early that morning. Even in a daze, she managed to dress in the strange clothes folded in her drawers and pack a few things to smuggle in her backpack.

Lilith stood at the door. She hugged Serena and called her Stormy again. This time Serena actually looked at her aunt. Her expression was so adoring that Serena's heart ached. When Lilith saw her, she really saw Stormy. It was in the warmth of her eyes and the gentle tug at her lips, so Serena allowed the hug. Lilith was such a broken woman, who was she to break her further?

Serena didn't look up at the covered window above the garage as she climbed into the SUV. She sensed Lilith watching from the kitchen doorway. Did she know? Was she a part of what Simon and Rosalie were doing? If she did know, then it was no wonder she blocked it out. It was spooky to see someone so far removed from reality.

***

Lilith watched Henry drive Serena down the driveway. Her 'vacant' smile fell away as she shut the door. She went to the phone and punched in the numbers.

"What?" Simon barked. "I told you not to call unless it's an emergency."

"She found the room."

"I'm on my way."

Chapter 49--Wednesday

At the bottom of the hill, Henry didn't stop. He pulled out onto the road and drove her to the school. If it weren't for the fact that she needed to meet with Jesse she would've enjoyed not being on the bus. A nagging feeling within her told her to write down what she wanted to say. She carefully pulled out the one textbook left in her backpack and scratched out a quick note on the back of a half-finished homework assignment. Just as they arrived at school she squeezed the book back into the bag. She sat up and kept her eyes forward so as not to give away who she was looking for even though Henry wasn't an idiot. He'd probably be staying on the premises, ensuring her captivity.

Jesse was pacing in front of her locker. "Finally!" he said. "I was getting worried."

"You should be." She punched in the numbers of her code. "Henry drove me here. I don't know if he'll be following me around school or just hanging out in the parking lot, but there's probably no way we're getting out of here." Seeing anxiety etched across his face warmed her soul.

He ran a hand through his tangled hair. "I know, I noticed Mr. Dawson in the library earlier. It was bound to happen." He sighed. "I feel like we're so close yet so far from getting you out of here. Give me your backpack." Her backpack was black like his. They exchanged the bags.

"There's a note in the bag. You have to read it." He picked up on her urgency and nodded his head. He had to go. They'd switch the bags again the following morning. So this was it for the day. "I'll miss seeing you."

"Me too," he said. His eyes said he would kiss her but there wasn't time. He slung her backpack over his shoulder and walked around the corner just as Mr. Dawson came down the hall.

She spun around to her locker and fiddled with the lock. Mr. Dawson was right behind her.

"Good morning, Serena." Mr. Dawson spoke quietly. Then he reached out and brushed his knuckle on the back of her hand that still clung tightly to the lock. She looked up, startled.

His hair was a downy white and his pale blue eyes were lined with white eyelashes. His fingers were too long as they grasped her hand, holding her still.

"Please, sir." She fought to keep her voice calm and spacey so he wouldn't pick up how alert and disgusted she was.

"You've been avoiding me, haven't you, Serena?" He spoke hypnotically, and she could feel a part of her mind relaxing under his tightening grip.

Serena! Pull away. Don't let him touch you.

The urgency in Stormy's voice dragged her from his entrancing stare. Their eyes were locked, but she didn't know what to do next. She couldn't pull away or he would notice she wasn't spellbound anymore.

Oh God, please help me!

She didn't know what made her cry out to God. She hadn't prayed since Dad had died. Dad believed in God, but to her He just seemed too far away. But now, at this moment, she knew God was the only one who could help her.

"Is everything okay?" Ms. Steele stood in the hall with a funny look on her face. It was enough of a distraction to break Mr. Dawson's hold.

"I was just helping Sto--Serena with her lock."

While he was distracted, Serena grabbed the backpack and began walking the other direction. She could get to her class another way. Her steps quickened as she rounded the corner until she was in an all out run. Another teacher yelled out behind her to walk, but she barely slowed down.

Henry stayed in the car the entire time, but the teachers watched them like hawks. Just before the final bell Jesse met her at the bathroom door.

"I got it," he whispered in her ear. "I have the papers we've been waiting for. Now we can get you out of here tomorrow morning." His eyes were both relieved and sad at once.

Her voice caught as she opened her mouth. "Wait, aren't you coming with me?"

He shook his head. "I can't. I'd put my grandma in danger if I left right now."

"Oh." She sucked in a sharp breath as she realized that saying goodbye to the horrors also meant she was saying goodbye to Jesse. "All this time I assumed you were coming with me. I can't do this without you." The tears she fought were beginning to flow.

"Yes you can, and you will."

"Will I see you again?"

"I'm planning on it." He wiped her tears off her cheeks. "Now listen, tomorrow you need to bring anything else you're going to need or want. I have a feeling we're down to the wire now. I'll park at the next driveway over so Henry doesn't see you and then I'll follow just to be sure you're okay. Be on your guard at every moment, okay?"

She couldn't answer him. He reached his arm around her neck and pulled her close. "You can do this Serena. You don't have a choice."

She nodded. He kissed her on the forehead and released her as the bell rang. Then he picked up his backpack and walked away. Shaking, she picked hers up and went the opposite direction. She focused on breathing slowly in order to calm herself. It worked. Sort of.

That afternoon she acted like everything was the same. She managed to only nibble her food so she wouldn't get the full dose of drugs, and then after a night of watching old reruns she went upstairs but didn't change her clothes. She needed to be ready early in the morning.

As she lay down the tinkling tune of the music box drifted down the hall, the melody haunting and familiar. She had heard it from somewhere else besides here. Suddenly a memory came back to her, taking her breath away. She sat straight up. She had found a music box in the back of her father's closet years ago. When she had opened it the same song rang out. Her father found her within a minute and slammed the lid down, explaining that he would tell her about it when she was older. And he did--on his deathbed. That night played over in her head.

That must've been the box he had told her to find! If Stormy had the exact one in her room, was the one her father had belonged to herself? If it was, and Stormy's was mysterious in some way, then was the other box also magical? Now she knew what her father had bound the magic to--the music box in the back of his closet. That had to be it! And she had to get therebefore Simon or Rosalie did. The house still belonged to her, she just had to find the key, which she assumed, were in Fred and Martha's possession. After she got to Portland she'd go home and get it. The last puzzle piece fell in place leaving her at peace. She finally closed her eyes and drifted off to sleep.

Chapter 50--Thursday Morning

Of course, Simon came home the day Serena was supposed to leave. The morning dawned bright with not a cloud in the sky. She woke before her alarm rang and since it was now nearly summer the sun was already rising. She lay in bed, her eyes and body still heavy from sleep. Her spider web of thoughts brought her out of the deep sleep that clung to her. So much had changed since she'd arrived in October. She almost didn't recognize herself, nor could she account for about a month of days and nights, but at least she was getting out.

A part of her felt like she'd grown and was shedding the skin of the girl she used to be. She didn't recognize this new girl, and she didn't think Dad would either. Was she more like the girl in the mirror now than her true self? Or maybe a combination of both. The grieving daughter was cocooned and waiting until it was safe to come back out. She wasn't sure that girl would know how to exist at this time. She had to be kept safe and buried. With her came fears and heartbreak, memories of her father, memories of a bittersweet life, faint memories of her mother and sister, memories of her home in Oregon. That girl missed her dad and was confused by her world and all that had happened in life. That girl didn't know how to handle life with Simon and Lilith. That girl went to sleep at some point and decided not to wake up.

But this girl. This girl, now named Ava, had to do the waking up. She was the one who'd get out of here. She was sure a psychologist would have a heyday with her. She was beginning to wonder herself if she had multiple personalities, but she didn't think so. She was still the same girl--the one sleeping as well as the one awake, but it was her job as the alert one to protect the one who couldn't face life.

"Do you know how crazy you sound?" Stormy appeared at the foot of the bed, her knees tucked up, her arms wrapped around them and her chin on top. She wore her dress, but now it was pristine white instead of dirty and her fair complexion was tinted with a hint of rose instead of ghastly white.

"I know." Serena sat down on the bed. "You don't think I'm crazy, though, do you?"

Her laugh was like a silvery chime. "No, but I'm dead."

"Do you hate me for leaving?"

"No. I wish I'd gotten out of here when I had the chance." Stormy paused before continuing. "But you don't actually think you'll get out of here do you?"

"What do you mean?"

"Simon is driving up the driveway even as we speak."

"What?" Serena sprang off the bed.

Stormy grabbed Serena's arm and pulled her back.

"What happened?" Serena's legs gave out and she sat down on the floor. "How did they know?"

Stormy sat on the floor beside her, "Oh cousin. They know so much more than you realize. You can't get away from them. My mother, she pretends to be in a daze, and in some ways she really is, but she can see things beyond our ability."

"What do you mean?"

"She's a trans-medium psychic."

Serena looked into Stormy's animated green eyes.

"She's clairvoyant as well as a trans-medium. She can read you, know what you're doing or find you if you go missing, and then she'll let my father know. Although she has had a difficult time reading you in particular."

"Is Rosalie a medium like Lilith?"

"Rosalie is in a class all by itself. She's a sorceress, a necromancer and is powerful in the art of lithomancy. She's one of the most powerful witches in Northwest America."

"What are those things?"

Sighing, Stormy said, "Basically she's a witch, a Luciferian witch, which is the most powerful kind. She can speak with the dead, they tell her things. That's just a small part of what she can do."

Serena gulped before she asked her next question. "Is that what I am? If I can see you and hear you?" she trembled.

"Yes."

"Why? I mean I never even knew these people before this year. How can I possibly be cursed this way?"

"You could say it's in the blood." Stormy gave a sad smile.

Serena shuddered. "Did my father know? Was he clairvoyant?" She couldn't see Dad as a warlock.

"Among other things, yes, but then he fought it. He didn't want it.

That's why he cut off our family, broke every connection he could with them. He didn't want them to get their claws in you."

"How did they then?"

"They were more powerful. They could do anything they wanted in order to get you, and that's what they did. You were supposed to go live with the Youngblood couple, but Rosalie has ties with important people. That's how she got you here, Serena."

"What if I don't want this?"

Stormy's eyes darkened as she cocked her head quizzically. "Why wouldn't you want it? You have been chosen and can be of much use to us."

"Us?" It was Serena's turn to be confused. "What do you mean us? You are helping me aren't you?" She scooted away from Stormy.

The sweet smile that had touched Stormy's lips all morning began to twitch and change along with her eyes. Her pupils narrowed, giving her a cat-eyed appearance, and her mouth twisted as she hissed.

"Help you? I was supposed to help you? What made you think that?"

"Because! You're my cousin! Because you didn't want me to die like you did!" she stuttered scrambling as far away as she could while Stormy dropped into a crouch, hands and feet on the floor like a spider, and crawled to her.

"I do not help you." Her voice dropped two octaves lower. "I help my father, I help Rosalie. You? YOU are nothing." Her hand flew out faster than Serena expected and caught her on the cheek, nails dragging along her face. Serena scrambled on her bed and under the covers, but Stormy grabbed her foot.

Serena turned and gripped the bedpost, coming face-to-face with Haley's skeletal grin. She dragged her bony fingers along Serena's arms as she held onto the bed. Icy pain sliced through her skin, and she nearly let go. Haley cackled as Stormy continued to pull on Serena's legs, and she thought for sure they would rip her in two. Haley suddenly disappeared, but her presence could still be felt in the room. The lamp and pictures of Lilith and Stormy levitated and began swirling into the air, crashing into each other, raining glass and pottery onto Serena's hair. Drawers opened and closed; clothing was yanked out and thrown into the air.

"LILITH!" Serena screamed, hoping she'd stop these wraiths.

She heard thumping footfalls, too heavy to be Lilith's, hurry down the hall. The door flew open and Simon stood in the doorway.

"HALEY! LEAVE!" Serena could feel Haley's substance vanish at Simon's command. The picture frames and lamp crashed down on

Serena's back, stabbing a half-inch from her spine.

Stormy tightened the grip on her ankle. Serena screamed in pain. "ENOUGH STORMY!"

The pressure released. Serena had to get out of there as fast as she could. Lilith stood in the doorway, and if she were the size of a normal person, she would've blocked Serena's way. Instead, she shoved past Lilith. Serena stood in the hallway, panting, not sure where to go or what to do next. Would they even let her out of the house?

Stormy's door opened with a gust of a hurricane wind, and Serena turned just in time to see her rush out, her mouth a gaping black hole. Her screams echoed through the house. Her dress hung in tatters over her skeletal body as her flesh literally melted in front of her. Serena backed up until she stepped on Simon's foot. He stood just inside her bedroom.

"Don't you see it?" she cried.

He wrapped his arms around her. She struggled and flailed to get away, finally pulling out of his arms. She faced him.

"You don't see that?" She pointed behind her at the banshee that continued to scream in her ear. Her finger went right through the ghastly face.

Simon's mouth stretched wide with an eerie grin. "Of course I can see her, Serena. I'm the one who called her."

Get out! Get out! GET OUT! Her own voice was screaming in her head. Her backpack sat next to the door. She would have left it behind, except it held pictures of her parents and sister. Simon lunged for her. She kicked him in the shin as hard as she could, and he dropped to the floor. She grabbed the bag and ran out of her bedroom door and through the ectoplasm that was her cousin. Lilith shrieked and sprang forward, but Serena shoved her away. She pinched Serena's arm as she tried to hold on, but Serena kept moving down the stairs. Lilith was on her heels, grabbing at her.

Serena's shoes were next to the door, where she'd left them the night before. She stooped to grab them. Lilith hopped on her back, knocking her over.

Frustration, fear, and anger came over Serena as she fell. She was going to get out of this house, even if it was the last thing she did. She elbowed Lilith in the nose as she reared up behind her. Lilith fell back with loud yell as blood gushed from her nose. The keys to the SUV were hanging on the rack. Serena reached up and grabbed them. Simon had arrived at the bottom of the stairs. He took two enormous steps and grabbed her arm as she pulled away. With the notched end she lashed the jagged end of the key at his face, scraping it along his cheek. He cried out but held onto her arm, trying to take her down.

Lilith's voice broke through the mayhem, a raspy, gurgling voice that wasn't her own.

"Take her! TAKE HER!"

She was still on the floor with blood pouring from her broken nose.

"No," Serena grunted, as Simon tried to yank her closer. She understood what Lilith meant when she told him to take her. "You can't have me!"

He smiled, a dark look void of everything a smile should be, and said, "I already did, Serena. I've taken you several times."

Sudden flashes of memory shot through her mind. *Body weight. Can't breathe. Slobber. Hot breath. Sore. Blood. Tears. Pain. Fingers pushing, prodding. Panting. Night. Darkness. Shackle. Ankle.*

She pushed him away, but he was stronger. "No!" she shouted. "Nooooo!"

"Oh yes, Serena. Yes!"

He pushed her up against the wall and she knew he was going to rape her again if she didn't stop him. Her mouth was close to his ear, she bent her head and bit into the cartilage.

He screamed and pulled away, but her jaw locked down. His hand came out and slapped her. She let go, and he stumbled back, holding his ear. Her eyes watered as she spit something bloody out of her mouth and gagged.

She wiped her mouth with her sleeve, slipping the key in her right hand between her first and middle finger, ready to jab him in the eye if he came back at her again. She knew this was as good a time as any. She grabbed her shoes and backpack and bolted.

Rocks bit her feet as if even they weren't going to let her get away. She didn't care. She was leaving. Henry's old jeep sat in the driveway where he parked it on Friday, already backed up and ready to go. Please let the keys be there she prayed. She yanked the door open to find her prayers were answered.

"Serena!" Simon yelled from the kitchen door. She heard a telltale cocking that brought her head up and back to him. He stood there, a handgun aimed at her head. She yanked open the car door and ducked in.

BOOM!

The shot echoed through the mountains. She slammed the door and turned the key in the ignition.

BOOM!

The backside window exploded. She hunched as she shifted into first gear and pressed on the gas pedal. Rocks flew behind her as she took off down the road.

BOOM!

BOOM!

BOOM!

A hole appeared in the windshield. Glass from the passenger side window was now all over the seat. How the shots missed her was a miracle. BOOM!

The bark from the tree beside her exploded, and she ducked down even further.

The car fishtailed as she skimmed over a pothole and missed trees by a mere inch. The road seemed longer than ever before.

"Please be there, Jesse!"

She was never so happy to see his truck idling at the end of the road. She screeched to a halt, turned off the car and took the key out of the ignition. Then she grabbed her stuff off the floor, slicing her fingers in the process, and slammed the door.

"What happened?" Jesse yelled.

"No time! Let's go!" She threw her stuff in the truck and jumped in. Without a word, he peeled out and raced for town. She brushed away the dirt and blood from her feet and pulled on her shoes. She was still dressed in her pajamas, but lucky for her, they consisted of yoga pants and a long sleeved t-shirt. She didn't look like she'd just gotten out of bed. She did, however, look like she'd been involved in "Fight Night" at the local bar.

She gave Jesse a shortened version of what had happened as she pulled down the visor and inspected the damage. Three red scratches stretched up her left cheek. Her heart chilled when she remembered how Stormy had left those marks. How could she have touched her? A little blood trickled from her nose, but it was merely a scrape, not anything serious. Little shards of glass twinkled in her hair as sunlight caught the gleam.

She pushed the visor back up and sighed as she leaned back. Jesse's hands were clenched on the steering wheel when they swung into a parking lot.

"What are we doing?"

"We're borrowing a car. Come on." They leaped out, and she grabbed her backpack and followed him to a little Geo Metro from the nineteen-nineties.

"Where's my stuff?" She glanced in the back of the truck, but it wasn't there.

"It's in the car."

The little car came to life before they closed their doors. "I realized," he explained once they were a couple miles down the road, "that if anyone saw us, they'd totally recognize my truck. Simon has spies everywhere, as we both know, so I borrowed a car."

"Good idea."

"Yeah, well, I wish I'd thought of it, but it was actually Frank, the one who's been working on your papers, who suggested it. He's done this a time or two before. One of my friends, Trevor, let me borrow it."

"I see." She glanced in the back and saw a tote bag with a manila envelope on top. She took it and opened it. A birth certificate, license, and passport, along with about a thousand dollars, were inside. It all suddenly became very real. She leaned her head back on the headrest and closed her eyes against the tears that abruptly welled. She could feel them slip past her lashes. Jesse's hand gripped her knee. When she jumped he let go.

"Are you okay?" Worry filled his voice.

"I will be." She swallowed. "Thank you, Jesse. For everything."

He didn't answer. She could tell he wanted to ask more about what happened, but there was no way she could describe all of the events of the morning.

They arrived at the bus station an hour later. They'd been listening to the radio to see if she'd been reported missing. So far she hadn't. They parked and then headed in together, neither of them ready to say goodbye. The duffle bag was small enough to keep as a carry-on. He gave her a little bag that posed as a purse too. She stuffed her new license in it along with some of the cash. Then he handed her a plastic grocery sack. Inside, she found a beret that looked like it belonged to an old man and a few miscellaneous items that looked odd to her.

Jesse motioned for her to follow him to an isolated spot near the locker area. He plopped the hat on her head and tucked her hair into it. There were some fake earrings and nose ring that he put in the right places. From a distance, a person wouldn't be able to tell that she was a poser. He even had some rub-on tattoos that he applied along her collarbone and arms.

His gentle touch sent a fluttering of butterfly wings along her insides and she hoped he didn't notice the gooseflesh on her skin. A brief flash of Simon's groping flickered through my mind, but she resolutely ignored it. He wouldn't ruin these last moments with Jesse. Besides, Jesse wasn't Simon.

"There," he said, as he applied the last tattoo, completely unaware of the war inside her head. "They'll come off once you get to Portland, but for now, you won't match any descriptions if they do put an all points bulletin on you." He winked and gave her a tremulous smile. "I wish things had been different," he whispered.

"Me too."

He pulled her into a long hug, and she fought the tears that wanted to come. Over the loudspeaker, they heard the announcement for her bus.

"Come on," he took her bag in one hand and her hand in the other. A few feet from the bus door he stopped. "I put my number in your envelope in case you need anything. Give me your phone."

"Oh my gosh, I think I left it at the house."

"That's okay, they can't track it to either of us."

"Are you sure?"

"Yeah. Just get another one when you get there but stay under the radar. No social media, okay? They'll be looking all over the computer for you."

The last call for her ride sounded overhead. He pulled off his leather coat and set it on her shoulders. The weight of the leather and the scent of Jesse was so comforting. She slid her arms through the sleeves. They were a bit long on her, but she didn't care. Jesse drew her into another hug, his arms wrapped securely around her waist, holding her tightly against him. "I'll miss you, Serena," he whispered against her hair, and then he kissed her temple. He put his finger under her chin, then he leaned down and kissed her lips, long and gentle. When he pulled away his eyes were wet. He swallowed. "Don't forget me."

"Never." She reached up and kissed his cheek, feeling the stubble along her lips. Then she turned and made her way to the bus. Once she found a seat she sat down and looked out the window. He stood outside, hands shoved deep in his pockets, watching her. As the bus began to pull away she raised her hand in a wave, and he did the same. She brushed away tears and wondered if she'd ever see him again.

Chapter 51--Thursday

Simon hollered as Henry's old jeep careened between the two large oak trees at the edge of his property. It would be hell to pay when he spoke to his mother. She wanted Serena dead last year and now she had escaped. Because of him, Simon. That's what his mother would think anyway.

How did she do it? He swore he had Serena under his control. He'd done everything to ensure it, including giving Lilith the medication to use in her food just in case. Even his bullets strayed from their intended target, spraying into trees, the windshield, back window and mirrors, but not Serena. He yelled again, but only his voice echoed back from the hills. Serena was long gone. No matter. All he had to do was call the police chief and report his car as being stolen. As soon as she was apprehended he'd take care of her like he should have months ago. He truly was foolish for thinking she was anything like her mother.

He thumbed the safety on his gun, turned and stomped back to his house. The cool spring breeze carried the scent of wilderness and wood. The grand home stood tall and imposing in this clearing, far above all those who lived on the mountain and small town below them. He opened the door to the kitchen to find Lilith sprawled on the floor, still in a trance-like state, her nose at an odd angle and blood drying on her lips and chin. She was going to be pissed when she finally snapped out of this state. He was tempted to step over her and leave her be, but he also had pride and didn't want a wife that had a crooked face. He planted his feet on either side of her legs, bent over and placed his hands over her nose. With a jerk, he positioned it correctly. She didn't react like a normal person, nor did she wake from the hypnotic state in which she had put herself. He wondered where her mind was when her spirit guide took over body. Apparently she had been working diligently on gaining her powers back because she acted more like herself today than she had in a long time. He was heartened to see it. Though she still had a ways to go on suppressing all of her emotion and acting purely on instinct when fighting her enemies, she was almost back to original self. Perhaps there was something left of his wife. He watched a single tear travel down her inexpressive face.

Simon swallowed the lump that suddenly appeared in his throat. Losing Stormy had just about killed Lilith. The tears that brimmed in her lower lids had nothing to do with the pain of her broken nose. It only had to do with Stormy. Something moved in the corner of his eyes and he turned.

Stormy floated an inch above the bottom stair; it was as far as he would allow her to come when he called her spirit. She wasn't watching him, only her mother.

"Stormy," he spoke her name and she looked at him. "Go back to your room. You've done enough damage today."

Stormy's eyes lifted to him, a fire behind the bright green, and shook her head. "One of these days, you won't be able to control me, you know."

"That's what you think. I'm far more powerful than you could ever hope to be."

The shrill ring of the phone interrupted him. That would be his mother. It rang again. They stared at each other, both knowing that it would not be a good conversation. It rang a third time.

"Get the phone," a gravelly voice croaked from Lilith's mouth, but it was not Lilith who spoke.

He couldn't put it off any longer. Might as well get it over with. He stalked over to where the kitchen counter connected to the wall and picked up the phone.

Stormy smirked at him, shaking her head. She was free of Rosalie, but he wasn't and they both knew it.

"What?" he yelled into the phone.

"Don't you dare speak to me in that tone!" Rosalie hollered. He winced and pulled the phone from his ear. "Where did she go?"

"I don't know, but I have to hang up and call the police. She took the jeep, so at least I can say it was stolen."

"I don't care what you have to say, get her now."

"I can turn her, you know that."

"NO! You can't, you've already tried it and it should have worked by now if it was possible for you to succeed."

"But Mother, you know she could be a powerful asset to us. Aza can sense these things and he wants to use her."

"I don't care what Aza says. You know the prophecy. Kill her before she kills me!" The line went dead. He hung up the phone on his end and then clicked the on button again and dialed the chief's number. The chief was a personal friend of his and would do what he could for him and the association. It didn't take long to describe Serena and the car and give explicit instructions that when he caught her, she was to be brought up to the house, not to the police station. He would take care of her, like he did with Stormy. When he got off the phone, he looked over to Stormy, who still hovered in the stairwell, glaring at him.

"You know she's stronger than you think," she whispered.

"Who? Lilith?"

"No. Serena."

"Believe me, I can still control her. I just have to get her under this roof again."

"You think raping her repeatedly will bring her under your control?" she glared at him, shaking her head. "You just don't get it, do you? She's stronger in the other realm, much more than *you* could ever hope to be. She will only become more powerful the longer she is away from you and she will kill you before you ever get a chance to hurt her again. If she doesn't, I will make sure you never get away with it." She spoke quickly and quietly, her voice carrying an air of truth, forecasting his future. They locked gazes, each daring the other one to break down first.

"Go. Back. Upstairs," he growled when he realized she wouldn't back down. "And stay up there."

She glowered at him as she slowly disappeared. When she was completely gone, the phone rang again, startling him. Frazzled, he answered gruffly.

"What?"

"Sir," the police chief spoke in his ear. "We found the car."

"Where is it?"

"At the bottom of your road."

Maybe one of the bullets had hit her after all. That will be messy to explain to the police if she was dead from a gunshot wound.

"Is she okay?" He asked.

"She's gone, sir."

"What?"

"She's gone. There's broken glass everywhere, and some blood, but she's definitely not here."

"She couldn't have gotten far. Make sure your guys search the woods, the entire mountain if you have to, and put an All Points Bulletin on her. She can't get away!"

"Sir," the chief's voice dropped down an octave, "is she important to the Monarch?"

"Yes, you ass, but you're not supposed to bring that up! Now get her back!" Simon hung up the phone, wishing for the old fashioned kind that you could slam down. Now they just had these stupid buttons you pushed, never giving you the satisfaction of leaving the other person's ears ringing.

Serena had to have had an accomplice. That would explain her sudden disappearance. Maybe that kid, Jesse. Simon had warned her to stay away from him, but maybe she didn't listen. He called the chief back.

"Make sure you look for that kid, Jesse."

"Yes sir. What's his last name?"

"Garris, I think."

"We'll get right on that. I'll call you back." They hung up again.

Upstairs there was a loud crash.

"Stormy!" he yelled. He ran up the stairs, two at a time. Serena's door was still open, the shackles lying lifeless on the floor, blood shimmering in the sun that came through the window. Another crash sounded, from his daughter's room. He walked down the hall, wondering what he was going to find when he opened the door. The key was jammed into the old fashioned lock. He turned it and opened the door. Haley's ghost rushed him, shrieking. He put his hand up and she halted a couple feet in front of him. Enraged, she clawed out at him, but her nails went through him, not leaving a mark. Stormy was the only one with the power to touch and leave a mark, and only on Serena. He had given her that power.

Stormy stood several feet above the floor. Then she spun in a tight circle, causing the air to swirl around them. Pictures flew off the wall, books fell from the shelves, the stool at the vanity began levitating in the air, threatening to fly at him. Instinctively, he put up his arms just as the stool flew at his face. He felt and heard his bone crack and he roared.

"Stop! NOW!" The whirlwind halted immediately. Stormy, her face stony and streaked with mud and blood like it had been the day she had been sacrificed, faced him directly, her eyes blazing with fury as she dared him to release her from his spell.

He wouldn't though. He would keep her. It was her punishment. He refused to hold his aching arm as he backed out of the room and shut the door. He jammed the key into the lock so it couldn't open from the inside, then he spoke quickly, leaving a spell to keep the door locked in the spirit realm, imprisoning his daughter in this room, for all of eternity if needed. That would teach her to act out against him again. Inside the room, he could hear her shrieking. She was trapped. Only Lilith could open it, but she was still in a trance, stuck in her own thoughts. She didn't know what he had done and wouldn't know to release Stormy.

The phone rang again. He raced down the stairs and picked up the phone.

"Sir," the chief said. "We found the truck. It's parked at the grocery store. We're going in and doing a search of the market."

"Good, I'll meet you down there."

He hung up the phone and then went into his room. He changed into a fresh shirt and jeans, grabbed his car keys off the counter, then stepped over his wife's legs. She looked up at him, dazed, but still vacant. He sighed and shook his head.. He locked the door on his way out. Henry stood a few feet away from him, glaring at Simon, ready to charge like a bull and probably wishing he had horns to spear him with.

"You have the house keys, right?"

Henry nodded.

"Good. Wait until Lilith wakes or she'll take you out by accident." He sighed. "Take care of her, Henry. Just do what you gotta do to keep her safe from Rosalie."

The silent man nodded yes.

"Whatever you do, don't allow Lilith upstairs to see Stormy."

At the sound of her name Stormy let out a banshee scream that echoed through the mountains. "And don't you go up there either."

Henry's face paled and he shook his head. He wouldn't dare go up there especially now.

Once in his car, Simon quickly glanced up at his daughter's room. She stood, watching him, wailing and pounding her fist against the pane.

He shifted the gears and sped down the road. He couldn't get away from this house, this property, or this mountain fast enough. He didn't spare a look back as he drove between the two oak trees. Lilith, Stormy and the house were dead to him now.

Epilogue

Two days and three stops later Serena finally arrived in Portland, Oregon. Jesse's friend, Frank, picked Serena up from the bus stop. He was chubby and middle-aged with thinning hair, but he had a dimpled grin that made him look twelve. He wasn't at all what she expected when she pictured the person that created a new identity for her. He told her to call him Frankie.

The studio apartment he had secured for her wasn't much to look at. Aside from a bed in the corner, it was empty but it was all hers. She used the cash to put down her first month's rent, and then he asked if she had any leads on a job. When she told him no, he said he might know of one.

They walked to a coffee shop down the street. It was crowded with people of all different hair colors, earrings, and tattoos. Those who noticed her nodded a hello and smiled. Frank squeezed them through. They sidled up to the counter and sat on a couple of bar stools that had just been vacated. A redhead who was barking out orders nodded to Frank and then went back to her customer. When she was done, she walked over to them. Her hair was pulled back in a high ponytail, and several piercings lined her brow. She had a retro pinup girl look to her and an easy smile.

"Hey Frankie," she spoke in a smoky, feminine voice. "What'cha got here?"

"Hi Yvonne, this is Ava. She's new in town, wondered if you're hiring."

"One of your stray cats you're always bringing home?" She winked at Serena.

"Yeah, you know me."

"Yeah, I do. Ya ole bleeding heart, you." She stepped a little closer and looked straight into Serena's eyes. She thought for sure the other woman would notice the fake piercings and tattoo.

"Do you know how to make coffee, sweetie?" she asked.

"Not yet, but I'm smart. I'm sure I can figure it out." She knew she had to be more gregarious than what came naturally, but she was surprised by how confident she felt. Maybe it was the sense of freedom of not being under Simon's thumb anymore. She didn't know for sure, but she was going with it.

"Okay, good," Yvonne said. "I like a little spunk. By the way, my boyfriend is a tat artist if you want a real one." She winked at Serena. "And I can give you real piercings if that's your thing."

"It's not."

"We'll see. I bet you'll change your mind when you've been here long enough. Come on, let's get you started."

Slowly but surely Serena began to make a life for herself. She filled her apartment with hand-me-down furniture, picture frames with stranger's faces. She shared her fake stories with Yvonne, and told others fake stories about her fake family and the fake memories she had of them. She wished she could be real with someone, but she couldn't. Every night she would sit on her ugly yellow and brown plaid loveseat, eat a TV dinner, and eventually fall asleep.

She tried to forget Colorado, but she couldn't. She was always on the lookout. And just in case, deep in the back of her closet there was a small duffle bag packed and ready to go at a moment's notice. Sometimes she would pull out the pictures of her real parents and sister and a small one of Jesse that he'd snuck into the manila envelope. In the bottom of that duffle bag held her memories of life before Colorado. A life with a good and kind father who loved her, a father who had left her a magic music box in her childhood home. She knew the Youngbloods had kept the house but she was afraid to go back, afraid of what she would find in that box and afraid Simon would be waiting for her.

The mountaintop house still haunted her dreams. She'd often wake nauseous and gagging with Stormy's voice or Simon's heavy breathing in her ear. Once the sun rose in the sky, though, the dreams melted, pushing Simon, Lilith and Stormy far away. She often thought of Jesse and wondered what he was doing, and then she tried to go about her day with work.

Yet, no matter how hard she tried, she knew it was only a matter of time before her past found her.

Acknowledgements:

There was a lot more that goes into producing a book than I ever thought and I would be remiss if I forgot to thank all of them, or at least as many as I can remember.

First and foremost, I'd like to thank my awesome husband, Josh, for your encouragement, patience, and sense of humor when I'd lost mine. I wouldn't have been able to do this without your support and I love you to pieces.

Thank you kiddos, for your help in watching over your baby brother when I was writing, for letting me bounce ideas off of you, and for cheering me on when I was having a low day. You guys are all so awesome and I'm proud to be your mama.

Jennifer Sawyer Fisher, thank you for your help and constructive criticism. Thank you for catching all of the grammar mistakes and a few of the holes in my plot. This book wouldn't be half as good without your help. You are amazing and I am so humbled that you believed in my book when I wasn't sure if I did. Thank you so much.

Thank you to my parents, Rick and Barbara Booye, and my sister, Kelly Goodson, for all of the years you encouraged me to continue writing and suffered through me reading to you, even when the stories were a bit juvenile. I love you guys!

Thank you to Laura Harrington, Aimee Norvell, Lisa Lee and Lexi Lee. You were all great as my trial readers. Thank you so much for your input and excitement!

And thank you to all of my online supporters and friends on Facebook and Twitter. You have no idea how much your cheers helped keep me going. You guys are so awesome.

And last, but not least, thank you God. You know I couldn't have done this without you!